Wicked Games
Twist My Heart
Wreck My Mind

u

Wicked Games

WRECK MY MIND

BROOKE TAYLOR

Wreck My Mind
ISBN # 978-1-83943-798-4
©Copyright Brooke Taylor 2022
Cover Art by Erin Dameron-Hill ©Copyright May 2022
Interior text design by Claire Siemaszkiewicz
Totally Bound Publishing

Published in 2022 by Totally Bound Publishing, United Kingdom.

Totally Bound Publishing is an imprint of Totally Entwined Group Limited.

WRECK MY MIND

Dedication

To my grandmother MJ for showing me the
world and inspiring me in so many ways.

Obsidian Protocol

"The most beautiful stories always start with wreckage." ~ Jack London

Chapter One

Coop

Aziza and I were not friends, we weren't enemies, and we certainly weren't lovers...we were liars. The biggest lie of all, the one I'd been telling myself for years, had become damn impossible to keep up. But the constraints of reality had never stopped me before, no sense starting on a boat speeding into the shadowed heart of the Amazon river basin at zero dark thirty.

Aziza

"You're *not* happy to see him!" I scolded myself. "You're just glad the stubborn, prideful, stupid...*man* isn't dead." Because if anyone or anything was going to kill Michael Cooper, it was going to be me!

I growled over the sounds of the tropical storm battering Marakata Cay.

Pulse punching, I scrolled back through the video capture dated nearly twenty-four hours ago. The heavily bearded profile blending into a small crowd of people before disappearing into the thin blue air of Rio de Janeiro most definitely belonged to an alive and well Michael Cooper.

What the hell are you doing in Brazil?

If he was even still there.

Twenty-four hours may as well have been a month. He could be anywhere now, even in a morgue. It wasn't like he hadn't made serious enemies working for Beryl Enterprises. As our Director of Defense and Specialized Operations, he contracted with major private sector corporations as well as notable governments for high-level security solutions. His teams were often called in to deliver asset reconnaissance and recovery, be it intel or high-value targets. And *occasionally* those clients required more direct and unconventional warfare resolutions. It was these uniquely focused, clandestine operations that often put Beryl Enterprises in the crosshairs.

Concerned for his safety, I'd boldly asked Coop to relocate his home office from Dubai to Marakata Cay — the crown jewel of Beryl Enterprises. I'd proposed it would help shield both him and Omar Zaki's private island. But it certainly hadn't been my main motivation.

I'd truly believed he'd felt the same attraction, connection, to me that I did for him. Sure, our relationship was primarily professional. But for the past year or more our virtual meetings had lingered long after all work talk had been settled. We'd joke and laugh, talk about life. What had started as fun flirtation had quickly turned into something special.

Oh fuck it, I thought we were in love.

How could I've been so wrong?

So foolish!

I'd risked much more than my heart and pride when I'd dared ask him to make good on the flirtatious dance we'd been doing for years. And what had been his response? To send Brecken Wolfe, his top operator, here in his stead. To take off on an indefinite vacation while avoiding all forms of contact. To go completely off grid while simultaneously evading all SIGINT — every CCTV camera and satellite surveillance mechanism known to man. To freaking ghost me!

Hint. Taken.

But *why* go to such great lengths to stay undetected? Was it to dodge me, or was something else going on?

Coop had been acting off for months now, and if it wasn't because he'd been fighting his feelings for me, then why? Someone else? Something even worse? Just because I hated him didn't mean I'd stopped caring. *Hoping.*

My nerves knotted tight enough to fray as I fretted over what I might discover. But I couldn't hide from the truth any longer.

Ignoring my heart overfilling like a balloon and bursting on every beat, I replayed the loop in slow motion. I should've been scanning the background for clues as to what exactly Coop was doing in Rio, and more importantly why he'd slipped up and gotten caught when he'd expended great effort the past month to stay off grid. Instead, my questions and frustration evaporated as I paused on the singular image of him. He looked just like when I'd first met him over ten years ago — a little angry and a lot tired. Hardened from too many tours in the sandbox. Handsome as sin. Hot AF.

Despite the shitty resolution, those deep, ocean eyes of his managed to steal my air and throttle my heart.

"I've missed you, *My-sharky*," I whispered on a sigh.

The pet name was his butchered reiteration of *mushaeghib* – the Arabic word I often called him in frustration. It meant troublemaker and it fit him as well as calling him my shark did.

He was my protector. My warrior. My worst freaking headache. I wasn't about to lose him forever and have him become my greatest heartache, too.

My gaze traced along his jawline. The carved edges were now covered by a thick, rough beard. He hadn't shaved in a month, but the dark mass cloaking those panty-melting dimples of his looked more like a year's worth of growth. Same with the wild, black licks of hair.

Licks...

My eyes drifted to the slight protrusion of his tongue. Suddenly it was if his lips weren't on my computer screen or thousands of miles away in Brazil anymore. They were here on Marakata Cay right where I wanted – *needed* – them. My conjured vision of him had blown through my bedroom door with the same force as the tropical storm pelting my windows.

Dear Lord! My head needed to be examined. I'd spent weeks terrified I'd never see Coop again. I was furious at him for inexplicably leaving. Frightened, confused, hurt...and though it was tough to admit considering we'd never even touched, my heart had been wrecked when he'd vanished without a trace. Yet a stupid screenshot of him could still completely derail me with delusions and desire.

How could one gorgeous, but frustrating – *infuriating* – man have such a massive effect on me? I was a capable, intelligent, task-driven professional. As Omar Zaki's right hand, I had authority over the Beryl Enterprises empire, which included multiple specialized operations teams full of cocksure alpha men.

So why couldn't I control my own thoughts when it came to one, very annoying, smoking hot, Michael *freaking* Cooper?

The man had a way of slipping up on me and taking over my mind the same way scents of plumeria and rain had slid beneath my balcony's French doors to saturate my room. Being unable to stop myself from jumping his bones was half the reason I'd kept him in the Dubai offices and far away from the island for so long. I had too much to lose to be getting sexually involved with anyone I had true feelings for.

Asking him to relocate had been reckless and impetuous.

Foolhardy.

The mere sight of him, even on a computer screen, melted my resolve and my body like butter on a beach. Now was no different.

I wanted him here—not *just* here...*here with me*—more than I'd ever wanted anything.

As I had so many times before, I imagined him on the island. Actual flesh and bone in my room...on my bed...against my body. His lips traveling down my neck, still wet from the rain as they slid across my skin. His hot mouth hungrily cutting between my breasts, leaving a buzzing trail of need in its wake.

I tugged apart the perfect little bow at the waistband on my pajama bottoms as I spread my knees. My body needed him even if it couldn't have him. Careful not to let my tablet fall, I gazed at Coop's image while turning my wicked imagination loose. Instead of the streets of Brazil, I envisioned those beard-roughened cheeks of his were buried between my thighs. Sliding my hand down, I let my fingers do all the things I wanted his tongue to do to me.

Wild images of Coop flooded my head. Lifting me, covering me, filling me. The gusting wind and slapping palm fronds of the real world muted. Sounding in my passion-fogged brain were the near-realistic hollow thuds of the bed knocking rhythmically into the wall followed by a husky voice, "*Aziza...*"

Imagining him saying my name sent me right up to the edge. Right out of my body. My strangled reply caught along with my breath, "Com...in—"

A very real, ear-splitting creak of the bedroom door jolted me out of the fantasy. Hard. I jerked upright as my eyes shot open to a large man's darkened profile coming through the doorway. *Coop? Here? For real?*

I scrambled to hike my pajamas back up and cover my lap with the sheets as a voice that did not belong to Coop speared my heart. "Sorry to bother, ma'am."

My tablet slid, crashing to the floor along with my hopes.

"Oh, shit." Brecken Wolfe flipped on my light. "You all right, Zee?"

"Yeah, yes, I'm okay. I just wasn't expecting you."

Before disappearing, Coop had sent Wolfe to Marakata Cay by promoting him to the newly created Chief of Island Spec Ops position. In other words, he was Coop's idea of a solution. Like Coop, most of the elite operators were tall, muscular, and looked like they hunted all their meals with their bare hands. But Wolfe's Nordic features, keen glacial eyes, and dirty blond, braided Mohawk gave him a distinct Viking flair.

"I mean, you surprised me. I didn't hear you..." Watching him salvage my computer from the floor, I grappled for the words. *Wait...* Had the bed knocking actually been Wolfe knocking on the door? *Ugh.* Clearing my throat, I removed a dangling AirPod from my ear. The other one must've become lost in my pillows. "Had my buds in."

"Sorry about that, I could've sworn I heard you say to come in."

Come in...coming... Same thing. *Good Lord!* I wanted to die of embarrassment. One of my employees had just walked in on me while I got off on the fantasy of another employee.

Seriously, Aziza? Seriously?

Thankfully my hand wasn't still down my pants as he handed the computer back to me.

It wasn't like it would've shocked him. Sex of all kinds abounded on Zaki's private island. At many times Marakata Cay was a hedonistic oasis. Two weeks ago we'd hosted a whole seminar series devoted to self-pleasure, for fudge sake! But...I was *me*. Between being much younger-looking than my thirty-two years, female, and having the black hair and olive skin tone of my father's Arabic roots, I had to fight for respect with the powerful people I worked with. Many of whom preferred to dismiss me as some glorified harem girl of OZ's.

Better than them knowing my real relationship to Omar Zaki, I supposed.

I dared a glance at Wolfe, knowing the heat from between my legs had shot to my face. From his stoic expression, I couldn't tell if he'd realized what he'd walked in on. "I was on a video chat," I fibbed.

Wolfe grunted. "I knew that bastard didn't take a vacation. Freaking workaholic barely takes a piss break."

Lowering my eyes, I realized my screen was still zoomed in on the man I'd been using every resource at my extensive disposal to basically stalk like a scorned ex-girlfriend. *Shit.* The cherry topping off my mortification sundae — Coop was not only Wolfe's direct supervisor, but they were also close friends and former SEAL teammates. If it got back to him that I'd completely disregarded his privacy and tracked him down...or worse, he found out I was clinging to some romantic notion of us when he so clearly didn't see me the same way... *Ack!*

Ruining our friendship was the last thing I wanted to do. *If* we were even friends. Nothing was certain where Coop and I were concerned. A lesson I seemed determined to learn the hard way.

I pushed out a thought-clearing breath. Before I could change the subject, Wolfe mused, "I knew something had to be up when he missed Will's funeral. What's the scoop?"

SEAL funerals were the only reason Coop had ever unexpectantly taken time off work, and even then he stayed in constant contact with me and our Intelligence and Activity department. Skipping his former teammate's funeral had raised red flags for me as well, but I wasn't ready to collaborate with Wolfe.

As OZ's figure head, I often had to think on the fly. While I wasn't proud of it, deception had become an art form for me. But this had to do with Coop. *My* Coop. *My-sharky.* And not knowing where he'd been for the past month had sent my normally functioning brainwaves into a swirling cat-five hurricane. I resorted to playing dumb, despite speaking English better than my native tongue. "Scoop?"

"Is something going on with the emerald mine?"

I narrowed my eyes. If it weren't for Sapien, the cutting-edge biometrics software suite Beryl Technologies had in development for the CIA, I might've never known where Coop had disappeared to.

"How did you know he was in Brazil from just one screenshot?"

Wolfe shrugged. "I didn't. It was just a guess."

"Good guess," I muttered, disappointed he didn't have more information than I did. But at least I had an angle to deflect him with. "We were testing the advances to Sapien and Mr. Cooper agreed to play hide and seek."

Mr. Cooper? Yeah, that didn't sound sketch. I doubted anyone had ever called him 'Mr. Cooper' in his life.

Wolfe hiked up his brows, but all he said was, "Must be magic if it caught the Ghost."

Ghost. Another one of the mythical Michael Cooper's nicknames. This one a throwback to his Navy days when he and another of his teammates, Nikolas Steele, had been MIA in the Hindu Kush, but how apt it was. The infuriating man sure knew how to ghost a girl! Figures, Navy SEALs did *everything* to the fullest.

I focused back on Wolfe. "You didn't *guess* Brazil. Or if you did it was an educated one. Show me what you saw."

Wolfe moved closer, bracing one hand on the ebony pillar of my four-poster bed as he pointed. "That sign there? It's in Portuguese, and Coop is wearing a Flamengo football jersey, the most popular team in the region. The only football Coop acknowledges is American-style, and the only team he roots for is the Texas Longhorns. The hair, beard, clothing... He's blending in as a local."

While I'd been impressed with Wolfe's competency as a career operator over the past few years, I hadn't worked closely enough with him to see this analytical side. No wonder Coop had entrusted his former teammate to keep OZ's private island secure in his stead — the eagle-eye SEAL didn't miss a detail.

His attention stayed trained on the screen in my hands as his fingers worked to zoom it out.

"Yep, two more men in the crowd are dressed just like him as well. See, the police shield shape is Santos, and that green one is another Flamengo. *And...*" Wolfe zoomed in again, this time on a woman whose backside extended a good foot and a half from her tiny frame.

It wasn't just big, it was...

"Looks like one of those balloon animals, doesn't it? Nowhere else on the planet will they do a butt-job like that, nor should they."

He straightened, towering above me. His cocky grin told me he knew I was impressed. "Sometimes it takes more than software to see the world."

I swallowed and glanced away. I hadn't realized it was so obvious how sheltered I was on Marakata Cay. My virtual reach might've been global, thanks to Beryl Enterprises' extensive technology, but physically leaving wasn't an option. Not even when I desperately wanted to chase after my runaway heart.

I glanced back. Wolfe's ice-blue eyes had dropped to my lap. The waistband of my flannel pajama pants gaped and the drawstrings dangled. I jerked my comforter over the swathe of naked skin, hoping I hadn't just flashed my *kus* at Wolfe.

He spun on his heel and headed for the door. With a throat-clearing cough, he grunted, "Send *Mr. Cooper* my apologies for interrupting your game of hide and seek."

Shit shit shit. I squeezed my eyes shut, blocking out his broad back as he retreated with a snicker.

Unfortunately, like everything I wanted, ripping my covers over my head and screaming would have to wait. I was just as much a workaholic as Coop. A slave to the island and a slave to OZ. And Spec Ops didn't make a habit of coming to my bedroom in the middle of the night unless it was important.

"Wolfe, stop. You needed something?"

"Oh shit, right." He shook his head as if to refocus. When he turned back, his professional expression was firmly in place. "We're getting notifications of a ship in distress. Colt's got a rescue boat almost there now."

I set my tablet aside. Had I really been so consumed with chasing after an unrealistic, unrequited crush that I'd missed a ship getting near the island?

"How close are they?"

"We're the only ones who can respond."

"*Exactly* how close? Coordinates."

Wolfe rattled them off and my mouth went dry. I swung my legs out from the covers, twisted my waistband in my fist and headed for the bathroom to change. "I'll let Zaki know."

"Is that necessary? It's kind of late."

Having only recently moved from Coop's lead team in the Dubai offices, Wolfe hadn't much experience working directly under Zaki. Typically all of OZ's directives went through the Intelligence & Activity branch, me, or Coop. But knowing OZ's exacting standards and enigmatic temperament, employees generally feared the reclusive billionaire. Big, tough Vikings were no exception.

I didn't have time to put Wolfe at ease, but I needed him focused on the situation and not on his employer. "Marguerite has been changing unused bed linens for days. Zaki isn't big on sleep. Trust me, he'd be more upset to be left in the dark."

19

"If you're sure. I mean, I've got everything handled."

I fought to keep the snap from my voice as I straightened him out. "No, you don't have everything handled. Unknown people are coming to the island. Have I&A get full background profiles of all passengers, surviving or not. I want ownership details on the boat, purpose of their trip, and what the hell they were doing in those coordinates. Advise Colton to do SSE and use Obsidian Protocol."

"Obsidian Protocol?" he asked.

While Sensitive Site Exploration, or the gathering of any intel, was par for the course on ops, the various protocols on Marakata Cay were not. Unfortunately, I didn't have time to explain. "Meet me in the war room in thirty."

"Yes, ma'am."

Chapter Two

Coop

Banking hard through a hairpin turn in the ever-winding river vein, my guide, Reynaldo, throttled the piecemeal trolling motor to its limits. Sensing we were close, I checked my GPS, then told Rey to kill the power.

"*Aqui não,*" Rey hollered over the motor. "Closer. I get you closer."

I swiped my fingers across my throat in an emphatic slicing motion. "Shut 'er down."

Rey shook his head, but cut the gas.

The murky water swelled against the low-riding skiff's bow, lifting me high. Just as quickly, it lulled me down, bringing the boat to an eventual stall. Without the rattling engine and whirr of wind, I half expected silence and calm as we bobbed in the dark river channel. Instead, a clamor of insects and wildlife engulfed us. The orchestra of throaty chirps and sawing cicadas served as a reminder of just how much the surrounding foliage cloaked. It wasn't just the forest's dangers like poisonous dart frogs and wandering spiders, jaguar and bullet ants. *Or snakes.* I shuddered. *Hate snakes.*

The dark jungle concealed something far more threatening — Marco Alvarez, the piece of shit I was being paid to take out.

The Alvarez Cartel's death grip on the massive river basin made information scarce. What intel Rey had managed to ferret out was sketchy at best. Meaning I could be serving myself up as croc bait for nothing. Approaching the abandoned village Marco was reportedly holed up in from a distance was the only way I could ensure Rey's safety. Not that the rusted-out skiff provided much of a getaway if things went south, but with the slight head start, the seasoned guide could navigate the river better than anyone.

Knowing the Amazon so well was probably why the round-faced native was eyeing me gear up like I was out of my ever-loving mind. He wasn't far from the truth.

Speaking in a low, hushed tone, Rey chided, "You must have death wish, SEAL boy."

Quite the opposite.

While swimming one of the deadliest parts of the Amazon at night did seem a bit extra, scuba diving in a river teeming with black caiman, anaconda, and piranha wasn't all that different from the missions I'd performed on the reg for the Navy. And risking Rey's safety by inserting closer to the target wasn't an option.

I lifted my head from my task of securing my MK 12, sheathed with a waterproof, shoot-through bag, and flashed him a smirk. "Don't you trust me by now?"

"I know, I know, boss. You only take *calculated risk.*"

I laughed, enjoying how he threw my old words back at me. Twelve years ago, Rey's intimate knowledge of the jungles and connections to the indigenous tribes had enabled my SEAL team to successfully retrieve missionaries who'd been taken hostage by the Alvarez Cartel, then run by Marco's father.

"But this feels like a different kind of mission, my friend."

Very different. I'd never been a killer for hire before — not when I was a Navy SEAL, not as a black ops contractor for the CIA, and not while playing scarecrow for Omar Zaki at Beryl Enterprises. It was a distinction I'd always been able to hold myself higher than, until now. But I doubted Rey split hairs as fine as I did.

My humor fading, I used one hand to slip a fin on as I motioned with my other hand for him to spit out his concern.

Rey leaned forward, pleading with his eyes for me to be sensible. It was not the first time I'd been on the receiving end of that look. And if I survived, I doubted it would be the last.

"You have no *A-Team*...no magic skybird."

I grinned at his choice of words, campy and tribal just like he was. When I'd first worked with Rey, he'd never seen a drone, much less knew what one was capable of. I gathered he still hadn't had much experience with them.

"No, how you say, que or eff, no er...*backup*?"

"QRF, quick reaction force. You have a good memory." Acronyms aside, I understood what Rey was getting at. Without my team to help me, a high-tech drone to be my eyes in the sky, or anyone nearby to save my stupid ass, I was risking more than I ever had.

But that didn't make my plan any less calculated. "Believe me, Rey, I wish I had those resources too."

I needed something else more important, though. Taking out Marco put me one crucial step closer to that end. Unfortunately, killing the deadliest drug lord of the century was the easy part of my plan.

Rey reached out to set a trinket in my palm. "Perhaps this can offer you some protection."

I closed my fingers over the protective medal and slipped it in my med pack. As a good Catholic boy, I knew the talisman's significance, but in the dark I couldn't tell which patron saint it belonged to. Not that it mattered really, I'd take whosever help I could get.

Rey whispered a quick prayer and crossed himself. Dropping my chin in silent thanks, I settled my underwater night-vision goggles over my eyes before seating the mouthpiece of a rebreather between my lips. Then I went through the requisite pre-breathing sequence to prepare my body for pure oxygen.

"You're crazy, Cooper," Rey muttered.

I shot him a thumbs-up as I rolled back into the deadly river.

Not crazy. Desperate.

Swimming below the surface, I kept my movements calm and my finning fluid to avoid attracting predators. Clandestine approaches to target via water had been the bread and butter of my early days with the Teams, and my muscles stretched with the comfort of memory. Being underwater came naturally. More than that, operating in the field again kicked my endorphins up to a very happy high. Something I desperately needed after the past few months. Unfortunately the invigoration of pulling on my old work clothes didn't last more than seven hundred meters. The slightest change in pressure from being underwater caused translucent lightning bolts to squiggle in my periphery. *Shit.*

Diving after too many concussions was risky, but I hadn't expected an aural migraine from such shallow water. I wrenched my jaw to relieve the pressure. Nothing. Frustrated, I scrunched my eyes a few times. The images refused to clear. Sometimes clenching my eyelids tight for twenty seconds helped. I squeezed them and started counting.

One, two, three…

On seventeen, something thick as an arm brushed slickly across my cheek. *Snake?* I thrashed like I'd just taken a spider web to the face. Before my awkward motions caught a croc's attention, I swiftly swam forward, only to get hard punch cold-cocked in the throat. I jerked backward, choking out a panting gasp while trying to be mindful enough to not lose my mouthpiece. I moved off again. This time the asshole squeezed round my throat. I thrashed, grabbing for my knife as I went to hacking. With each slash, I feared my blade would slip off and cut through my own flesh.

Managing to get a solid cleave, I started sawing. As fast as my heart was racing and as eager as I was to be free of the slime-coated bastard, I had to be careful not to slit my own throat or my equipment. Finally I spun free.

I'd expected blood and body parts to chum the waters. But as I sucked in oxygen, I realized the giant constrictor I thought I'd killed had been nothing but a looping vine. I suppose that was the good news. A chopped-up anaconda would've attracted more predators than my no-holds-barred wrestling match already had to have. Still, it was way past time to get off the X.

The bad news was I'd managed to swirl up a storm of particles in the water, clouding it completely. Any referencing signal from the landscape had vanished. Foliage and downed logs could've come from above or below. With the rebreather there were no oxygen bubbles to rise to the surface and help me regain my bearings.

The spot behind my right ear pounded. Electric red sparks flashed in my periphery. My blood pressure spiked. My forehead tightened. My mouth tasted like it was full of sand, and I'd tasted a lot of sand in my life — from Coronado to Qatar. But this shit tasted just like Fallujah sand. *Fuck.* So not what I wanted the last thing I tasted to be.

If I was going to pass out and die, I wanted the taste of Aziza's plump lips on my tongue.

I spun up the memory of that beautiful pout of hers, the one she'd flash when she was irritated at me. And I *always* irritated her just so I could see it.

Six seconds into our virtual convo, I realized that pout of hers was flush with color and extremely shiny. Zee wasn't a makeup kind of woman, didn't have time. Or need, in my opinion. No, it wasn't makeup making those lips of hers look like she was trying to signal a rescue plane. They'd been swollen up and stained from having been kissed all night.

I wrenched my suddenly tight neck. No. Couldn't be. She didn't have time for that either.

Thank God.

Besides, any man with half a brain was too intimidated by her connection to OZ to make any sort of serious move. Which was fine by me. Neither of us needed the distraction.

Sixty seconds in, her top lip was legit looking like a duckbill and turning the color of strawberry pulp. "You okay, Presh?"

"*Yeah, fine. Why?*"

"*I think you've got something on your lip.*" I ran the tip of my tongue along my upper lip to show her where.

Her eyes widened. I had an impressive tongue, or so I'd been told.

"*You're looking a little flushed.*"

She tried to hide her mouth, all casual like, behind her hand. Those slender fingers of hers couldn't do a damn thing. Her lips were ballooning at an alarming rate.

"*Sure you're okay?*"

"*I'm fine.*" She ducked her head, but the shiny curtain of black hair she hid behind wasn't able to cover her typically even-toned, olive skin before it fired in a peach blush.

I couldn't help my smile. And I certainly couldn't help imagining bringing her whole body to blush like that.

"*Not a little peaked?*" I flicked my eyes down to my own heated reaction. "*I know I've been feeling peaked myself lately.*"

"*I...I...I gotta go!*"

I chuckled as she scrambled to cut our session off. In her haste the video didn't disconnect, and I caught the best view of her gorgeous round butt in short-shorts as she hustled from her bed to the bathroom. Despite losing sight of her, I could hear her frantically splashing water. My lips stretched in a grin as I eavesdropped on her grumbling, cursing, and wailing. "*Great, Zee. Try to attract a guy with lip plumper and end up having to jam an EpiPen in your thigh!*"

Attract a guy?

My neck stiffened enough to require muscle relaxers.

What guy!

"*Oh yeah, this looks real sexy...if you want to seduce Ronald McDonald! Or Pennywise. What kind of name is that for a clown anyway? Why is this shit not coming off?*"

Who cares about clowns, Zee! Tell me who this fucking guy is so I can kill him!

"Now the only thing Coop's going to notice is that you're a freak."

Me? I was the guy she wanted to seduce? Talk about a battering ram right in the feels. Certainly as shocking.

Did Zee really think I hadn't noticed her? The woman had had my full attention, complicated as it was, from day one.

Months later and about to drown from stupidity, I still didn't understand what an intelligent woman in her prime wanted with a beat-up old man like me anyway. Hell, my shredded body had been stuffed back together so many times the seams barely stayed sewn anymore.

But *if* this body could somehow be put back together just one more time...then *maybe* I could find a way to be worthy of her.

First I had to get out of this river alive.

Aziza

A chill crawled up my spine as I approached the war room's vault doors. When I'd first come to the island as a child, the underground bunker had been a crude, cruel prison. A fact I had a hard time forgetting, considering it could've easily become my own.

There was a good chance I would still find myself locked up or worse if anyone got close to the truth. And getting too close was exactly what had me waking up top Intelligence & Activity personnel for a virtual situation meeting with OZ.

I entered through the class-five security vault doors and flipped the heavy circuit breaker switch to bring the cavern to life. The other three sides of the war room were walled with coarsely chiseled volcanic stone, which kept it as cold and hard as the empire's king.

A thick marble slab conference table inlaid with emerald chips from Zaki's prized Brazilian mine filled the center. Surrounding the table were six high-backed chairs, the contours of which were more suited for luxury racecars. They were crafted in exquisitely supple, cream-colored Chanel leather and quilted in the brand's famed diamond pattern. Replacing the legendary linked double-C logo on each of the headrests were Omar Zaki's ever present initials in the requisite deep emerald green color. The pervasiveness of the OZ logo made for an efficient moniker as well as a constant reminder.

Whether one was on Marakata Cay or in any of the global office complexes, forgetting whose empire you lived and quite possibly died for was damn near impossible. The reclusive billionaire's presence filled every room, even the ones he'd never set foot in. The so-called war room was certainly no exception.

Wolfe stopped in the entry, appearing to debate which chair to take. Typically confident and decisive, he gave his ear an awkward scratch. Admittedly, I'd dropped the ball getting him fully integrated into his new role. The sucker punch of Coop's rejection had kept me from investing any energy into his substitute. I couldn't. Wolfe was a walking, talking reminder of what I wanted so badly, but would never have.

The memory of the night I'd asked Coop to move here returned—as it did nearly every day. I'd been begging for him to give me one definitive clue to how he really felt about me. Just one.

"What is it you want? Tell me."

"I want it all on the table." His voice was clear and certain, but his words were cryptic and coy. It was just like him to be ambiguous whenever I needed a straight answer.

"What *do you want on the table, Coop?"*

"Everything." *He seemed to study my reaction through the computer screen for a beat. Then he flashed his dimples as those sapphire blue eyes of his sparked. "Especially you, Presh."*

"Sharky!" *I exclaimed with a shocked laugh. I could never tell if his innuendoes were serious or not.*

His deep voice sanded down to a gritty whisper. "Yes, Princess?"

Princess? My momentary happiness tripped over the unusual nickname.

Presh or Precious were his go-to endearments for me and it was just like him to distract me by playing mind games. Going in circles was wrecking me. He wanted everything on the table? Well, there was only one way to do that.

"Come to the island."

I could still feel how my heart had wedged in my throat when I'd waited for Coop's response, how I'd choked on the poor, dead thing when Coop had finally told me Wolfe would be a better fit for me.

'Better fit'?

What did that even mean? What had anything he'd ever said to me meant?

Chapter Three

Aziza

"Princess," I muttered, still feeling as tripped-up, blindsided, and confused as I had over a month ago. I shook my head to clear it. Thinking, *believing,* that anything Coop had ever said to me had been more than playful teasing did me no favors.

I forced my attention back to the war room and caught Wolfe grinning at me. "What?"

His smirk deepened. "Did you just call me a princess?"

Dear Lord! I had to get my head in the game. Insanity had stolen my focus for too long.

"Pre-steps. Sorry, was thinking aloud. Go ahead and take a seat."

Wolfe shifted from one booted foot to the other. "Does OZ care which one?"

Ugh. Had to rip the Band-Aid off sometime. I motioned him toward the chair left of the table head.

I refused to dwell on the fact that Coop always 'sat' there when he'd join virtually. Or that I really needed him here for this. I'd hung onto the hope that he would realize he missed me, wanted to be with me, longer than he deserved. I didn't have the luxury of wallowing in self-pity anymore. Certainly not right now, and quite possibly never again if I was right. And the sinkhole my gut had collapsed into since learning about the distressed ship told me I was dead on.

I took my place across the table from Wolfe and pressed a button on my armrest. It lit up a wall of computer screens where various heads of the I&A branch were being conferenced in. Other screens produced an onslaught of sifting data or connected with live feeds from inside the rescue boat.

As Wolfe sat, his eyes volleyed between the screens and the open vault door like he was spectating a championship tennis match. He'd been privy to virtual war room meetings from the Dubai offices, but this time he wasn't leaning back in his chair, reviewing intel, and mentally preparing a confident plan of action like I'd witnessed many times from him in the U.A.E. But then, he'd never been about to come face to face with the great OZ. His apprehension was understandable.

So was mine. I hadn't had to deal with a potential threat of this magnitude before. If Coop were here he'd know what to say and do to calm me down... *But he isn't.*

Luckily the next best thing, the head of Island I&A, was. Vivian McQueen sauntered down the corridor toward the war room as if it were a runway in Milan. She had no doubt learned the walk from her mother, an elite supermodel who'd been discovered by Ralph Lauren when he'd been on safari in the Mara of Kenya.

Having grown up in England, thanks to her Guinean father who'd been a famed midfielder for Manchester United, Vivi had had everything going for her to be an even brighter star than both her parents, but she wanted to be a spy. Luckily, MI6 was too narrow-minded to use her for anything more than a honey trap.

I flicked my eyes over Vivi appreciatively. The bright pink of her pencil skirt and blazer, like a neon highlighter, contrasted boldly with her midnight-black skin. She looked gorgeous in everything she wore, even the things she hated, like the Obsidian Winds uniform.

As she approached, she shot me an elegantly long middle finger. I couldn't blame her. We both knew getting her goat was entirely why I hadn't replaced the required outfit.

"You look very bright, very Caribbean." *Pink.* "Festive."

As she slid into the seat next to me, she growled, "I look like bloody Botswana Barbie."

"I didn't think there were any Maasai in Botswana?" I asked.

"No self-respecting Maasai would be caught dead in *this*. Actually '*dis*... Tiday, mi ah Jamaican mon. Nuh worry, lass, everything irie!"

Her grousing attempt to morph her velvety British accent into a Jamaican patois had me laughing. The sound bursting from my lips surprised me as much as the feeling of Vivi's hand briefly covering mine. I met her eyes. From a glance or a distance they were bold and black and sometimes a bit too hard, but up close they were warmed by a hint of rich brown depth.

"Good to hear your laugh again, love," Vivi said under her breath.

I hadn't realized just how much I needed the levity of our rapport. Reminded me I still had friends despite having lost my best one. The fact she'd donned the ridiculously pink uniform without a fight meant someone still had my back.

I swallowed down my emotions as I scooted closer to the conference table. With a subtle press of a button, I closed the vault door, sealing us inside.

Wolfe shifted, keenly regarding the empty seat at the head of the table. "Zaki not coming?"

"Don't you know, love? Zaki's already here," Vivi said with a wink.

But Wolfe didn't know. Most people weren't privy to the full extent of Zaki's reclusiveness, not even some of his longtime employees. I ran my palms along the armrests, then pushed out a steadying breath as my fingers found the controls to initiate his entrance.

Wolfe turned toward the head of the table where Zaki appeared. Though the chair at the table's head was kept free, he always stood, or rather floated a foot from the ground, appearing just a smidge larger than life.

"Oh." Wolfe pushed out a low huff. "From Dubai he looked real and—"

Before he could expand on how Zaki looked shorter than he'd expected, I smiled tightly and reminded him quietly, "He is real and he *can* hear you."

"Shit." Wolfe's muscular frame seemingly shrank five sizes as he sat deeper into the chair. He kept his stare on Zaki, who wore the traditional Arabic attire of a white kandura and a head scarf, called a keffiyeh, which was kept in place with an agal. His keen eyes, like two black holes, seemed to take in everything and nothing at the same time.

Holographic or not, Zaki's arrival never ceased to stir a whirlwind of emotions, good and bad, inside of me. I'd trained myself not to let any of them show.

"Welcome, sir. As you're aware, we've initiated Obsidian Protocol. Focusing on the positive, the rescue team succeeded in retrieving all of the passengers. There was no loss of life, which is obviously the most important thing. No deaths also means we will be able to downplay the rescue and avoid media attention. Nor should there be any investigations."

I glanced at the live feed of Colton's rescue boat, catching the distressed wreckage burning in the background before it exploded in a giant fireball. Shock, fear, and relief to be alive played out on the young survivors' faces. I turned back to OZ. "As you can see, our new guests are en route. They will be evaluated for any medical needs and given five-star care. Vivi's team is prepping for their arrival. Pilot is on standby to fly them to Nassau as soon as it's appropriate. Naturally, I&A is running thorough backgrounds and biometrics."

My fingertips twitched, knowing what Zaki's response would be.

"Why were they here?"

"We're working on that, sir," Gracelyn "Gray" Bauer, I&A's crackerjack cyberstalker, piped up from her screen on the wall.

Even at this hour of night, the southern belle's coppery chestnut hair had curled-for-church ends and her monogrammed, chambray blue oxford PJs were wrinkle-free. I'd bet money she was already sipping a tanker of sweet tea, knowing this would be an all-nighter.

"So far, I can tell you the boat belongs to a charter company in Nassau which specializes in extreme diving adventures," Gray continued. "They also have a solid history of discovering shipwrecks and bringing up artifacts."

"Colton's already reported his initial site exploration," Wolfe jumped in to say. "There was diving equipment and a side scan sonar on board. He was able to retrieve computer equipment."

"Get it to me, we'll have the techs get on that ASAP," Scott Hayes, Director of I&A, spoke up from his home base in Washington D.C. From the way he was wedged up close to the table, I was pretty sure he was wearing a button-down and tie on top and boxers below.

"Thanks, Hayes, I'll go ahead and handle it on this end," I volunteered, albeit not altruistically. I wanted a crack at the data before anyone else could see what, if anything, the sonar had picked up.

"Thank you, Zee," Scott said. "We'll be getting more information once the storm passes Nassau, but it's possible they'd simply been blown off course via strong current systems."

"I don't believe in coincidences," Zaki reprimanded.

I didn't either, not given the distressed ship's precise coordinates. Plus a sonar meant they were looking for something very specific. It could've been schools of fish, could've been shipwrecks, could be something more. But lightning wasn't prone to striking twice in the same spot.

"Of course, sir," Hayes quickly amended. "We aren't ruling out any options. And, sir, since we have you, I wanted to alert you to the presence of a possible new invisible working the Amazon region. Not sure yet if this is a narco or human trafficker exactly."

I grunted. "Just when I think I know all the spiders, along comes a new one."

Flamboyant drug barons and infamous kingpins were a thing of the past. New generations of narcos operated in the shadows and off most everyone's radar. Hence the invisibles moniker. They were clever masterminds of business and technology. Even the US government had given them the distinction of DTOs, Drug Trafficking Organizations, as a testament to the stability of their business structure. Their empires were diversified and imbedded with legitimate investments, and they had power and profits that made most Fortune 500 corporations look like lemonade stands.

"Alvarez will take care of them," Wolfe said, his usual confidence settling back in. "Nice thing about trash is it likes to take itself out."

"Someone's taking out the trash, but it's not Marco Alvarez."

"Not Marco?" I asked. With the emerald mine in Brazil, Beryl had been forced to co-exist alongside of the Alvarez Cartel. We didn't work *with* Marco, but we didn't work *against* him either. As long as we stayed out of each other's way, we had a tenuous version of peace. But our concord looked to be coming to an end, and not because of Marco.

Hayes nodded and continued, "Rumint coming in suggests that in the past three days, several of *Marco's* top men were eliminated by a highly specialized *sicario*."

"Shit," Wolfe muttered, echoing my own thoughts.

Rumint. How much was rumor and how much was actual intel was always a concern. But Scott Hayes rarely, if ever, brought intel to Zaki that wasn't actionable. He likely had dangled the trinket of information as a way to soften the blow of Zaki's earlier reprimand, but still, Hayes had to believe a *sicario* single-handedly dismantling Alvarez's cartel had some credibility. My mind could scarcely wrap around how, though. Marco's top men, his cousins, ran a tight ship and were excessively brutal. For them to fall like dominos? Very few people had the skill *and* the balls to pull something like that off so quickly.

A devil I didn't know was never a good thing.

"Who's the *sicario*?"

"Good question, Zee," Hayes said. "Hitman's currently ghost status too."

Ghost. The only one I knew of worked for us and he was on vacation...*in Brazil*.

The room blurred as my mind attempted to process what my heart couldn't. Had Coop gone rogue? Was he working for this new entity? Had he turned? *On me?*

Sensing everyone's eyes focused my direction, I schooled my expression. Afraid the quiver in my heart would come out in my voice, I looked pointedly at Zaki. Below the table, my fingers twitched.

"We don't trade in invisible. We trade in intelligence." OZ's terse words drew the rest of the room's attention away from me. "Please ensure anything — actionable or not — finds its way to Aziza before anyone else. Dismissed."

And with that, OZ's virtual presence vanished.

I forced my focus to what I had control of. "Vivi, the guests will be arriving shortly."

"I'm on it, love." She uncrossed her long legs and gracefully stood, adjusting the vile uniform. Before she left, she pinned me with her eyes. They were everything Vivi herself was — elegant, cool, and dangerous from a distance, but up close, all heart.

In that regard, she reminded me of Coop. Most people dismissed him as brash and cold, as well. I knew better. *At least I'd thought I had.*

Her slender fingers buttoned the bright pink blazer and straightened the silver name tag that read Vivian McQueen, Director Hotel Operations, Obsidian Winds

Resort. "But, darling, this *will* be the last time I don this hideous getup."

"Just think how smashing it will go with the new pair of Kenkazi earrings I'm going to get you." I smiled, knowing she couldn't resist her current favorite luxury designer.

"Best add a matching pendant." The ping of her high heels echoed, signaling the end of negotiations.

Wolfe stood, planting his palms on the table as he leaned forward. "Now might be a good time to fill me in on Obsidian Protocol."

Hard as it was, the time had come for me to start treating Wolfe like he was here to stay. Especially if Coop really was working for someone else.

"It's a proactive measure only implemented on Marakata and only for very specific circumstances, like this, when visitors arrive unexpectedly. In other words, unvetted. Our new guests will be told they're being taken in by a resort called the Obsidian Winds. The staff caring for them wear the bright pink uniforms and none of OZ's logos appear anywhere. The guests won't be required to sign NDAs and they won't have access to any part of the island other than the bungalow where they will be sequestered. Any communication devices will be jammed or intercepted and they will be flown out at night so no identifying parts of the island can be seen. For all intents and purposes, they will have never been on OZ's island."

"So Colt...?"

"Scuttled their boat. Made it look natural — storm damage, gas leak explosion. Left no reason for them to return, nothing to recover or investigate." I paused, watching Wolfe process the information, seeing the concern weighting heavily in his pale eyes. "Just say it."

"There's a big difference between being proactive and being paranoid."

Perhaps informing him about the DNA samples, which would be procured during the guests' medical evaluations, could wait. Life on Marakata always required a bit of an adjustment, which was why everything was on a need-to-know basis.

"Omar Zaki is a very private man. This is his home. The heart of our organization. Our resources are invaluable and our clientele are confidential. Beryl Enterprises, our entire business, is *nothing* if the emerald island, the *crown jewel* of our organization, can so easily be breached."

Wolfe nodded and stood, but hovered in the doorway like he had more to say. Career operators typically didn't have qualms about our more invasive measures, like detaining and deceiving possible innocents or even with blowing up a boat or two.

Maybe Wolfe wasn't as good a fit for the island as Coop had thought. Best to find it out now, before he learned anything more. "Is this going to be a problem for you?"

"No," he replied absently. He peered down the hall before returning his attention to me. "Sorry, I was just stalling until I was sure we were alone."

"We're as alone as we're going to get," I said, knowing Vivi was long gone and I'd disconnected the room from I&A.

Wolfe approached me until he stood close, with legs a bit spread as he crossed his arms over his chest. Keeping his voice low, he said, "Coop's in the Amazon and I don't believe in coincidences either."

Okay, maybe he fit *too* well. But that didn't mean he needed to know everything I was thinking yet.

To be a convincing liar wasn't so much about concealing the truth, but crafting a new reality. "You were right about there being a scoop."

"Let me guess, Coop's there looking into it for you. Should've known you both would be on top of it already."

It always helped if your subject crafted the reality they wanted to believe for you. "Please keep this under wraps."

"Of course."

I waited for Wolfe to clear out before elbowing the table and pressing my face into my palms. If three of Marco's men had died by Coop's hand, the Alvarez Cartel would most certainly draw a bullseye on Beryl Enterprises.

What have you done to me, Michael? To us?

Chapter Four

Coop

> *Get control.*
> *Focus forward.*
> *Work the problem.*

Like a pilot in zero visibility, I had to rely solely on my instruments, namely the depth gage and GPS. Maneuvering blindly, I got back in line with my intended coordinates. Then I worked to stabilize my breathing.

I studied the dive computer. My PO2 levels were significantly higher than expected, given the short, shallow dive. While it wasn't exactly a mission concern, it still served as a reminder that I wasn't in as good of shape as I let on — a crisis which would have to wait.

Thankfully the part of my brain that sharpened my focus for fight or flight was unaffected by whatever chaotic hell was brewing in my skull.

Time to fight.

My planned insertion point on the bank promised greater danger than the river. I was an easy strike on the shoreline for a croc and odds were strong I'd attracted at least the attention of a couple by now. Then there was Marco and his remaining goon squad. Seeing as how I'd eliminated three of the highest-ranking members of Alvarez's organization, it would be naïve to think he wouldn't be prepared.

The list of snipers capable of taking out his men in the fashion I had was a short one. He also had it out for me — the man who'd killed his father. Another reason I'd opted to insert from a safe distance.

After one last hit off my rebreather, I surged out of the water like the Creature from the Black Lagoon. Head on swivel and senses fully heightened, I kept my rifle positioned to take out anything that came between me and my goal. Surveying the jungle, I mentally calculated and cataloged various routes and paths, all the while scanning for potential traps like trip lines and sniper hides.

The dense air smelled of earth, leaf decay, and snake musk. *Fuckin' hate sn —* A scream ripped through the canopy, launching my heart through my chest. Whether the howler monkey had alerted his troop to my presence or to something hunting me, I couldn't let it put me on tilt.

I centered my attention downrange. The shoreline mud sucked at my boots, as I moved off. But I couldn't shake the feeling of something stalking me from the river. I held up, listening for any atmospheric shift at my six.

Within milliseconds of hearing the change in the water's flow, I spun and squeezed off a round. With suppression, the singular shot hitting the water sounded like a heavy drop of rain. *Ploop!* The croc who'd had me on his dinner menu heeded my generous warning, splashing and churning the shoreline water as he swished away. Turning back to my own prey, I strode into the heart of the jungle, becoming one with its familiar darkness.

Thick greenery slowed my progress, but after two clicks in, I started picking up wafts of burning trash. To my right I noticed a worn path a little wider than an animal trail. As much as my legs would've preferred a smoother track to picking through the roots and rock, my plan wasn't to walk right into Alvarez's camp. I was one man who could be up against at least five and up to fifteen narcos. I needed to find some higher ground to get some recon in.

Through the heavy foliage I caught sight of some huts and a large structure sided with scrap metal. Just beyond that would've been a small tributary of the river. I knew it would be guarded by sentinels, which was why I hadn't inserted there. But I maneuvered with it always in my periphery. If Alvarez was going to escape, that was where he'd squirt out.

Sighting a young male making rounds, I held position. He had an AK hanging off his shoulder, but was more concerned with his phone. After walking past me, he came to a halt barely a foot from my hide. With one hand he kept texting or whatever. With the other he undid his jeans, whipped his dick out, and started relieving himself. He was so close I could pick out nuances in his urine. Despite my cover and camouflaged face paint, I was certain he could have seen me if his pupils hadn't been contracted tight from the bright phone screen. I wrapped my hand around the handle of my KA-BAR knife, but willed him to turn away. I didn't want to have to use it.

Shit. I doubted the kid even had fuzz on his balls.

I'd had to kill young men, boys really, just like him in Iraq and Afghanistan. Kids who'd been strapped down with explosives meant to blow up US troops. But this wasn't war and mine was the only life in immediate danger. I also wasn't a mile away on some rooftop looking through my scope. I was heartbeat to heartbeat and he was just a dumbass mixed up with the wrong people.

The boy slipped the phone into his back pocket as he threw his head back and concentrated on squeezing out a few more squirts of piss. He grunted, looked down, and gave his dick a couple of shakes. His pupils would be expanding now, adjusting to the darkness. Again, I prayed he wouldn't lift his gaze.

"*Entra. Entra,*" a comm-check came through over his radio.

Turn around and answer. Please don't make me do this.
"*Entra,* Miguel!"

Fuck. We even have the same name.

The boy zipped up, then grappled for the radio hanging off his belt. I watched the whites of his eyes grow as he stared into the four monoculars of my panoramic NVG's. *Shit.*

His hand shook as he dropped the radio and sloppily went for the AK. I slammed my grip down on his wrist while I spun his body so his back was against me. Clasping a gloved hand over his mouth, I held my knife to his carotid artery. He tried to scream against my palm.

"*Callate, Miguel,*" I hissed in Spanish since my Portuguese was shit. "*Tranquillo.*"

I backed us deeper into the foliage as the radio squawked again.

"Entra. Entra, babaca!"

It would've been much safer to have slit Miguel's throat. Smarter, even. But thankfully not necessary. After relieving him of his AK, I left him in a warm embrace with the nearest tree thanks to a set of zip-tie handcuffs. After shoving his T-shirt in his mouth, I grabbed the dropped radio and headed back into the jungle.

Confident Miguel would relay which direction I'd gone, I doubled back before changing directions. Then I tried to find a suitable tree to climb, avoiding kapoks as they were covered in thorny spikes. The smoother trees all had extremely long trunks before branching into their canopies. Even if I wasn't too tired for a hundred-foot shimmy, I was way too old for a hundred-foot drop.

Over Miguel's radio, I heard Alvarez's men put the camp on blast. I turned the volume as low as possible then wrapped the column-like trunk of a suitable tree with a doubled-up rope from my kit. Clamping the inside edges of my boots so my big toes almost touched, I scurried up.

I'd honed the skill after spending a couple summers in Oregon with my uncle, who was a regular pole climber at the Lumberjack World Championships. Admittedly it had been a lot easier at thirteen, when I'd had barely any muscle tone to weigh me down and a hell of a lot more energy. I was still heaving in air as I laid out on a bough thick enough to hold my weight. I positioned myself belly down with legs flopped to each side like a jungle cat taking a nap. Leveling my rifle, I used the limb to help stabilize it, then bumped my NVGs up, trading them for my rifle scope.

The tree served as a comfortable sniper hide except for two factors. One, my nuts were crushed. Two, after I took Marco out, I had no idea how I was going to get my old ass down without attracting his men.

I scoped the camp, hoping to surprise Alvarez with a nice quick head shot. But he wasn't about to make it easy for me. In fact, he had a few surprises. The first RPG came wheezing through the open camp, landing right where I'd doubled back from. *Thank you, Miguel.*

I held tight as the concussive thunder shook the tree. Debris rained down through the cloud of smoky haze. Not exactly the kind of weather pattern the rainforest was known for.

Another RPG launched, this time nearly taking out the speedboat waiting at the dock. I would've laughed, but compromising my cover and falling to my death didn't sound all that appealing.

I scoped the village, waiting for Marco to squirt out toward the river during the distraction. But the first explosion still had my head ringing. Now the aural migraines were back and I couldn't manage to get in focus.

I tried changing my visual angle a bit by scoping along the forest floor. Alvarez's men were picking their way through the maze of tree roots toward me. I could probably knock off three or four of them before the virgin rocket launcher could clue in on precisely where to lob his load. But there was only one man I'd come to take out—Marco.

It was imperative I finished the job without additional bloodshed on my hands.

Hearing another grenade launch, I locked my legs at the ankles and held tight. I didn't think I'd actually take a hit, but even a blind squirrel occasionally got a nut. This one landed so far from my location the leaves barely rustled.

Speaking of nuts, I shifted position. Not much relief, but wasn't like my future was destined to include having children.

As the men below got closer, I spotted Marco making his move. *Shit.* My one chance at getting the guy came with losing my cover. I lined up my shot. Just as I was preparing to exhale and squeeze, two things happened simultaneously — the aural migraine completely knocked out my vision and an RPG launched right for me.

Chapter Five

Aziza

Forget sleep. The remaining few hours of the night I spent with my gut twisted, my heart punched, and my mind positively blown.

In my private wing, my office had four auxiliary computer screens feeding live video capture from the surveillance cameras in the Obsidian Winds bungalow. I trusted Gray's team would be scrutinizing them, so I dedicated my main two monitors to drilling down into Coop's recent endeavors. It was a toss-up which situation was more disastrous for Beryl Enterprises or more dangerous for me personally, but my mind fixated on the one I couldn't understand.

I'd never thought Coop would hurt me. *Ever.*

I questioned everything between us over the past few years. What had I been to him? Certainly not a friend. Was I a mark? Some kind of long con he'd been running?

Whatever I'd been, I felt like the biggest sucker in the world. It wasn't even the highly confidential intel we'd exchanged or that I'd entrusted him to strategize on critically sensitive dealings for Beryl. Those things may have branded me naïve, but it was the intimate, personal conversations we'd had which had given him the power to crush me.

I'd trusted him because he'd shared with me too. I knew about all his failed marriages, of which there were a few. All the nightmares he'd gone through, of which there were too many to count. All of his successes and all his regrets.

He'd trusted me with everything. Why had I not known this side of him?

Obviously he didn't share *everything.*

Thankfully, I hadn't trusted him with everything, either. But, oh, how close I'd come to laying it *all* out on that table he'd claimed to want to take me on. *Too close.* Stupid me thought he'd wanted my heart, at the very least my body, but turned out he didn't want me at all.

Or if he did, it was to fuck me in a completely different way.

His going rogue, possibly even turning on me, had chilled my battered heart to the point of rib-crushing, physical pain. I might've been a lovestruck fool, but like hell was I going to let him string me along and leave me in the dust when he was done. Whatever he was up to, I was bound and determined to find out.

I&A hadn't identified him as the hitman in the Amazon, and I certainly wasn't about to enlighten them. *Yet.* I'd have to soon. Beryl Enterprises had to be prepared for Alvarez's retribution. But for now, I was too raw.

Coop's activities felt entirely too private to share. How could his actions not be personal? The man I'd loved and trusted as my *muharib*—my warrior—had basically declared war on everything I'd so desperately needed to protect.

Well, *I* would protect myself now, even from him.

I'd never accessed Coop's accounts before. Not even when I'd stupidly feared he'd been hurt or worse. Despite my unique livelihood, I had a great respect for both freedom and privacy. It was only after he hadn't shown up at his former teammate's funeral that I'd even started running biometrics to locate him. It'd been *so* out of the ordinary for Coop. Something had to be really wrong.

Well, gone were the days of my compassion and consideration where Michael Cooper was concerned. Now that the emerald-colored glasses were off, so were the gloves. I had zero qualms about using every hacking, cracking, and tracking trick in my bag.

Since I&A was confident the hits had been a hired job, there had to be a money trail. I began by running financial forensics on all his accounts. Coop was a workaholic and not a spender. Everything he needed, Beryl Enterprises provided, including a very healthy salary. He should've been sitting on millions with no need for a side-gig. So I was prepared to find one of two things—a flush account, if I'd completely overreacted, or an empty account, if he'd turned on me.

Unfortunately, for both of us, his accounts came back with just a few thousand dollars.

Drilling down deeper, I fully expected to find his money had been siphoned out right before he'd gone off grid. Which it had, but my gut started cramping when I realized the transaction amounted to less than a year's salary. This wasn't some rash decision he'd made, running from his feelings for me. No. Coop had been planning this getaway for a while.

Numbly, I stared at the long string of consistent withdrawals that went all the way back to when he'd first started at Beryl. Without delay, I traced every single one. I expected to find it had all been pulled out as cash. My gut had been wrong this time.

Each year the bulk of Coop's income could be traced to a laundry list of fallen SEALs' family funds as well as a couple of veteran's organizations and even a rehoming program for retired military K9s. Each donation was legit, and over the years had accumulated into a few million. Not only was his money all accounted for, but the contributions had been made 'in memory of' or anonymously.

I sat back in my chair more confused than ever. He took credit for none of them. Nor did a single donation show up on his taxes for the deserved deduction.

Here I'd been so quick to vilify him. How could someone who gave so much to so many, and for zero recognition, be capable of double-crossing me?

At six a.m. sharp, I gave up the ghost. Literally.

After responding to Zaki's various correspondence, I reviewed and handled any new intel on all of the other hundred balls Beryl Enterprises had in the air. Then I headed downstairs and stood for an iris scan to gain entry into OZ's private corridor. My eyes were so bleary I was shocked the scan greenlighted.

Outside the entrance to Zaki's suite, a breakfast cart waited to be cleared away by Marguerite. OZ may've been worried about other people's germs, but I wasn't worried about his. I poured a cup of coffee from the carafe, giving myself a much-needed shot of wakey-

wakey. Then I lifted the sterling warming lid and snagged a corner of buttered toast with one hand and gathered up the plate, still heaped with food, with my other.

As I took a bite, I swore somehow the butter OZ got was better than any other on the island. Perks of being the king.

Heading toward OZ's private entrance to the zoological conservatory, I paused for another retinal scan, and entered. Like other eccentric billionaires from the Arabian Peninsula, Zaki had a thing for exotic animals, notably big cats. Golden tigers, white lions, leopards, and cheetahs, as well as many other species like elephant, zebra, and giraffes, and even critically endangered ones like rhino rounded out his collection.

Balancing the breakfast plate, I put in my code on the lock for El Hambre's cage. The golden tiger's low chuffle sounded like a garbled purr or happy growl as his nearly five-hundred-pound body curled around me. He rubbed his cheek against my leg, scenting me.

"Who's my hungry boy?" I murmured as I set the plate down and pulled off the silver covering to reveal an untouched, rare sixteen ounce ribeye and four fried eggs. I picked up the remaining corner of toast and passed the rest over to El Hambre.

At the sounds of the head veterinarian and zookeeper preparing their breakfasts on the front side of the observatory, the other big cats started pacing and chuffing, letting their impatience show. The metallic scrape of passthrough doors opening sounded as each cat got fed along the row. El Hambre's tongue made one last swath across the cleaned china plate before trotting toward his own breakfast, with his primordial pouch swinging.

"Stop spoiling that cat, Zee! He's fat!" Dr. Miller Walsh called from the other side of the passthrough where he'd slid in El Hambre's actual breakfast.

"OZ orders it for him. I don't make the rules!" I hollered back. Then before I forgot, I added, "No swimming today. Obsidian Protocol."

"Roger that."

I picked up the empty plate and headed back down the corridor, ultimately disposing of it on OZ's service cart.

I swung through the kitchen and picked up a fruit smoothie before heading out to the stables. Working closely with the Arabian and Akhal-Teke horses Zaki bred had always been therapeutic for me. Considering last night's events, therapy was desperately needed. But after a few short hours, I'd been kicked and had rope burns on both hands. Not to mention, I'd been thrown three times from as many horses.

With my back flat against the arena sand, I cursed and hollered. But the beast responsible for this particular ejection, a pure white Arabian stallion named Altabashir, was staring down at me with his dark globe eyes. The spectacular stallion's nostrils puffed out wide as he blew warm breath over my face. Was Bash worried about me? Sorry for pitching me through the air? *Doubtful.* His eyes told me I should've known better.

His pink tongue jutted out as he lapped at my cheek like a fricken' golden retriever. "Ack, *Mushaeghib!*"

My-sharky. Ha. Another one. Obviously I had a type.

Dr. Walsh strode past as I dusted my butt off. With a self-deprecating grimace, I waved. Miller was easy to dismiss as a pretty face. He looked more like a movie star than one of the world's leading veterinarians.

Billed as the James Brown for endangered animals, he'd once been featured in a documentary for his magical ability to seduce hard-to-breed, near-extinct species to get their groove on and conceive in captivity.

Miller looked like an ad for cologne as he propped his foot on the fence rail while he waited for me to lead Bash to the arena gate. Though 'led' was entirely the wrong word. The Arab stallion danced around me, never seeming to have more than two hooves touch the ground at any one time. I might as well have been flying a beautiful kite in a tropical storm. The tether, while fragile, took all my strength to keep hold of. Reminded me of my connection to another stud I knew. I shook my head.

Yep, I definitely have a type.

Miller maneuvered to open the gate for us and asked, "What's going on?"

The stallion skittered around like the gate was hot-wired. "With Bash? He's just spooking at ghosts." *Ghosts…of course.*

"No, with *you*. He's sensing your mood. He knows you're wary of him. How can he trust you when you don't have faith in him?"

I had to remind myself he was talking about the horse. It made sense though. Horses were incredibly perceptive and intuitive, especially the highbred ones we raised. I rolled my shoulders, trying to work the tension out of them.

"Just stressed. Zaki's not happy about unexpected guests," I hedged as Miller fell in step with us.

"*Obsidian Protocol*. Right. You carry too much, Zee." Miller gave my shoulder a squeeze and a friendly pat before lengthening his stride. "If you get a chance, swing back by the conservatory. I've got some good news for you."

"You're the only one who ever does! Can you tell me now? I could use some good news and today's going to be a long one. I'm already running late to meet Vivi for a lunch brief on the unexpected arrivals."

"Long story short, Ivory is not only doing great, but the additional supplements worked."

"What?" A month ago we'd almost put the rare white tigress down. Her liver enzymes had been extremely elevated and hadn't seemed to be improving. I feared she'd just go downhill from there and couldn't bear to see her go through the pain of acute liver failure. The only niggling thing was, other than having a bit of a bellyache, Ivory hadn't even started showing the signs of liver damage that her off-the-charts numbers warranted. Miller had suggested we wait, treat her current issue, and if other symptoms showed up we'd assess her quality of life then. "*I treat the animal, not the numbers,*" Miller had advised.

"So her bloodwork?"

His toothpaste-ad smile broadened. "Came back great, better than I'd hoped."

Squealing, I threw my arms around Miller's neck, spooking Bash. The stallion let out a full-bodied nicker while dancing around me. "Sorry. Sorry. Whoa, boy."

"Looks like you have your hands full." Miller laughed as I detached myself from him to tend to Bash. "I'll keep you posted."

"Thank you so much!"

Miller gave a wave as he headed farther down the barn's aisle to do checks on the pregnant mares. I rinsed Bash off in the wash stall and returned him to his paddock. Then I headed out to my green 1975 Bronco to keep my lunch meeting with Vivi.

With the top removed on the vintage SUV, the breeze whipped at my hair. Hopefully it improved upon the mushed hat shape my riding helmet had given it. I pulled out of the stable lot onto the road traversing the high ridge of Marakata, which ran from OZ's estate to my favorite casual dining restaurant on the island, The Lizard & the Lime. The pass had expansive views of the ocean as well as the calm bay created by the island's curled shape.

I drew in a deep breath. The air was so crisp and fresh from the storm, it was reviving. Which was good, because the work never stopped, and before I got to the restaurant my phone was ringing.

I listened as Gray gave me the details she'd been able to investigate as of this morning. Sounded like the guests were going to clear security and be able to go home. But I wasn't about to let my guard down, not until we knew more about the company who'd sent them.

"Oh, before I let you go—Hayes was asking if you'd had a chance to check the sonar feed."

"Not yet."

"He offered to take it off your hands since you've got a lot on your plate already."

I already knew this because he'd sent Zaki a private message stating the same.

"I'll be fine. Besides, it's not much of a priority for OZ since the guests checked out as legit," I lied. Truth was, it was no longer a priority for I&A to know what the sonar had captured, but it absolutely was one for Zaki.

Chapter Six

Aziza

The Lizard & the Lime was perched atop a cliff, affording it amazing vista views. On a beautiful day like today, Vivi and I would be dining on the balcony that hung right off the edge, seemingly floating over the ocean.

As I headed into the restaurant, Vivi was pulling into a parking space with the pink golf cart she'd driven. It was the only vehicle on the island that wasn't painted in some shade of green and made her look even more Barbie-ish. She caught my laugh and flipped me the requisite bird.

As I approached the table, it was her turn to chuckle as she informed me I still had half the arena dirt smeared on my cheek and in my hair.

"We make quite the pair." I settled in across the table from her while attempting to look more presentable.

"Yes, love. Just a couple of lassies living the dream, we are."

"At least we are living *in* one," I conceded as I took a moment to absorb the beauty of the vast ocean and feel the sun's kiss.

"We don't even need the emerald-colored glasses, today," she teased, referring to our inside joke about life in OZ's emerald empire not always being the paradise it appeared. In fact, the view from the dark side of the rainbow was very different from the idyllic one before our eyes.

Willa, a Caribbean native and the restaurant's curator, made her way to our tableside and chatted a bit before taking our orders. Then, getting down to business, I asked Vivi, "How are things going at The Winds?"

"Just peachy, Zee."

"Don't you mean *pinky*?"

She arched a perfected brow at me. "Don't you have some online shopping to do? Because my ring size is six."

"You really think I've forgotten your size already?"

Vivi broke into a laugh. "You do seem to owe me more and more these days."

"Oh, just wait. *This* day is far from being over," I muttered. I flexed my shoulders and stretched my neck.

"Sorry, love. I know you pulled an all-nighter too." Vivi caught the bartender's eyes, which wasn't difficult, seeing as how Alex had been ogling her since we'd gotten here. I watched curiously as she used sign language to order us two Outbreak Energy drinks.

"I see you've learned more than just the bad words in ASL. Are you and Alex...?"

"We're friendly," she was quick to say. But the sparkle in her eyes told another story, as did Alex's fingers stroking against hers when he hustled over to set her drink down.

I glanced away, partly to give her privacy and partly because of the jealous pang in my heart. I wanted the sweet exchanges, the learning of another person's language, the nights tangled up in each other's bodies... I coughed before my thoughts went the way they had last night.

Was that really just last night? Seemed like a week ago.

As Alex walked away, we both signed thank you, but Vivi's looked more like blowing a kiss than mine did.

Vivi caught my grin. "He's a great communicator."

"He can't hear or speak."

"He doesn't need to." Vivi closed her eyes and made a happy humming sound. "Everything he needs to tell me he can do with his hands, and he's *very* good with his hands."

"Obviously." I'd never seen Vivi so blissful. It made my heart happy.

"And it's so peaceful and quiet."

"My best spy wants peace and quiet? There's no hope for me now." I laughed out of pure exhaustion.

Vivi tilted her head with a smile. "No, you never bring me peace nor quiet, but I still love you, darling. And I adore this job, I do, but we all need some decompression time. Even you."

Avoiding the subject of my needing a break, I asked, "Did I tell you I just got a request from Gillikin Records? DV8 wants to bring a full entourage to the island to shoot his next video."

"Please tell me it's the collab with Lil' BayBay. You know I love me some BayBay!"

At my nod, Vivi did a little chair dance version of the San Francisco bay area rap sensation's most popular moves. "Think he'll let me be in the video?"

"Not if you do *that* in your audition," I said, choking on a laugh. Vivi was good at a lot of things, but dancing was not one of them. "Tell you what, I'll let you arrange all the I&A on it."

"Let me? Isn't that already my job?"

"I'll send over the details." I took a long swig of the energy drink. Then I asked, "How are our guests this morning?"

"If by guests, you mean immature, vapid soul-sellers? They're pretty shaken up, but harmless."

On my drive to the restaurant, Gray had informed me they were all young, hard-bodied twenty-somethings who'd signed up for an adventure competition slash reality dating show called *The Love Triangle*. The premise of which tasked pansexual relationship seekers with solving the mysteries of the Bermuda Triangle.

Basically they were just a bunch of kids excited for a once-in-a-lifetime experience. While they were at it, they could grab a little attention, a bit of fame, and maybe love, but mostly social media followers. Which meant each of them had an extensive online presence. In other words, they were not invisibles. Not even close.

"Don't worry, Viv, they'll be out of here at nightfall. All their backgrounds checked out, but Gray's still digging through umbrella companies to determine if the production company's legit."

Or more accurately, finding proof that it wasn't legit and, more importantly, who was behind it.

I smiled and thanked Willa as she brought out our plates. She could tell we were talking business, as we often did, and didn't linger. As I took my first bite of romaine-wrapped Caribbean jerk chicken salad, I let my gaze travel across the cerulean blues of the ocean. The surface gave nothing away about what lay beneath. Never did.

Before taking another bite, I asked, "Did they tell you specifically what secret they were tasked with discovering?"

Vivi swallowed a bite of her crab risotto. "Said it was supposed to be a dive to a shipwreck. Some yacht that disappeared en route to Escobar's private island. They were simply to explore the wreck and get some video footage to analyze."

There *was* a shipwreck in those coordinates, but it hadn't been in route to Norman's Cay, the island that was once instrumental to the Medellin Cartel. No, the ship forty-five meters below the surface of the Atlantic had gone down on its way to Marakata Cay over twenty years ago. I knew, because I had been on it.

The depth wasn't suitable for recreational divers, even skilled ones, as it was what was considered a deep dive. In addition, the waters protecting it were heavily inhabited with sharks. Plus, the wreckage was highly unstable. It could shift or collapse with no warning. Legitimate production companies would never risk the lives of contestants so blatantly. "Are they even SCUBA qualified? Experienced with diving on wrecks?"

"As I understand it, they were given a crash course. Two had certifications, but admitted a dive like this would be beyond their limits and were relieved when they didn't end up going down."

"Why on earth would they agree to go out with a storm approaching?"

"Honestly, I don't think they had any idea what they'd gotten themselves into. All they cared about was beefing up their social media presences and parlaying the experience into a quasi-career. Production was on a tight schedule and pressured them to get at least one dive in. They assured the kids they'd be back on solid land before the storm affected them, but then it changed course and quickly became a dangerous situation. A helicopter was sent to retrieve everyone, but the crew took the first ride back. The storm intensified, preventing the helo from returning. Via radio, they were told they'd have to ride it out and not to worry. That as soon as the weather cleared, the crew would come back. That was the last communication they received."

My stomach dropped. Those kids had been left to die. That had been the 'production company's' plan all along—use the kids to get intel on the wreck without risking their own lives then dispose of them. And for what?

Money? Treasure? *More?*

I quickly sent Gray a message to arrange for the kids to sit with a sketch artist if the ship's crew hadn't been located yet. I also approved hotel, flights, and any other expenditures for them to get home safely to their families. If the supposed production company had dumped them once, they were bound to do it again.

Wouldn't be the last time they tried to come for my secrets, either.

If not these people, someone else. And while I didn't give a crap if some modern-day pirates died chasing treasure or on some witch hunt for proof of my past, I did care about innocent people being sacrificed for my sins.

I couldn't sit by and do nothing. Not knowing these kids could've died.

"You all right, love? Not hungry?"

I stared at my plate halfheartedly. The food was absolutely delicious, but now I'd lost my appetite. "Last night is just catching up with me, sorry."

"Zee. Go. Get some rest. We've got things all taken care of here."

I nodded and made a show of following Vivi's advice, but instead of going to my suite, I headed straight to the war room to view the sonar footage. The equipment wasn't sophisticated and coral had started a decent covering, but the video clips showed enough for me to recognize the ship as the *Esmeralda*. The image took me right back to those final moments.

The circular orange raft careened as it hung from the yacht's side, an awkward kite rising and plummeting from the sheering gusts. Tethered only from above, safety dangled and swung like an out-of-control pendulum. I gripped the railing, staring at the space between the raft and yacht as they pitched out of unison, pulling wide from each other before bashing together. Any misstep threatened to break my legs then drop me down into the violent seas.

"Where's the rest of the crew?" I hollered over the storm.

"They launched already." The captain reached up with a knife as he sawed at the last tether securing the raft to the yacht. "Now or never, Princess."

I scrambled over the rail and leaped onto the slick rubber floor, slipping and grabbing for anything to hold onto as the bottom of the raft dropped out from under me. We hit the water hard.

The rough waves bashed us into the yacht a few times before spitting us out into open water. I hung onto whatever I could just to keep from getting pitched out. Weeks before, we'd hit rough seas around the Cape Horn. One of the crew members had taught me to focus on the horizon, so as not to get seasick. There was no horizon now, only darkness and the shadowed shape of the Esmeralda. Soon the storm bore down fully upon her, predator on prey.

The wounded yacht pitched and bucked like a wild zebra refusing to be taken to the ground. The harsh slap and crack of waves. The onslaught of rain. And lastly a wave larger than anything I'd ever seen, even in a movie, came up over her — a lioness pouncing and sinking its fangs into her withers, severing her spine. Down she went, buckling into the sea.

Then the wave came for us.

I studied her there on the ocean floor. The storm may have taken her to the ground, but she'd given one hell of a fight and kept all her secrets.

Now it was my turn.

I pressed the button to close the war room door, ensuring I had complete privacy. With a deep breath, I initiated a conference with Zaki.

Waiting for Zaki's holographic to appear, I felt compelled to break down and cry. To scream. But I wouldn't do it here. Not in the place where suffering much worse than I'd known had taken place.

Besides, antics like that would do nothing to change the past, and certainly not Zaki's opinion of me.

I closed my eyes. I'm so sorry. I tried my best to make you proud. To protect you. Protect us.

When Omar Zaki appeared, I pulled it together and regarded him from a place of strength. He didn't say anything as we stared at each other, nor did I expect him to.

"It's time to initiate Ozma Protocol," I said.

The silence was expected, but I rushed to fill it. "We're going to want to bring Coop back in. He's capable of a deep dive. He can handle the demolition. He needs money." At this point I was more thinking aloud, justifying what exactly I was proposing. Needing. Miller and Vivi were right, there was just too much on my shoulders to carry alone. "I can't do this without him."

But can I trust him?

My fingers twitched and paused. *If* Zaki could convince him to take the job...and if Coop *had* turned, he'd have whatever leverage he'd need to finish us off. There was no way I could let him leave the island. I'd have to have him—

I swallowed.

Don't even think it.

I shook off the grim thought. This was *my* Coop. My-sharky. How could I even suspect him of turning on me? Of wanting to hurt me?

Because he did *leave you*, I reminded myself. *He* did *hurt you*.

Recalling it tore through me all over again. But it wasn't his fault my heart had been shattered, I was the bull in that china shop. *And...*rejecting me didn't make him a traitor. But the only way I'd know for sure was to bring him to the island. Keep your friends close and your enemies closer and all.

Or maybe I just wanted Coop closer, no matter which he turned out to be.

I closed my eyes, gripping the armrests. "I need your help to convince him."

"Can you trust him?" The question slipping from Zaki's lips was the very one I'd been asking myself. But somehow it carried a bit more weight coming from him. My answer would also make me accountable.

Yes... No. *Maybe...* I offered up an option, more to convince my own heart and mind than Zaki's. "If I can't trust him, I'll..."

I shakily drew in a deep breath. Was I really suggesting...? *If his life threatened mine, I'd have no choice.*

I clenched my fingers and listened as Zaki affirmed my offer.

"*You* will be the one to get rid of him."

Ozma Protocol

"Brains are an asset, if you hide them."
~ Mae West

Chapter Seven

Three weeks later...
Coop

After shaking three pills from a prescription bottle into my palm, I grabbed a cold drink from the Gulfstream's wet bar to wash them down. Like everything on the luxury jet, the specially labelled water bottle bore my billionaire boss's initials—O.Z.

As cool as I was playing it, I was completely unnerved to find myself here. For one, I hadn't intended to be going to Marakata Cay—*or seeing Aziza*—so soon. It wasn't the right time. There were important things I hadn't put in place. And two, I still couldn't believe I was alive.

Three weeks ago I'd awoken from a coma. I hadn't remembered Alvarez or the explosion. Luckily those things had since come back to me. Rey had had to fill me in on the rest. Like how the mishandled RPG had actually taken out most of Alvarez's remaining men, the others had fled, and I...I had fallen out of my sniper hide in the tree and lost consciousness. Thank goodness Rey had heard the explosion and mobilized. How the little guy had gotten my two-hundred-and-twenty-five-pound ass out of the jungle and back to his village shaman, I still hadn't worked out. But I was forever in his debt.

What I did know was I needed another concussion like I needed another rock in my head. I couldn't afford to remove the one fucking mass I had growing there now.

While I knew Beryl Enterprises would provide me the best medical attention available, the last thing I wanted was to be sidelined indefinitely in some sort of pity position. Like hell I'd become another one of OZ's pampered pets on Marakata Cay. Aziza would do it, too—care for me like that overweight pet tiger of hers. Then we'd both live in a cage.

That first morning waking up in Rey's remote village, I hadn't had time for worries or ego. The only thing filling my mind had been the ringing coming from an encrypted sat phone that had been left on my chest. How Aziza had managed that trick, I may never know. I'd just desperately wanted to hear her voice one more time. Maybe if I had, I'd have told her how I really felt about her. But when I'd answered, it had been Zaki.

If that didn't tell me exactly where I stood in her eyes!

Fuck. Even three weeks later, I still burned from the salt of it.

Of course Zee didn't want to talk to me, I'd abandoned her. She had the same hard pride I did.

For her to put her stubbornness aside and make the first contact with me, even through Zaki, had to have been a tough pill to swallow. Perhaps even harder than it'd been for her to summon the courage to lay her beautiful, fragile heart out to me when she'd asked me to move to Marakata Cay.

God, if only I didn't have one foot in the fucking grave...

I shook off the self-pitying thought and replaced it with a mantra from my SEAL days. *Never out of the fight.*

And this job was my only ticket back in.

I still didn't understand the sudden need to recover something that had rested on the ocean floor for over twenty years, but I owed it to Zee to listen to Zaki's proposition.

Little did she know I would've taken any job she wanted me to for free. *If* she'd asked me herself. But for Zaki? My acceptance took the five-million-dollar payday and the assurance I could bring along my old Teammate Nikolas Steele and my little brother, Leo.

Nik and Leo were my best friends. If I was going to die, I needed them with me. And a deep dive with my history of concussions *and* this rock in my head could easily be a suicide mission. I needed Steele there to ensure the job would be completed. And I wanted to spend some time with my brother, just in case it was the last.

I wanted Aziza by my side as well, but knew better than to ask God for another miracle. Just being alive and getting to see her one more time was more than I deserved.

Originally the plan had been for Nik and me to meet up at Leo's, then travel to Miami, where we would be meeting the ship to sail directly to the dive site. Which meant originally Zee had no intentions of seeing me at all.

By a literal twist of fate, a tornado to be exact, my boy Nik had fallen heart first in love, postponing our trip several days and strapping Thea Gale and her German shepherd, Titan, to our manifest. This caused us to, also literally, miss the boat. The only option left had been flying into Marakata Cay.

In less than thirty minutes I'd have boots on the ground in the most important battle of my life. The objectives — stay alive and figure out a way to tell Zee exactly how I felt about her.

The odds were not in my favor.

Despite the sudden jostle of turbulence, I maneuvered easily around the executive jet. Sensing I was being watched, I cut my eyes across the airplane's spacious interior, catching Thea's stare. The perceptive blonde had been keeping tabs on my every move since I'd emerged smoothly shaven from the luxury airplane's restroom. After carefully stepping over Titan's sprawled body, I dropped to sit across from her and next to my snoring brother.

I jutted my chin toward a sound asleep Nik and grunted, "Don't let him catch you."

She shifted more upright in the luxurious leather seat. "Catch me doing what?"

I smirked and whispered back, "Staring at me."

Joshing with Thea was fun. She often took the bait, but never took my shit.

"As if I'd been making a secret of it."

Secrets. The very reason Aziza had avoided bringing me to the enigmatic island my entire career with Beryl Enterprises. But here I was speeding six hundred miles per hour toward Marakata Cay with my own head full of the bastards. I scowled at the reminder.

"I'm not a secrets kind of woman," Thea continued, undeterred by my glowering. "I have plenty with my amnesia, no sense creating more."

I eyed the fat file sticking up from her bag, which contained a very thorough background on her. One I'd had Zaki, which really meant Aziza, compile. "You could rectify that, you know."

Her only reply was an unimpressed huff.

The tornado had stolen her memories, and Thea had no intentions of retrieving them. In fact, I was surprised she hadn't already lobbed the file into the nearest trash can.

Plucking a bright red gummy bear from a black vitamin bottle, I nipped its head off before swallowing the rest whole. "You're still staring," I muttered with a freshly sharpened edge of annoyance.

"Sorry, I'm just not used to this version of you." Her amber eyes flicked over me.

Clothed downright sartorially, I was perfectly in step with the opulence of Omar Zaki's G650, the most luxurious private jet on the planet. The chop of dark waves on the top of my head barely hinted at what had been an unruly, wild mess in the jungles of the Amazon. Now it was short enough to knock out the whorls on the slicked-back sides.

The only remnants of the old me, aside from my blue eyes, were a few scars. They stood as a reminder that despite the exquisite cut of my suit, I wasn't afraid to get bloody.

I'd given myself the makeover in Denver, because I couldn't very well show up to Aziza's island looking like some caveman who'd just spent the past month in the jungles of South America taking out cartel leaders. *Almost* taking them out. Even though I'd softened his forces and his hold on the Amazon basin, Marco Alvarez was still my problem to handle. The faster I could get my head back in the game, the sooner I could tie that loose end up.

So, yeah, Thea was right—I gave the impression I was the millionaire executive director in OZ's empire that I was supposed to be. But under the surface, as she was no doubt also aware, I would never really be as civilized as all that.

Still, she'd agreed to follow me on a dangerous job I'd yet to divulge any details of, to an island she wasn't allowed to talk about, all while a woman we still had no clue how she'd wronged was out to kill her.

Well, technically Thea hadn't followed *me*. She'd followed Nik. For all I knew, Thea hadn't let go of her distrust of me.

I steepled my hands and flashed a smile which I knew showcased my innocent looking dimples at her. "Still think I look like a bad guy?"

She grimaced in apology. Seemed forever ago, not days, I'd attempted to intimidate her with hostile bravado. It worked well when I'd been a SEAL, but didn't scare Thea.

"Not *bad*, per se. More like…too good to be true."

I couldn't hold back a wide grin. "Touché."

She held up her cell phone and flashed an image of OZ's private paradise. "So does this island you're taking us to."

There was a scarcity of information on Marakata Cay because all visitors were required to sign lengthy non-disclosure agreements, just as we had before boarding the jet. But that didn't mean people hadn't speculated.

The emerald island was alleged to be everything from a player's paradise to nothing more than a mirage, an inglorious scam of epic proportions. Online searches produced phrases like *hedonistic, mystical,* and *spellbinding,* yet none of the stories provided substantive detail. Just like there was no proof that JFK Jr. had faked his death so he could live on the island in blissful anonymity. Or was it Elvis this week?

"Seems to be just another means for the influencers of the world to separate themselves from the mundane," she read off her phone.

I recognized the quote from a write-up on the yearly Meeting of the Minds held on the island. Much like Google Camp, Bilderberg, and other summits like them, high-profile celebs and global activists converged on Marakata Cay to discuss world issues. From the scant reports, the Meeting of the Minds looked more like a billionaire boat party.

As always, the truth lay somewhere in the middle.

"An internet search about OZ or the island isn't going to tell you what you really want to know. Just like avoiding the file I gave you but Googling your own name won't tell you who you really are, Theadora Emelia Gale."

She glanced down at the cell phone, where she'd spent just as much time researching herself as the island we were headed to. "How'd you know?"

"You're using the jet's Wi-Fi. I know everything you've searched."

Her eyes went wide as she realized what else I'd caught her looking up.

"*Those sites,*" she scoffed, "just popped up when I was looking for something else."

I gave my chin a skeptical tilt, fully enjoying this rare moment of having one-upped her. "For the record, Nik would love being woken up with that one thing you *accidentally* watched five videos on."

Her jaw dropped. But she snapped her mouth shut, no doubt realizing she looked exactly like the women in the videos she'd watched. At the deep blush to her cheeks, I splayed my lips in a devilish grin before a robust laugh busted out.

She grumbled, "I see you're back to being the brash rake I'm used to."

My brother, Leo, roused. "Leave her alone, Coop. You're just jealous no one is waking you up like that."

"Ain't that the truth," I grunted. Aziza was more likely Googling ways to blow me away in my sleep than how to wake me with a blowie.

Despite my puckish attempt to move the conversation away from the island, Thea pressed on. "I'm more curious about where exactly you're taking us."

"Look out the window. See for yourself."

Chapter Eight

Coop

After miles of nothing but clouds and water below us, there in the distance was green, lush earth — an emerald jewel set in a sapphire sea. The mountain island rose up high in a crest and curled around itself like a sleeping dragon, the jagged-toothed snout and spearing tip of the creature's tail almost touching. Nestled in the center of the nearly circular isle, the pale turquoise water was clear enough to see through to the sandy ocean floor. The narrow inlet gap where the land almost connected was called the Cut.

The plane's initial pass took us high above Marakata, *and Aziza*, before gliding over a darker stretch of water. Among the mottled light blue patches of sea, black outcroppings punctured the surface.

"Coral reef nearly surrounds the island. Few early explorers ever survived getting close enough to see land. For much of its life, the cay existed only as a myth amongst pirates," I explained to Thea and Leo. Nik was still passed out, as was his habit while flying.

The plane banked in a slow arc while I pointed out remnant bones of wrecked ships. Some were just scraps below the surface, others looked like animal carcasses picked clean and left to bleach in the sun. They stood as omens to others. A warning of what would befall you if you came too close.

Or maybe they were proof that what lay ahead was worth dying for.

Even in modern times, the remote island continued to perpetuate mysterious legends. This time as OZ's private Eden.

But even Eden had a snake.

Hate snakes...

Thea's eyes homed in on a small aircraft nose-down just below the surface.

"That one was from an electrical storm a few years back," I explained. "Given today's weather, we're safe out here over the water. It's when the plane goes through the Cut that our chances of wrecking are highest. This is the largest airplane able to fit through and still stop on the runway. With this crosswind, the pilot has to be perfect or..." Instead of finishing the thought, I twisted my lips in an ominous grimace.

"I knew this was a bad idea." Leo tunneled his fingers through his dark hair. "Freaking Bermuda Triangle."

"None of the wrecks have anything to do with superstitious bullshit. It's science, bro. Physics. Weather and currents, hidden coral reefs. Tangible things."

"Whatever the reason, it's freaking dangerous out here."

"Well, I can't argue that." I went on to explain how, in order for the pilot to make a final approach to the short landing strip, the plane would basically need to belly surf across the water's surface as it edged through the narrow gap between the stony dragon's nose and tail.

On cue, the plane dropped low, too fast for my stomach to follow suit. Titan scrambled to stand and balance in the aisle. I reached out and wrapped my arm around him, bracing his chest in my palm and hugging him to the side of my seat.

As both wings skimmed within a hair's breadth of the narrow rock opening, Leo slammed his eyes shut and Thea drew her arms in tight. I chuckled at them both as Nik stirred, still peacefully asleep.

We popped through, coasting safely over the pale lagoon. My eyes sliced sharp and keen along the sandy crescent beach, honing immediately in on the gorgeous, dark-haired woman astride an equally breathtaking horse.

Aziza.

As the runway approached, the plane's jets first kicked out waves then sand, blurring my view of the exotic horse and its equally captivating rider in a cloud of white. Aziza managed to keep her seat as the powerful animal spun and skittered in a sidestepping canter.

With a bounce and bark of the tires, the plane touched down. We were immediately pitched forward with enough force to cause our seatbelts to dig in and Titan's body to press heavily into my palm as the pilot fully engaged all the various braking systems.

The beach no longer in view, I turned my attention back to the cabin. As the aircraft lurched nearer to the abrupt end of the runway, Thea's eyes widened. She dug her nails into the armrests while thrusting her heels into the floor. As if she could help bring the powerful machine to a stop. Marring the wall of rock's surface were several colorful smears and scars — evidence of the variety of planes that hadn't stopped in time.

But the aircraft never stopped. Instead it swerved hard, cornering like a very awkward race car.

Leo braced for the wing outside his window to crash into the solid barrier. We all watched as it sliced cleanly through the air instead.

"It's okay, Tiggs, this is normal," Nik murmured sleepily to Thea as he blinked, awakening.

Leo gritted out on an exhale, "Nothing about *this* place is normal!"

You got that right, brother.

Having thwarted death, Leo and Thea both slumped back in their seats, relieved. I let go of Titan and adjusted my suit as if this were just another day at the office. Then I nudge-kicked Nik in the shin. "Time to go to work, Sleeping Beauty."

Leo shook his head. "We almost died and you slept right through it!"

"Always do," Nik said with a satisfied yawn. Airplanes were the one place insomniac Nik could be counted on to fall asleep.

"I never really believed you slept through a plane crash until now."

Thea tilted her head and made wide eyes at Nik. "You were in a plane crash?"

"It wasn't a *crash*, Tiggs," he assured as he adjusted his seatback more upright. "We just didn't land on a runway."

"Or in one piece...or in the country we were supposed to," I added. There'd been no end to the wild adventures Nik and I had been through as SEALs.

"At least you finally got some rest." Thea patted his chest, her fingers lingering a bit longer than necessary. "You needed it."

I dropped a pair of gold aviators over my eyes as I stood up. "Thea's right. I need you bright-eyed, bushy-tailed, and ready to blow some shit up."

Waiting for the plane to taxi back to a parking spot, I leaned down to scan out the window, automatically seeking the white beach. But it stretched out deserted, as if both horse and rider had disappeared in the whirlwind. In a way, it was like Aziza had never been there at all.

I recalled the way sunlight had reflected off the stallion's unusual silver coat, giving it the most spectacular pearl sheen. Still, it couldn't compare to the glow Aziza had radiated.

As if reading my mind, Thea lifted her chin and asked, "Was that horse for real? I mean, do horses really come in that color?"

"They do on this island. He's a rare breed called an Akhal Teke. They're world-renowned for their metallic coloring. Zaki breeds them as well as many other unique and even endangered animals."

"And the woman?"

I swallowed. *The woman* was a one of a kind. And whole story unto herself. "Aziza. She's Zaki's right hand. *And left.* I'm sure she's headed this way now."

It irked me that I couldn't keep the apprehension from lacing my tone, or my heartbeat from ramping high. Since when did meeting anyone, female or not, make me this uncertain? As much as I wanted to see her, I'd begun to dread it, too. Because where I was eager to see her, I knew she hadn't wanted to see me.

I mused aloud, "She'll need to debrief me before we head out to the dive site."

More like dress me down, and not in the way I wanted.

"Debrief, huh?" Thea smirked. "Figured you were more of a commando guy."

Thankful for the levity, I curled my lip and deadpanned, "You really have to stop staring at my brief-less ass, Thea."

"You wish," Nik growled.

"Nik's right. I only have eyes for his gorgeous, tight, round—"

"Got it," I grunted.

The plane shimmied as the pilot made his final adjustments into a parking spot. I looked out the window again. Still no Aziza. Couldn't she put everything aside for one fucking moment?

Maybe she isn't rolling out the welcome mat because this isn't your fucking homecoming, dumbass. You turned down that offer. Remember?

I also remembered why.

I needed to get my head on straight in more ways than one. This was a job. Pure and simple. And Aziza was my boss—not my friend, not my family, not my lover. Until I got rid of this rock rolling around in my skull, that was how things had to stay.

Thea's sudden jolt and gasp spun my attention back to the cabin. Titan had nearly leaped in her lap, his nose poking her head, his tongue lapping her cheek. I narrowed my eyes—Titan had done something similar to me back in Colorado. His snout had poked me right where my tumor was.

"Scared me, boy," she said as she gently eased his front paws from her legs to back him off.

"You okay, babe?" Nik asked as he scrubbed his fingers through his hair on the tail end of a yawn.

Thea was pressing her fingers into her eyes, like I did when a migraine would be coming on or when I had trouble clearing PTSD memories.

"Thea?" Nik asked louder. Her lack of response must've worried him, too, or he'd have called her Tigger. A nickname I still didn't fully understand, but then, I didn't understand half of the gooey-ooey, lovey-dovey stuff ol' steel-hearted Nik had suddenly adopted.

Thea flinched, jerking back as Nik squeezed her shoulder. The spooked look in her eyes made me suspect she'd had some sort of flashback. Probably from the kidnapping.

"You okay?" Nik asked again.

"Sorry, I'm fine," she assured. "You just startled me."

"Let me see your eyes." Nik tilted her chin to look into her pupils. As a corpsman he could always be counted on for being fucking annoying about the medical shit. I usually humored him, because he'd also saved my ass on more than one occasion.

Thea wriggled away. "Just have a headache," she said, but her voice lacked conviction.

Nik flexed his jaw. "I knew it was too soon for you to travel."

Fearing he'd start carrying her everywhere on the island, just as he'd carried her aboard the aircraft in Colorado, I grunted. "Here, take one of these." I lobbed my prescription bottle across the cabin. Nik caught the pills in one hand and the water bottle that immediately followed in the other. "It'll help her with the migraine from the concussion."

Nik eyed me. "You having trouble with migraines, Coop?"

"Nothing I can't handle," I said before he got the idea to jam a penlight in my eye. I grabbed up a large tactical duffle packed with weapons and explosive ordinance and slung it over my shoulder. "Time to make things go boom, Steel."

Chapter Nine

Coop

Warm sunlight, wafting fresh air, and the lapping of ocean waves surrounded us as we descended from the jet to solid ground. We were all a little speechless as we looked around, taking the island in.

Tall, tubular palms lined the landing strip, their crowning fronds swaying in the floral-scented breeze. I visually traced the origin of the fragrance to a vibrant, thick blanket of red. The flowers draped over the volcanic rock ledges that had been blown out and chiseled back to make room for the runway. The flora hemmed an evergreen jungle where high in the canopy gold monkeys chattered at the rainbow-colored birds looping among the branches.

I'd seen the island many times and from many angles, in the highest definitions of color no less, but being able to feel and smell it was like everything before had been in black and white.

"This place is magical," Thea exclaimed as she stared off toward the bay. Along the stretch of sand where Aziza's mirage had dissipated, Miller was playing in the calm surf with two large white lions. Most every day Dr. Walsh took various big cats out for a swim and elephants for hikes, like they were children at camp.

Everything about the island had been designed to make it appear fantastical, and even though I'd seen it a million times through the lens of surveillance, I found myself awestruck by the reality of it.

Staff members as richly varied as the island's topography emerged as if on parade to assist us with our baggage. Most of the faces held some familiarity. I viewed them often during routine observations. But one in particular was more like family. Vivian McQueen. I couldn't help but smile as she exited the thatch-roofed pavilion, all legs and a smile.

"If it isn't the cowboy with the bluest eyes in Texas! *Finally*," she teased as she pulled me into a hug. "Thought you might never find the pathway here."

"I know, I know. I took the long road." Even in Vivi's embrace, I found myself glancing over her shoulder, unable to hold back my disappointment. "Where's Zee?"

Vivi leaned away, her eyes narrowed with mock confusion. "Well, did you knock?"

"Did I what?"

She pointed to a sign below a brass bell on the pavilion's entrance that erroneously instructed visitors to knock instead. The Oztralians, as the rest of Beryl Enterprises called those who lived on Marakata Cay, enjoyed spouting cryptic inside jokes. But I wasn't in the mood for their Ozzie humor. I just wanted to see Zee.

"Oh, Cooper, smile or we'll make you wear the emerald-colored glasses." With a playful swat to my biceps, Vivi turned her joviality on the others. "Welcome to Marakata Cay. I'm Vivian McQueen, but everyone calls me Vivi. You must be Leo. I've heard so much about you."

Vivi eyed the younger and prettier of us Cooper boys. Even with his wild mane of hair and scruffy five o'clock shadow, his calmer nature had a way of peeking out from his brawn. She turned to extend her hand to the next in line. "And, Mr. Steele..."

"Please, call me Nik."

"Nik, of course," she said as she shook his hand. "We're honored to have you helping Michael with this project. And..."

Vivi looked around, finding Thea had wandered over to one of the squatty miniature palms flanking the pavilion. The tree was short enough for her to reach up to fondle the pair of hairy brown balls dangling from it. She curiously glanced back at us. "What do you do with these?"

I couldn't help but exchange a look with Vivi, before saying, "Oh, darlin', you just keep doing what you're doing."

"And you, love, *must be* Thea."

Thea turned with wide eyes and dropped jaw as she openly gawked at Vivi, stammering, "You... You're..."

Thea's amnesia had not only stripped her of memories and experiences, but also of any social filter, making the otherwise intelligent and savvy woman come off as a naïve ingénue.

"I'm what, dear?" Vivi asked with a gracious but reserved smile.

Even with a supermodel mother and a soccer star father, I knew Vivi had been bullied through school due to the extreme length of her legs and the rare onyx depth of her skin. I braced for Thea to stick her foot in her mouth on some aspect of Vivi's dramatic appearance.

"So...beautiful! And your accent! What is it?"

I released my breath as Vivi's trepid smile turned into a hearty laugh. "The same as the Queen's, love. And you gave us quite the scare. So glad you and Titan are well. I understand you weren't prepared to come to the island. OZ asked me to arrange some clothing and toiletries for you. They are in with the supplies."

"Thank you, Mr. Zaki's generosity has been overwhelming already. I don't suppose he would agree to meeting with me? I'd really like to thank him in person."

"Oh, *nobody* sees OZ in person. Not nobody, not no-how," Vivi said with a laugh. "But I will relay your thanks. It's truly his pleasure to take care of those who come to stay with us. Speaking of, I imagine you all are starving and ready to eat, yes? We've set a buffet for you. Right this way."

We followed Vivi into the open-air, beachside pavilion where the tables looked more like parade floats with their rainbows of berries and vegetables spread out around artistic fruit carvings. Other tables had vast selections of meats and cheeses along with intricate ice sculptures. Beyond them, several manned stations for made-to-order entrees to suit anyone's tastes awaited.

"You do know there are only four of us? Six with the pilots?" I asked.

"You think we put out this kind of spread for *you*, Cooper?" Vivi said with a laugh. "Lil' BayBay and DV8 are flying in right behind you with full entourages. They'll be staying for the week to shoot their collab video."

"Don't let them see you dance or you'll never get a cameo."

"Go eat, brat," she said swatting me toward the food.

After going through the buffet, we settled at a long table with plates piled full. Even Titan was served a bowl of raw meats and fresh water with artisan ice.

"After your brunch, OZ will brief you gentlemen privately on the job requirements," Vivi announced. "Thea, I know Michael arranged for you to have excellent medical care before coming here, but it wouldn't hurt for you and Titan to be checked again. I also have scheduled our chiropractor and acupuncturist to look you both over."

Thea choked down the delicate croissant she'd indelicately crammed in her mouth. "Um, Titan, too?"

"Yes, Michael mentioned he'd had some trouble sliding down the cliff during your rescue. OZ would prefer having our vet make sure he's okay."

"I'm sorry, who exactly is *Michael*?" Thea asked, causing the whole table to laugh.

"Michael Cooper, nice to meet you," I said as I dipped my chin toward her. "All the animals here at Marakata Cay have access to stellar care."

"Not *just* the animals, Michael," Vivi corrected. "Thea, I've also booked you a few hours at our spa facilities so you can get tidied up a bit after your travels. If that meets with your approval."

"Oh yes, thank you so much!"

"I'll have Django meet you in the salon for your hair. And your masseur, Adrian, is a master with his hands. Be prepared for your body to be taken to heaven!"

"Adrian? Django?" Nik piped up. "I don't know about this..."

"Is this going to be an issue for you, Steele?" I asked, noting Nik's flexing jaw.

I'd be laughing at his obvious jealousy if I weren't having my own fit of it. What or *who* was more important to Zee than seeing me, anyway?

"It's just..." Nik growled low. "We don't know any of these people."

He hadn't been apart from Thea except to go to the bathroom since Clay had abducted her. If Thea and Rebecca hadn't already killed the motherfucker, either one of us would've enjoyed doing the job. But that was in the past and right now Nik needed to keep his focus forward and not on his lady love getting rubbed down by another man.

"Thea's safe here," Vivi said reading the situation semi-correctly. In a feathery soft tone, she assured, "OZ has matters well in hand. Security on the island is top-notch. Michael has made sure we have the best protection available. And I believe you do know Brecken Wolfe, our Chief of Island Spec Ops."

"Wolfe's here?"

"Yes, he's prepping for the arrival of our next guests, but I can see if he can accompany Thea?"

Nik's jaw flexed again. He probably was recalling Wolfe's Nordic brawn and how the women in

Coronado would lap that whole Viking look of his up. "Thea doesn't know him."

Thea, who was typically plucky and confident, also seemed just a bit unsure. I didn't blame her. The last time she'd gone off without Nik, it had been with someone she'd thought she could trust—me—and I'd screwed her over. I scrubbed my face with my palms, realizing I'd been making a bad habit out of letting women down in that regard.

"I'll stay with her," Leo suggested before Nik backed out of the whole mission. "You can fill me in on anything I should know after."

"You sure, man?" Nik asked.

I clapped Leo on the shoulder. "He can endure some froufrou pampering. You don't get to be the prettiest MMA fighter out there without a little luxuriating."

"I got to be the prettiest MMA fighter by knocking out my opponents before they could touch me, asshole."

"Glad we got that settled," I announced as I stood from the table. Zee had had her fun by making me wait, sweat it out. Set it up so I'd have to come to her and not the other way around. And maybe I deserved it, but now I *was* going to see her. "Vivi, let Zee know we're on our way."

"Unfortunately, Zee must sit the meeting out," Vivi informed me. "She's not feeling well."

I held back from yelling, *"Bull-fucking-shit!"* I couldn't believe what I was hearing. She'd never missed a meeting with me before. And she'd certainly been feeling good enough to go freaking horseback riding on the beach.

Zee was avoiding me. I dropped my sunglasses over my eyes to hide the hardness I knew had formed. I bit back a frustrated growl.

You want to play games with me, Princess, bring it on.

Chapter Ten

Coop

The entry to Zaki's home looked more like the white marbled entry of a high-end hotel or resort. Which made sense given the mansion was run like a business, not a residence. Though, as I explained to Nik, several of the higher-up employees, like Aziza and Vivi, as well as the house staff, lived in the mansion's many suites. Zaki's quarters were only accessed by a select few and it had been years since he'd stepped outside of them.

"Why live in paradise if you're going to lock yourself away and never enjoy it?" Nik mused as we followed Vivi down a hallway to the bunker-style war room.

I was still stewing about Zee snubbing our meeting and wasn't in the mood to delve into all of my theories. I relayed the most publicly accepted one. "The shipwreck was rumored to have left him disfigured and I guess that was the final straw. But Zaki's always had a touch of the Howard Hughes. Already a notorious germaphobe, his obsessive-compulsive disorder eventually morphed into a full-fledged fear of a global pandemic. Doesn't seem as paranoid now as it did back when he withdrew completely."

A search on Zaki's family would yield a long history of tragedy and death—from the mysterious illness which took his youngest daughter at an early age and his wife's subsequent suicide to a deadly kidnapping of his oldest daughter and daughter-in-law. The final straw had been the shipwreck that had taken the remaining family members.

Oddly, Zaki's reclusion had become one of his best career moves, as it gave him a platform to endorse Beryl Enterprises' ground-breaking metaverse projection system called Portal. The AI advances to Portal allowed users to flawlessly project lifelike holograms that could be used in normal ambient light environments without the use of headgear or goggles. Beryl had already completed an AI profile and a series of holograms using OZ's likeness for demos, but initially hadn't had any takers for the expensive new tech.

Zaki had set out to prove he could run a global empire from the immense luxury of his island mansion by attending multiple conference meetings on different continents in the same day as effectively as if he'd been there in person. By not using heavy fuel consumption for travel, corporations could also save money, time, and the environment.

With the success of Zaki's program, it didn't take long for Beryl Enterprises to become the industry leader in modern business solutions. Soon Beryl started diversifying the AI experience, expanding into more nuanced biometrics as well as taking on counter hacking. That was when first-world governments had come calling, and when my services had become necessary.

"Gentlemen," Vivi said as she opened the oversized vault with a retinal scan followed by a long string of characters as her credentials. The security system not only took into consideration the user's physical attributes, like fingerprints, but also compiled other biometrics, like finger pressure and speed of entry on a code. If the user behaved out of the norms learned by the system, the vault would not open.

"I'll let OZ know you're here."

Nik whistled in appreciation at the wall of computer screens relaying not only views of the island, but also around the world. "Shit, man. This is some next-level surveillance. Reapers? Real-time NSA feeds? UN satellite footage?" His attention shifted as he homed in on the one of island's camera blocks, specifically the one of Thea and Leo in the salon.

I shook my head at the footage of my little brother blissfully leaning back in a massage chair while one person worked on his feet and another buffed his fingernails. "Getting his fucking paws done, while sipping champagne, no less."

Meanwhile, an Asian male hairstylist with shiny black hair that resembled a cross between modern art and an origami swan appeared behind Thea. "Wish I could hear them," Nik muttered.

I touched the screen to zoom in and turned the microphone on so we could eavesdrop. Nik huddled in closer.

In a thickly Australian accent, the short, wiry man explained, "My birth name was Johnny Lee, but I prefer

Django, because it means 'I awake' and *your* hair, doll, is in desperate need of waking."

Eyes wide, Thea cautiously asked, "My hair won't be as awake as yours, will it?"

I laughed. Django's hair looked like it was on its fifth energy drink, and not the Outbreak Energy drinks Leo endorsed, either. More like the extremely potent Rip Its we used to chug before missions while in the sandbox.

Django waved his hand, dismissing Thea's concerns. "Darling, your cheekbones could never pull this off. Leo's, on the other hand…"

Leo, engrossed in his own beauty ritual, didn't realize his rangy mane had been eyed for takeover. Lucky for him, Django's attention swung a hundred and eighty as his assistant brought in a small tray with two large shot glasses on it. "First we drink, then we create!"

After setting the tray down, his assistant balanced two spoons, cradling a cube of sugar each, over the green liqueur. Absinthe shots were another one of those Ozzie novelties cultivated to add to the mystique of the island.

As the assistant turned to face the camera, I recognized her as Michelle Lovelace. Everyone called her Mickie. She was casually dressed in ripped capri jeans and a simple white T-shirt, but paired it with full makeup and retro pin-up girl hair. Her platinum bangs were dyed purple and rolled into a tube wave that rivaled the Banzai pipeline.

Where most Caribbean resorts went the traditional route of tropical-colored uniforms and conservative, cookie-cutter staff, Ozzies valued creative displays of individuality. It was a drastic contrast to Zaki's formal traditions, which he himself appeared to hold onto.

Django motioned to Mickie, who proceeded to lower the lights for added drama. After some machinations, she handed the now-flaming green shots to Thea and Django. Upon knocking his back, Django let loose a warrior's cry. Mickie took the cue to brandish two miniature samurai swords that had been sheathed in her lavender-colored bun. She presented them to Django, who immediately began slash cutting Thea's hair like a crazed samurai.

"Oh, *hell* no," Nik growled. Wheeling to go save his girl, he collided with Omar Zaki's image. Nik spun, slicing the visual with some decent jujitsu moves. "What in the actual fuck?"

"Chill," I said with a laugh. "It's not a spiderweb, Steele."

Nik spun back around, swiping through the visual again, this time more slowly. "What the fuck is it?"

"It's a hologram."

"But he looks so real?"

"Stop groping it, perv." I slapped his hand back before he sliced it through Zaki's stomach again, then hit the button to turn the spa mic off. "Sir, I want to introduce you to Nikolas Steele. As you're aware, he'll be accompanying me on the dive."

Zaki's image turned to Nik, who had semi-regrouped. "I've heard many good things about you. Thank you for coming to my island and working this job with Coop."

"Sorry about...uh, yeah... Pleasure is mine, sir." Nik reached out to shake the lifelike hologram's hand before awkwardly stepping back with a nod.

"Please have a seat, gentlemen. I'll get right to it. As you may be aware, many years ago I was aboard a yacht that went down near the island. Several lives, including those of my son and granddaughter, were sadly taken. In addition, some irreplaceable cargo, most notably a rare emerald, was lost.

"I've had mixed feelings about retrieving the gemstone and disturbing what has become the last of my family's resting place. I'd hoped the emerald's disappearance had escaped notice. But, given the notoriety of such a jewel, and certainly its value, it would seem it has attracted attention. Someone who wishes to risk the heavily shark-inhabited waters to steal it. Worse, they have already shown they are willing to endanger innocent lives. I can't have that happen."

"No offense, sir, but trying to find a singular gemstone at the bottom of the ocean will be a hundred times harder than looking for a needle in a haystack," Nik interjected. "Currents, ocean floor movement... It may not even be remotely close to the wreck site."

"This particular emerald is no needle."

I pushed out a frustrated sigh, still not understanding why I'd been brought in for the mission. Certainly my skills weren't required to recover a fancy piece of treasure before some modern-day pirate could nab it. And even if they were, I knew OZ wouldn't put my life on the line for an expensive bauble lightly. Not that anyone besides Leo knew about the tumor growing in my skull or that diving deep put me in more danger than any shark. Nor was I planning on sharing it. But there had to be more to this, because even OZ wasn't crazy enough to be paying us five mill to play Marco Polo with some fancy piece of jewelery.

I clenched my teeth. "Why don't you just tell us *exactly* what we're here to recover?"

"The main extraction is going to be a two-hundred-thousand-carat emerald."

Nik choked. "I'm sorry, did you say two-hundred *thousand*?"

"Yes. The Ozma Emerald is the world's largest, assuming it was not damaged during the wreck, that is. It weighs nearly one ton. Not only is it larger than the Bahia Emerald, it is of infinitely better quality. Potentially worth half a billion dollars or more."

Following the information in the electronic dossiers Vivi provided us, Zaki continued to discuss the job specifics, including the topography of the shipwreck and layout of the ship before it went down, as well as extraction options for the emerald. We also went over instruction on safely bringing something of this size to the surface.

"If the watertight vault used for its transportation wasn't damaged, it would be the safest means of bringing the gem up. Though it will double the weight."

"We can make an educated call at the site," I suggested. Now that I understood the magnitude better, my mind rolled through the op details, already calculating what would be necessary to retrieve the asset, be it blasting through potential walls or floors, or cutting through the hull of the ship with underwater torches.

"And if the vault can't be raised? I'm guessing the locking mechanism will be compromised after all these years underwater. How do you want us to get the emerald out?" Nik asked.

I leaned back in my chair and smirked. "Have you ever robbed a bank?"

"Not one a hundred and fifty feet below sea level."

Turning away from Nik, and back to Zaki's image, I said, "No worries, we'll get the job done. I just have one more request."

"Whatever equipment you require will be provided. I've taken the liberty of packing the necessary items and listing them on the manifest in your dossier," Zaki assured. "Vivi will take you to the weapons vault for any additional ordinance and gear, if you have specific preferences."

"Not equipment." Still reclining in my chair, I clasped my hands. "What I require is a person."

"Another hand?"

I wet my lips. "Hands, legs, lips, *breasts*..."

Nik eyeballed me across the table.

"You want me to provide you...a *woman*?" Zaki asked.

I couldn't miss the disgust sounding in the last word. Perhaps I'd laid it on too thick, but I was enjoying this moment a little more than I'd expected to. In fact, it was hard not to let loose a chuckle. "But...not just *any* woman. Aziza."

"Impossible," OZ snapped.

I decided not to correct the assumption that I'd just requested Zee be provided as sexual companionship for me and instead mirrored Zaki's firm assertion. "Nothing is impossible for the great and powerful OZ. And certainly an employee as loyal as Aziza would willingly do whatever you ask of her." I could barely contain my smile, knowing that wherever Zee was hiding out, she was listening and probably shaking in her knee-high equestrian boots. "If you want me to go down in shark-infested waters and liberate your precious gemstone, you *will* make this happen."

"She isn't available."

"Then it looks like we came a long way for nothing."

Zaki appeared speechless. I happily took advantage.

"In fact, I'm going to need to...*consult*...with her before we go. Just to ensure we're on the same page."

"I'll let her know your... offer," OZ said.

"The offer's only on the table for ten minutes." I turned my attention to Nik. "Vivi will take you to the vault. Please let her know Aziza will be accompanying us and to arrange whatever skimpy swimsuits she might need as well. We'll meet up with you when we're through *consulting*."

Even Nik, who had been well hazed by my bullshit over the years, was hesitant to push back from the table. He gave me a look of the *what the fuck are you doing* kind, but slowly stood and strode out the room. No doubt glad to get as far away from the developing shit show as he could.

I leaned back in my chair and unbuttoned the first few buttons on my crisp white dress shirt, then rolled up the sleeves. I shook my wrist and glanced at my watch then at OZ. His hologram disappeared so fast I half expected a poof of smoke and an explosion.

Your move, Princess.

Chapter Eleven

Aziza

Where the hell do you get off! I paced back and forth, fuming as I glared at the live stream of Coop looking oh-so smug as he waited for me to be delivered to him like a present.

Why did he have to be so fucking handsome when he had the upper hand?

Cocky bastard. I hope a shark does take a bite out of you.

He relished being stubborn. Getting him to budge on the ludicrous idea of my accompanying him to the dive site would be impossible unless I at least spoke to him.

But talking wasn't what kept flashing through my mind when I looked at him.

How could I be turned on by such an annoying man? I shouldn't be attracted to him at all. He'd blown me off. In spectacular fashion, no less. *This* was exactly why I hadn't wanted to see him.

Dear Lord! How was I going to go through with...
Killing him, Zee. That's what you'll have to do...
I still hadn't revealed my suspicions to Scott Hayes, Director of I&A. With most of Marco's inner circle taken out, the cartel would have to rebuild in order to come at us. It gave me much-needed time to figure out if Coop truly had been responsible for the Alvarez hits.
If?
How could I still have doubts? When I'd found Coop he'd been holed up in some village with an Amazonian shaman nursing his wounds just a few miles downriver from where Alvarez's hideout had been decimated. He'd insisted on bringing his own team, of sorts. Then proceeded to delay the job several days while harboring a potential fugitive. Granted all intel pointed to Nik and Thea's connection being completely coincidental and she'd turned out to be on the side of good, but I'd run out of red flags to raise.

I headed down the corridor, eager to get this over with.

I found Coop pushed away from the conference table. He leaned back in his chair with his legs spread, looking like he was waiting for a lap dance. While his large body didn't fill the room, his presence certainly dominated it.

Too bad. The war room was *mine* to rule.

In the same way I'd cue one of my stallions to charge into battle, I clenched my abs and drove my hips forward. With a straightened spine, I strode purposefully toward Coop as if my heart weren't punching straight through my skin.

I tried to keep my view blurry by looking through him, not at him. And it worked well until a loud clank behind me signaled the vault door locking shut. I'd heard it latch hundreds of times, but this time the shock of the metal bolt sliding into place jolted through me. My stare sharpened, fastening onto his deep blue eyes. They didn't hold the anger, or fear, as I was sure mine did. Instead they lured me in closer, making me thankful for the solid conference table between us.

He tilted his chin and quirked his upper lip. I prayed he wouldn't smile. Those dimples of his stole my breath and made me stupid.

My heart jumped at the sudden loud rapping of his knuckles on the table.

"Knock. Knock." The gravelly rumble of his voice, unobstructed by technology, strummed across my nerve endings. The vibrations fluttered in my stomach. My starved heart ached to leap into his hands.

Dear Lord! I was nowhere near prepared for this.

I eyed him with the same caution I'd give any wild carnivore. "Who's there?"

"Vivi said I had to knock to get you to come. Did it work, Presh?"

I swallowed and flashed him an exasperated grimace, hoping my sensitivities to all things Michael Cooper wouldn't show. I brushed off the innuendo in his question, trying to keep things professional when I felt anything but. "You did more than knock, but here I am."

The fact my voice came out as clear as it did was a miracle.

"Here. *You.* Are," he drawled. His eyes made a languid descent, dropping below my belt. I felt naked, despite wearing tan breeches and riding boots. "And yet you're still so far away. Aren't you going to come closer, Presh?"

I hadn't actually decided whether to stand, sit, or run for my life. I could barely keep his wicked grin, or the endearment I loved so well, from rocking the walls I was fighting to keep up.

His voice lowered just enough for it to lose the toying quality that always clung to it. "Have a seat."

Figuring sitting would be far less sexually charged than my other options, I moved forward. Fingers twitching, I took hold of my seat back, but Coop *tsk*ed me. "Eh eh eh. Not there."

I glared, half expecting him to pat his thigh and beckon me to sit on his lap. I probably would've. That's how strong a hold he had on my sanity *and* how little a grip I had on it. Thankfully, his hands clenched the armrests as he slowly rose with an annoyed sigh.

Before I could drool over the intricacies of his straining tendons, muscles, and veins—*Hello, forearm porn!*—he'd pushed up to stand. *Whoa.* So much taller than I'd realized and growing even larger as he moved right in front of me. I felt the need to take a step back to keep the whole of him in my focus. Instead I froze, letting him shadow me.

"I believe I was clear that my offer was *on the table.*"

My pulse sped from hard, distinct pounds into something closer to static, crackling just beneath my skin.

He wrapped his hands around my hips, his wide fingers pressing through my breeches and into my flesh like he was branding me with his prints. I gasped and grabbed for his shoulders as he hoisted me up as if I were nothing more than an empty box. When he deposited my ass at the head of the conference table, the chill and hardness of the marble stunned my skin through the thin cotton.

From the thrill in his eyes, I was no mere package. I was a Christmas present he couldn't wait to tear into and play with until it broke. And damn my professionalism to hell, I wanted to be his favorite toy. *Ho ho ho.*

Kicking Zaki's unused chair aside, he wedged his body between my knees. Eye to eye, trading breaths, his physical presence became more potent to me than I knew how to deal with. I was toast.

His lips parted.

Buttered toast.

How was I ever going to be able to kill him if he kissed me? And if he kissed my lips, I knew I would want him to kiss everything.

"I want everything on the table, including you..."

I panicked and spat out, "I'm seeing someone."

Coop's forehead dropped as he dramatically collapsed down to his elbows. He made some sort of noise I couldn't decipher, then I realized he was laughing. *Laughing!* I wanted to kick him, but his face was in my lap and my fingers ached to stroke his hair and keep him there.

He rolled his eyes up to look into mine. "*Who* are you seeing, Princess?"

Princess. Realizing I was still gripping his shoulders, pressing them down to keep his face hovering near my *kus*, I gave them a shove.

Coop pushed up on his palms, locking his elbows straight as he treated me to a sliver of fresh air and plenty of rope to keep hanging myself.

Swallowing, I slipped the proverbial noose over my neck. "Brecken."

"Wolfe?" he repeated in an incredulous tone.

I nodded. "Yes. We've gotten very close the past couple of weeks. It's still new, but you were right, we're a good fit."

He heaved an annoyed sigh, then leaned in. My pulse pounded against my eardrums as his lips hovered close.

"Liar." He ground the harsh word out as if he were crushing it—and my heart—through his clenched teeth.

I stiffened with indignity. "Why would you say that?"

"Because, *Princess*, I told him if he touched you, I would cut off his hand and make him wear it around his neck, *Game of Thrones* style."

I narrowed my eyes. "You did not!"

"Oh, I did."

"Why?" I spat. When he didn't respond immediately, I slid off the table.

I brushed Coop aside and hit the remote to open the vault door. "You know what, I don't care why. I'm tired of playing games with you."

"Says the woman who's making me jealous with her imaginary boyfriend. Tell Wolfe you'll be on the runway in a half hour for his goodbye kiss. This I gotta see."

I started to spin back on my boot heel and growl, *'I wasn't trying to make you jealous!'* when I realized what he'd finally admitted to me. "You're...*jealous*?"

Coop

I'd had my doubts Zee would actually come on the dive with me. To my knowledge, she'd never left the island. She'd have little choice in speaking with me in person, though. The power of OZ worked to my advantage there, and I had zero qualms in using his influence over Zee. Especially as I watched her walk toward me.

There was a moment where she sharpened from still being the mirage from the beach into reality. My heart stopped. Not long enough to kill me, but enough that I thought it might.

I swallowed as I took her beauty in. She was as elegant and mysterious as her island home. Twin strips of black hair bracketed her forehead while the rest fell in a thick, lustrous braid over one shoulder. Beneath the graceful column of her neck, her loose-fitting white blouse billowed open. A generous swath of olive-toned skin showed across her collarbone and chest. The breeze from her anger-propelled stride flirted with revealing more, right up until she came to an abrupt halt inside the doorway.

Fuck me. This woman was going to kill me before the tumor even had a chance. I blatantly gawked at her before reminding myself that the room still had oxygen and I was long overdue to take a freaking breath.

I clicked the remote to seal the vault door shut, just in case she changed her mind about talking to me. When the lock bolt clanged, she looked like she wanted to hit a panic button and run. I couldn't blame her.

Close up, the slight divot in her plush pink lips gave her a hint of vulnerability. It matched a larger dimple in her chin. Her eyes were rimmed in onyx, or maybe her lashes were as thick and black as her hair. Either way, her dark eyes showcased her keen sharpness. All things I'd admired through the various lenses I was used to seeing her through, but Aziza in real life... I'd never wanted to touch anything or anyone more.

I could scarcely hold myself in check, right up until she lied to me. *Again.* Hypocritical of me? Yeah. I'd own that I was hiding things from her too.

Damn, aren't we a pair?

Maybe that's why I had laughed when she'd claimed to be seeing Wolfe. Well, that and it wasn't even a good lie. I'd forgive her another deception. *For now.* But only until I was ready to come clean with my own secrets. It might've been the stupidest line in the sand I'd ever drawn, but it was my stupid line in the sand.

Didn't mean I wouldn't give her shit about Wolfe just to watch her squirm.

Calling her a princess had been instinctual suppressive fire. She may have hated the endearment, but it fit her as well as her cream-colored breeches. Which I couldn't help but notice were tightly stretched over her shapely thighs and perfectly cupping her ass as she started to storm out.

Shit. She's getting away.

I hadn't been paying close attention to what I was saying, I'd been too captivated sparring with her and more than a little punch-drunk from having my face in her lap. But then she'd pushed me away and now she was leaving and I didn't know what to say to get her to return. I'd started to yell *"Stop!"* when, as if reading my mind, she halted abruptly in the doorway.

"Why would you be jealous?"

I almost snapped back with some quip about not being jealous of Wolfe, but taunting her online had been a lot easier than having her close enough to devour. Besides, I wasn't sure if I'd ever get another shot at telling Zee how I felt about her. I might've been an idiot in most ways, but I wasn't going to die with this being one of them.

"*Are* you with Wolfe? Truth."

"No," she admitted quickly. After waiting a beat, she added, "But if I was with him or anyone else? Would you be jealous? *Truth*."

I pressed the button to close the vault door again as I walked up behind her. Cupping her shoulders, I lowered my head, letting my lips hover over the skin at the back of her neck, just behind her ear. Wanting so desperately to kiss her, I ground out the most honest thing I'd ever told her. "*Insanely*."

Chapter Twelve

Aziza

My heartbeat scattered along with my thoughts. One minute I was about to faint from the tickling stroke of Coop's breath across the nape of my neck and the next he'd spun me around and hoisted me back onto the table. Was this really happening? It couldn't be. *Could it?* I reached out and pinched his chest.

He growled.

Shit. He's real.

His eyes cut a harsh line to mine and I wiped the smile from my face. "S...orry."

Flames seared his pupils, like fire dancing over the ocean. His fingertips skirted up the outer edge of my arm, but my nipples tightened painfully, as if he were stroking them. "Don't worry about it, Presh, because..." His husky voice trailed off as his eyes dropped. He continued his thought, idly whispering to one of the sensitive peaks straining toward him, "I plan on doing much worse to you."

My body quaked with full-on awareness. I forced a deep breath through my nose. But his scent was like some crazy mixture of ocean, wind, rock, and sky. How could a man dressed straight from Savile Row show up here looking to take me like a warrior while smelling of star dust and sea mist?

I shakily drew back.

I was imagining him again. This *couldn't* be reality.

Yet live stream videos relayed real-time current events. Nighttime traffic flowed like a bright kaleidoscope around Seven Dials in West End. The POTUS waved from the south lawn of the White House in D.C. before getting ready to take off in Marine One. A haboob had blurred out most all of Dubai's outside cameras throughout the day, but the dust had started to settle as night had fallen. Here on the island, a German shepherd was getting an acupuncture treatment. Little pins speared out all over his black and tan head, but his tongue lolled from his mouth like he was drunk and in love.

All the screens and monitors powered off. The room darkened, now only lit by the glow of the conference table's emerald-colored undermount lights.

"*Presh*?" Coop drawled, before setting the remote back on the table. "Just you and me. The rest of the world can wait for one goddamned minute."

I reached out and let my fingers trace his face. His skin felt smooth. My heart sped dangerously. "The beard suited you."

Coop's hand went to his jaw, his fingers meeting mine and stroking against them. A sensual tremble ripped through me despite the gentle maneuver. "I'll grow it for you. Give me a couple of hours."

"You were off the grid longer than a couple of hours." I hadn't been able to keep the disappointment from my voice.

"I know." The tender tone accounted for both his disappearance, as well as the hurt it had caused me.

"We're going to have to talk about that."

"I know."

"Are you really here, *Mushaeghib*?"

His slow nod acknowledged just how heavily loaded a question it was.

"Pinch me again, if you want," he offered with a manly chuckle. His laugh changed to a low growl when I took him up, squeezing a little harder for leaving and for not letting me know he was attracted to me.

His eyes flared, as if I'd been disobedient for actually following his directive. "Is that so, *Precious*?"

He grabbed my hips and hauled me flush with him, like being pressed up against his masculine body was somehow a punishment. So solid. So...*hard*. The thin fabric of his slim-fit dress pants left nothing to the imagination. And even my active imagination couldn't have done him the justice God had.

My eyes bulged as much as his pants did. "Is *that* so, Sharky?"

"Is what so?"

I tilted my hips, rocking myself pointedly against his thickened length. So *very* rigid. "Already?"

The inferno blazing in his eyes pulled oxygen from my lungs. His grip tightened, restricting my rocking motion to a grind. In a voice rough with gravel and lust, he asked, "Did you really think you were the only one who imagined this day? Us together?"

Yes!

"When I asked you to com—"

His mouth roared against mine like a rogue wave slamming into the shore, our tongues eagerly tumbling together like white water. *Whoa.* He tasted like warm, masculine sin. Definitely not just my imagination. No, this was real in a way that went beyond anything I'd ever felt before. But then, the feelings I had for Coop went way beyond anything I'd ever experienced.

"You're thinking too much," he growled as he gripped my braid and pulled it back, drawing my lips harshly away from his and silencing everything but the feel of him. He kissed down my chin, then pulled my braid back another inch to bare my neck to him. Sucking hungrily, he moved his lips and tongue down, insatiable for my flesh.

I'd never had anyone who wanted me with such powerful intensity. Even my own fantasies had been lukewarm compared to this inferno. And still I spurred him faster. I tunneled my fingers through his hair, drawing him closer and pulling him in. Even his shampoo smelled wicked.

As he ran his tongue and teeth along my collarbone, I clasped my legs around him, opening my hips so our bodies could meld. His thick cock rocked right against my clit, knocking a whimper of pleasure from my lips.

A low and rough moan sounded as he glided his hand up my side. His wide thumb strummed the outer curve of my breast in silent question, as his whisper became more husky demand, "You owe me a pinch."

Unable to find my voice to acquiesce, I leaned back onto my palms and arched my back. Coop nudged the white cotton collar of my shirt. When the gap didn't reveal enough to please him, he gripped the edge and ripped it aside. Hearing threads snap, I sucked in a gasp. Pearl buttons skittered across the marble table. Instead of being pissed at one of my favorite blouses being ruined, I was so turned on I could scarcely see straight.

He easily released the front closure on my bra with the snap of his strong fingers.

"God, Zee," he growled with appreciation.

His thumb stroked back and forth over my peaked nipple before he joined his forefinger with it and squeezed. Like a match being struck, my blood combusted and a throaty groan escaped my lips.

My nipple remained trapped in the vice of his fingers, while his stiffened tongue teased the captive bead mercilessly. The sharp stabs of pleasure shooting straight to my clit were more than I could take. My hips wriggled and jerked in a desperate attempt to both satiate and escape. We were grinding so hard together our breaths were already coming in pants and gasps.

His tongue kept up its hungry assault, even though my whimpers were getting loud and pained. Desperate to cling to something, I clawed for the back of his neck as I arched and came with a fraught moan peppered with girlish squeaks.

"Fuuuck," he ground out, gasping for air along with me as our bodies stilled.

After a few shallow breaths, he laughed. His lips softened as they tracked over to my other breast. "I didn't even get to talk to you, sweet thing," he lamented as he dropped a kiss on my other taut nipple, setting off an aftershock.

I palmed the sides of his square jaw with both hands to urge him away from the now hypersensitive area. With a grumble, he adjusted my bra back over me and latched it closed. His eyes lifted to mine as he cupped my chin and kissed me deeply.

I ran my hand between us to help take care of his needs as well, and realized he was good. *Very good* if the wet spot was any indication.

"Is *that* so?" I teased, still breathless.

"Four years of foreplay does that," he admitted sheepishly. "Never happened before, not even as a teen. I'd be embarrassed, but at least I lasted longer than you did."

I laughed, swatting him. "By a second!"

"Two. *Two* seconds. I'll take at least twice as long when we get to the boat, promise."

I started to laugh, then stiffened. *The boat.* The dive. Leaving the island. "I can't, Coop."

"Can't or won't?" he asked, his voice a mix of disappointment and frustration.

"It's not that simple," I hedged, my post-orgasm brain completely abandoning me as I tried to navigate the lies which bound me here.

"Why? *Truth.*"

Suddenly this intimate moment had morphed into a very dangerous game of truth or dare.

A hundred reasons filed through my mind, but I couldn't share any of them honestly. Not yet. A thousand fabricated excuses hovered on my tongue, but I didn't want to lie to Coop anymore. Not now. I drug my lower lip through my teeth.

I'd kept him from the island because he made me long for things I couldn't have. I'd fought my feelings for years, telling myself it was just girlish infatuation. But even from the first day, I'd known better. I'd known he would be the downfall of everything I'd worked so hard to build.

And maybe a part of me was starting to secretly long for that too.

It was only a couple of days.

Barely a few miles away.

Was it even really leaving the island if I wasn't going to another country?

Not really.

The helo would be back to Marakata tomorrow. If all hell broke loose, it could pick me up and return me on short notice.

Before I could change my mind, I lifted the corners of my mouth and chose dare.

"Give me an hour."

* * * *

I scurried around my suite, shoving a few necessities into a bag. Okay, the sexiest PJs, underwear, and swimsuits I owned may not have been necessities, exactly. But the closest thing to luggage I owned was a yoga bag. Skimpy clothes were all that would fit.

Knowing we'd be skydiving, I jammed my legs into a pair of fuchsia capri leggings and pulled on a matching formfitting sports tank.

I took a deep breath, making yet another quick mental catalog of the preparations I'd made. Forgetting even the smallest detail could be disastrous.

I still couldn't believe I'd shuffled the schedule around enough to clear a few days. *Three* full days to feel somewhat normal. For as long as I'd lived on Marakata, freedom had only been glimpsed a few hours at a time on a horse's back. Even less when scuba diving. Scant minutes while falling through the air on a skydive.

I'd been good at convincing myself that living on an amazing island with every luxury at my fingertips wasn't a cage. I'd even gone so far as to tell myself this life had been my choice. In some ways it had been. But eventually the day had come when I couldn't pretend any longer. The day I'd wanted to leave and couldn't. The day I had met Michael Cooper.

I sucked on my lower lip to taste him again. Replaying our kisses made the corners of my mouth stretch wide. Imagining three whole days with him had me flopping onto my bed dizzy with laughter like a teenage girl. A *normal* one, not the one I'd been.

I closed my eyes and visualized a montage of fun and flirty dating antics like I'd seen in the many romantic movies and series I'd watched over the year — playing in the surf, kissing, riding horses, sharing meals, more kissing, torrid sex in every position and every corner of the island. I screamed happily into my pillow.

I didn't have time to bask in my folly. I had ten minutes to get to the airfield.

I took one last look around my suite before turning off all of my monitors. Was this what being taken off life support felt like? Because it took me a minute to find my breath. Even my heart jostled erratically before settling into a rhythm again. This was good though. My aunts would be proud.

Jogging, I hurried out the door. Just as I made it to my Bronco, a call from A&I came in.

I slung my yoga bag into the backseat as I answered. "Gray, what's up?"

"Zee, oh my gosh. We just got your message about heading off the island for a couple of days. I'm so glad I caught you," Gray rushed to say.

I balanced my cell phone between my shoulder and ear as I swung up into the driver's seat. "Everything okay?"

I reached for the keys, which were always left in the ignition, and with a quick twist, I turned the engine over.

"I've got a lot— Oh gosh, Zee, I'm feeling as lost as last year's Easter egg. I don't even know how or where to begin."

"Maybe with not so many sweet teas?" I said, glancing over my shoulder as I backed out. "What's up? Something with the reality show production company?"

"Well, yes, I did find out whose umbrella it's under. Checked out as a pet project for the Austin heiresses."

I shifted into drive. "The Winkie twins?"

Olivia and Ophelia Austin had been born into a family fortune built largely on their grandfather's famous popcorn. But the heiresses had broken into stardom on their own via a kid's show called *The Winkies*. Each of the show's characters was a human version of an emoticon—smiley, frownie, sleepy, etc... The twins played the leads, which were the only two duplicate emoticons in the show's world. Both were winkies, but Olivia always winked with her left eye, while Ophelia winked with her right.

When the Austin twins had hit puberty, they'd outgrown their stagnant roles and tried to move on to tween TV shows and movies. But the young twins had struggled to keep fans happy when all they ever wanted was for the twins to make their respective winking facial expression for social media photos. Instead of rebelling, as kid stars tended to, they'd parlayed their fame into a multimillion-dollar line of eye makeup.

"Doesn't sound like their norm," I mused.

"Yes, yes. Exactly." Gray pushed out a breath then started right back full throttle, which wasn't easy with a southern drawl. "Well, something didn't smell right to me. I mean, the Austin twins are diversifying, but a reality show just doesn't fit into their trajectory. They've clearly wanted to be seen as grown-up, to be taken seriously, so a show about sexuality makes sense, but the pansexual focus, while certainly relevant, comes off as..."

"Reaching?"

"Yes! And I mean, it's not the first time a young actor or actress was heavy-handed when asserting their adulthood, but this show didn't seem to be run with their usual attention to detail, so I thought I'd check it against any other recent projects, and I fell down the proverbial rabbit hole. I traced the entire corporate maze of shell companies and get this... Not only are there no other projects of this nature, but there are *two* entities under the Austin heiresses' umbrella that have common touchpoints to the trafficking ring trying to get a foothold in the Amazon."

"Ring? You mean human trafficking?"

"Yes! Might be a coincidence but..."

"OZ doesn't believe in coincidences."

"Exactly!"

Neither did I. Nefarious pirates were snooping around my wreck site at the same exact time that a potential human trafficking upstart was systematically taking down the drug cartel which controlled routes in the Amazon. Both of these entities traced back to the same corporate umbrella. Question was, how else were these two things connected, because it certainly didn't all hinge on The Winkies.

"Great work, Gray." I pulled out onto the ridge road, heading toward the airport. "Send me everything you have and I'll put fresh eyes on it."

"I will, but there's more, Zee. The part I don't know how to tell you. Are you sitting down?"

It wasn't like Gray to be evasive. "Just say it."

"It's about the *sicario* taking out Alverez's cartel."

I pressed my foot on the gas as if I could outrun this news and make it on the plane before it ever hit my ears. The wind whipped at my hair as my stomach cramped.

"Zee, I'm sorry. It was Michael Cooper. I know, I know, I didn't want to believe it either. We all love Coop. But there's proof."

Chapter Thirteen

Coop

Late-day sun beat down on the runway as I scanned the asphalt roads leading toward the airfield. The Twin Otter skydiving plane had become stifling as we wedged together on the bench seats. Titan's panting sure as hell didn't help.

"Dude, she's not coming," Nik grunted from the opposite end of the fuselage, made even more crowded thanks to the large storage trunk that was getting dropped with us. We'd been loaded up and ready to go for the past twenty minutes.

Not only was Nik irritated and impatient, he was still side-eyeing me for my antics in the war room. Returning with my rumpled dress shirt yanked out to hide the wet spot on my pants certainly hadn't helped prove my innocence. Embarrassing as it was, I couldn't hold back my smirk. God, that sexy woman had managed to get a gallon out of me with just a little dry humping.

Thankfully, I'd changed into a clean pair of shorts and a T-shirt. But I could still taste Zee's sweet mouth, feel her body wrapped around mine, smell her on my skin. *Mojitos*, that's what her scent reminded me of — an intoxicating mix of sweet mint and lime, and just as easy to get drunk on.

"We're losing daylight," Nik muttered, ruining my daydream. "Let's go."

I didn't respond. I wasn't ready to admit she'd bailed on me, but it sure as hell looked that way. She'd told me she needed an hour. It was now bordering on another half past that.

I'd spent some of it researching what I could on Zaki's shipwreck to refresh my knowledge of the events. But like all things OZ, the information was scarce. The mega yacht *Esmeralda* and her crew had departed Salvador, Brazil, carrying Omar Zaki, his son, Sheikh Malik, and his ten-year-old granddaughter, Zamirah. While en route to Marakata, the *Esmeralda* had become disabled on one of the many outlying coral reef systems before being hit by tropical storm Oscar. Due to the violence of the waves, the damaged ship had swiftly taken on water.

The majority of the crew, Sheik Malik, and Zamirah had abandoned ship in the tender, leaving Zaki and the captain to barely escape via life raft. But the captain had been pitched from the small raft before it could make it to a nearby island. The tender carrying all the others had been decimated by a rogue wave. The rest was speculation and rumor, fueled by Zaki's refusal to be seen in public.

Knowing there'd been more to the story, I was eager to get down to the wreck site and see for myself.

"Coop, do you have any more of those headache pills?" Thea asked.

I glanced over at her. "Everything okay?"

"Yeah, between the heat and those flaming green shots my head's spinning."

"You weren't supposed to have any alcohol," Nik chastised. He'd had a stick up his butt concerning Thea's safety since her kidnapping. Seeing his reaction to her had kept me from telling him the whole truth about my own medical situation.

I fished out two pills for myself and handed another over to her.

Despite looking stunning after her spa day, Thea appeared tense. Her wide-eyed gaze darted around the plane. Due to her amnesia, this qualified as her second time ever in an airplane, and she was going to have to jump out of it. Tandem with Nik, of course. I planned to take Titan as my strap. Leo had been under canopy solo a handful of times thanks to Nik and I making him dive with us in the past. He'd been a fairly competent jumper, enough to make the beach drop zone we were headed to. But it had been a while since our last go, so Leo wasn't what I considered current on skills.

Nik had already reviewed the basics with Leo when he'd taught Thea how to position herself for the freefall. But I reminded, "COA every few seconds." Circle of awareness was a constant cycle of checks to ensure safety. I tossed a helmet into his lap. "You'll be fine. Put this on."

A drop of sweat pilling along his hairline fell as he glanced down at it, unsure.

"Don't tell me—you're afraid of ruining your new hairdo?" I mocked. Django had slathered a fair amount of product in Leo's hair, but the cut did give the kid some much-needed edge. Short on the sides and curly... Why was it *so* curly on top? *Did that fucker get a perm?*

"More like ruining my brain," he fretted. "How is this supposed to protect me in a fall from ten thousand feet?"

"Your pretty head will be just fine, brother." *Mine, on the other hand, needs a hell of a lot more than a hard hat.* "The helmet is so Nik and I can comm with you if you need."

Leo glared at me from his cramped seat in the plane's tail as he clenched his stomach like he might puke. He didn't like taking risks the way Nik and I did. If we didn't get wheels up soon, I knew my little brother would wuss out.

Where the hell was Zee? Had she bailed or flat lied? Maybe this was payback for abandoning her. Teaching me a lesson.

After admitting how badly I wanted her...tasting the rawness of her beautiful desire...her absence now felt like a RIP round to the heart.

If this was how I'd made her feel, I deserved every painful bit of it. Maybe it was good this was a suicide mission. If she wasn't hurting me, I knew I would ultimately be hurting her.

"Let's go," I barked as I rolled down the garage-style jump door.

Jessie, the pilot, turned the engines over. While she taxied the plane to the rock wall, Titan leaned into my right side and poked his nose into the tender spot just left of my sternum. I smoothed the fauxhawk the groomer had given him down as I dropped a kiss on his forehead. "I know, boy. It's breaking, isn't it?"

I really didn't blame Zee for backing out on me. It'd been too much to ask her to leave the island, even for a few days. It wasn't even like I'd expected her to say yes. My goal had been for her to meet me in the middle, which she had when she'd come to see me in the war room. But my hopes had gotten so high up when she'd said yes that the crash hurt like fucking hell.

The plane's engines spooled up as Jessie prepared for takeoff.

I popped two gummy bears from the pouch in my pocket as the plane picked up speed. Knowing I might never see Zee again, I closed my eyes, trying to engrave her image on the backs of my eyelids.

We all pitched forward when the plane's acceleration dropped sharply off and the brakes engaged.

"What now?" Nik groaned over the squelching brakes.

I craned to look out the cockpit window. In the small opening between Jessie and her copilot, Peter, right below the rearview mirror upon which a pair of fuzzy emerald green dice dangled, I could see the hold up. A vintage Bronco stopped right across the runway. The driver flagged her hand toward us. Satisfied she'd caught Jessie's attention, Aziza pulled out of the way.

"Looks like we're picking up a hitchhiker," Peter hollered back to us.

I scrambled to roll up the door, smiling as the most beautiful soul on the planet sprinted to the plane with a bag over her shoulder and her rig pack in her hand.

"I didn't think you were coming," I said over the engine noise as I reached out to help her with her things.

Locking forearms with her, I hoisted her easily up the few feet into the fuselage. "Last-minute intel I had to take a look at. Then I couldn't find my lucky chute and had to pack a new one."

I mentally kicked myself. "Sorry, I should've made sure there was one ready to go for you."

I signaled to Jessie that we were good to go again. After rolling the door back down, I turned to watch Aziza stow her personal belongings in the supply chest that would be dropped with us. She then quickly and awkwardly introduced herself around as the plane repositioned itself to take off again.

I squeezed over to make more room on the bench. "Aziza, here."

Distracted, she muttered something about her rig pack, then bent down to grab it. The plane swung into position, knocking Zee off balance. She'd barely righted herself when Jessie accelerated for takeoff.

I cursed under my breath as I rose up, grasping Zee's wrist. "Sit. Now."

The sharp liftoff caused her body to collide against my chest as her rig fell back to the floor. Her tush dropped, settling her weight on my thigh.

"*Mushaeghib!*" she hollered, as if I'd orchestrated the whole thing.

She grasped for her dropped pack as it slid down the aisle, but my arm wrapped around her kept her safely in place while the plane continued to sharply climb in altitude.

Her body stiffened as I held her close. Not like in the war room when she had eagerly molded herself to me.

Hmm. I dismissed her changed behavior as nerves about leaving the island or because she'd been scrambling to get to the plane.

I tucked my nose behind her ear, enjoying the smell of her shampoo. Delighting in the fact she'd used her hour and a half to do more than clear her schedule and look at last-minute intel. "Thank you," I whispered.

Her breath stuttered as her eyes, dark and conflicted, met mine. "For what?"

"For trusting me. For being here. For finding me devastatingly handsome."

Her laugh sounded cautious. Now I was certain something had changed since we'd parted ways leaving the war room.

"Two outta three's not bad," I conceded.

"Coop. What happened earlier...was earlier. And right now? We're on a job. I'm still your boss."

"And I'm very good at following orders," I whispered against her nape, even though the rattling of the fuselage and humming of the twin turbo props kept our conversation private. Not that either of us noticed anyone or anything else.

I stroked my pinkie across her temple as I tucked a wayward strand of her hair behind her ear. I couldn't help but thrill at her shiver. She might've cooled off since the war room, but she wasn't frozen. *Yet.*

"I mean, we need to keep boundaries," she said in all seriousness.

"Well, *boss*, you're sitting in my lap, and your thigh keeps brushing against my dick like you're playing a violin concerto. I don't think *you* should be lecturing *me* about boundaries."

Flustered, Zee shot up and squeaked as her hand went straight to my crotch, fingers curling around my stiffy.

"Yeah, boundaries probably aren't your thing," I suggested.

She jerked her hand away as if she'd been burned. I chuckled, calmly supporting her elbow to stabilize her as she stood between my legs. She pulled away from that touch as well.

Did she really think she could keep her body from mine? We were like magnets and metal. But okay, might be fun to play along.

I spread my thighs wide, giving her more room. "No touching, I know," I said as I leaned back and crossed my hands behind my neck.

Her eyes narrowed at my champagne room pose. She tried to snarl at my antics, but her gaze snagged across the underside of my biceps. Her tongue jutted out like she wanted to lap up my trident tattoo. Between her distraction and the turbulence, she pitched forward. My instinct was to catch her, but she didn't want my help. I kept my fingers laced at my neck as her soft breasts gracelessly, and a little painfully, collided with my face. I didn't hate the slapping dance they did across my nose as she tried to right herself without help.

Bracing both palms on my pecs, she pushed up and attempted to hike a leg over my thigh. It was almost elegant until the turbulence knocked her forward again. She rode my thigh as her body thrust against me.

I snapped a fake nip near her ear. Scoffing, she scrambled to stand, this time turning around. She promptly went down again, all the way to the floor. Gripping both my thighs, she heaved herself back upright. Her ass cheeks brushed up my hardened crotch and I groaned.

"Just help me, please," she barked.

With a sigh, I unlatched my hands and easily lifted her by her hips into the seat next to me. "You were just getting the hang of it, Presh."

"Could you please treat me like a professional?" she hissed as she straightened herself. Her eyes darted around the cabin, worried about who'd been watching, but Nik and Thea were too busy cooing over each other and Leo was too nervous about the jump to care. Only Titan returned her eye contact, and he wasn't buying it.

"Professional? Right, my bad." I grimaced as I shifted my hard-on into a more comfortable position. "I didn't bring any dollar bills, but if you have change for a five—"

"I'm serious, Coop." When her glare met mine, I realized I wasn't the only one erecting things. The walls in her gorgeous, nearly black irises had gone up, locking me out of her beautiful mind.

I'd been wrong. Boundaries were very much her thing.

"Whatever you want, *Princess*."

Chapter Fourteen

Aziza

What I wanted was for Coop to stop calling me a princess. But what I needed right now was my rig. I hollered over the engine noise to get Leo's attention then pointed to my pack, which had slid into him during takeoff.

He tossed the rig. Coop caught it and started to hand it to me.

"Actually," I said, "I think the kit you packed has my lucky chute. Would you mind trading?"

Coop narrowed his eyes. "You don't think it's unlucky to swap rigs once in the air?"

"I'll take my chances."

"You're the boss." He groaned, shrugging the rig off. As we traded gear, he asked, "You pack this?"

"Yes. Why?"

"You were rushed, running late. You seem very distracted. On edge, even."

On edge? That was rich, considering the razor he'd been playing on in the Amazon.

Distracted? Hell yes, I'd been distracted. Coop taking out Alvarez's inner circle had been a different beast when it was only me and my suspicions. Now I no longer had total control of the dissemination of any information — or the outcome.

It hadn't just been Gray, either. As I was packing my chute I'd been alerted to a correspondence between Scott Hayes and OZ.

SH: We can't trust Coop.

OZ: Aziza's handling it.

SH: Is she? Aziza hasn't exactly been on top of things lately. She's not thinking rationally. Coop might even be playing on her emotions.

OZ: Aziza brought me this information several weeks before you and your team did. So when I tell you she's handling it, it's because you didn't. Aziza will *do what she has to do.*

At least I still had Zaki on my side. But for how long?

So hell yes, when I'd been packing my chute, I'd been preoccupied.

"I'm worried about you, Zee."

"Don't be," I snapped, knowing I was being overly sensitive.

It wasn't uncommon for Hayes to communicate directly with Zaki. In fact, I'd long suspected he preferred to. His need for 'man to man' discussions had triggered some of my best eye-rolls, but he'd never thrown me under the bus until now.

Bitch of it was, I couldn't even refute it. It *wasn't* rational for me to leave the island, to pack a bag full of sexy clothes for a mission my very existence depended on, to still be stupidly in love with a man I had hard proof had gone rogue, or to—*Dear Lord!*—let him bring me to orgasm on the war room conference table!

Hayes was right to worry about my mental state. I just had to focus and not let my attraction to Coop distract me from the facts or keep me from the job.

"Here, give it back. I'll gladly take the chute packed by a distracted, on edge, *woman*."

Coop scrutinized me until I gave him my full attention. "Zee. You know that wasn't what I was saying. Of course I trust your abilities, you."

You shouldn't. I grimaced, not wanting to think about the reality of that.

"Zee." Coop's voice was as gentle as the hand he wrapped around my arm.

I had trouble meeting his eyes, considering one of my objectives was to potentially put him down.

"I respect the hell out of you. You're the most capable person I know, and I know some pretty fucking impressive people. Many, if not most, are women."

"Thank you. It's just, I wouldn't have been rushed if—" I clamped my lips together. Several thousand feet above the ocean was not the time to get into the whole Amazon betrayal. Mainly because I didn't trust myself enough not to push Coop out of the airplane before he finished rigging back up.

"If?"

I stepped into the loosened leg straps of my lucky pack. As I hiked it up, Coop suddenly was directly in front of me. I swallowed and tried to remember what I'd been saying. "Um…I hadn't planned on you—"

I sucked in the rest of my sentence as Coop's large hand reached between my thighs.

"Let me help you with that." His deep blue eyes flicked down to mine as his fingers brushed just shy of center. He curled them under the bunched nylon strap, stroking it smooth as his heated breath teased across the nape of my neck.

He wrapped the tail of the strap in his fist and yanked, testing the clasp. The force rocked my body forward into his solid one. "You hadn't planned on what?"

"You…" I held my breath as he started repeating the intimate sequence on the other leg. I feared he'd feel the evidence of my body's reaction to him as his hand slipped between my legs again. The intense passion between Coop and me, even during the simple act of rigging up, was undeniable.

After he tugged again, he repeated the question with a knowing smirk. "You hadn't planned on me doing what exactly, Presh?"

I stuttered out a moan as his ribbed knuckles swiped over my hardened nipples while he thoroughly adjusted the chest strap. He turned me around and checked from behind, then swatted my ass to let me know he was finished with me.

So much for keeping it professional.

I whipped back around to face him, determined to resist his annoying charm and panty-dropping sexuality. "I hadn't planned on you…strong-arming me into working this job with you."

"Strong-arming?" He pressed his lips together and scrunched his brows in a doubtful grimace. "Is that really what I'm doing to you, Presh?"

My mind flashed back to the war room and the deliriously intense orgasm he'd given me. My *kus* throbbed, eager for more.

"With the job," I clarified. Everything else I'd been eager and willing and excited for. Even my active imagination hadn't prepared me for our connection in real life.

Maybe Hayes was right to bypass me and go straight to Zaki. My head clearly wasn't in the game and hadn't been for a while now. For all I knew, my panties weren't the only thing Coop wanted me to drop. Was it like Hayes thought? Was Coop using my crush on him, my body's overreaction to him, to get my guard down?

"How exactly did I strong-arm you, Presh?"

"You knew what you were doing. Going to Zaki."

"Oh! *He's* the reason you came. *Right.*" Coop quickly geared himself back up.

I was thankful he let the conversation drop, because I sensed we were getting close to the wreck site. I could feel the nervous energy buzzing in my bones. A muscle memory of sorts.

Fragments of the past shuffled quickly through my mind like a deck of cards in a dealer's hands. *Fighting. Gunshots. Death. An out-of-control amusement park ride. Blood. Darkness. Soaked clothing. Soaked skin. The smell of the slick orange rubber life raft. Hands reaching for mine. Drowning. The intense taste of salt. The certainty of death.*

A flash of red brought me back to the plane with a start. The light by the exit door.

"Two minutes to DZ," Coop called out, breaking my trance. "Check equipment."

Coop scooped up Titan and clamped him into position on his chest, then slipped the dog's goggles over his eyes. I stroked the shepherd's forehead, then Coop and I double-checked each other's rigs while Leo and Nik buddied up on theirs.

Thea looked scared but excited. I shot her a thumbs-up and said over the helmet comms, "Don't worry, you're going to love it!"

The light turned yellow, signaling we were a half mile to the drop zone. I crowded up alongside Coop, like a kid cutting in line for cake.

"Going first?" Coop laughed as he rolled open the door.

I nodded.

"Be safe," he said as I turned around to exit backward. He motioned with two fingers from his eyes to mine, to let me know he'd watch my back. I'd always been able to count on him, which was why this rogue shit didn't make any sense. But right now all I wanted was to shed the weight of worry from my shoulders.

Jessie backed the propeller speed and torque off. "Exit, exit, exit." Her voice carried through the fuselage as she turned the light to green.

I launched with my gaze hooked on Coop. Dropping away from the opening in the Twin Otter, I felt weightless. After I watched Coop shove an unappreciative Leo out the hatch, I laughed and spiraled away.

During free fall there was always a sense of motionlessness, the air simultaneously holding me while also speeding past. But really it was the air that was motionless as I fell toward earth at over a hundred miles per hour. Moving much too fast to think, time stood still, the Earth stopped rotating. I arched my body, twirling and dancing in space.

Total freedom would barely last a minute or so before I'd have to pull the ripcord on it.

Below me the gold strip of earth waited. Not far was the yacht we'd be working off of. And somewhere deep below the ocean's surface were all of my secrets.

They all could wait a couple seconds longer.

Chapter Fifteen

Coop

Once Nik and Thea had cleared the plane, I readied Titan and shuffled back to the opening. The copilot, Peter, stood by to launch the storage bin behind me. I glanced down, expecting to see Zee's chute deployed by now. She was still in free fall. *Shit.*

"Zee, pull your chute now," I commanded over the comms as I launched. I made as aerodynamic a beeline toward her as I could with Titan strapped to me. She wasn't technically in trouble. *Yet.* But she wasn't playing it safe — blissfully enjoying her little sky ballet while leaving zero room for error. "This isn't a pleasure dive, Zee. Pull now!"

Fuck! It was my stupid fault she was on this dive in the first place. If anything happened with her chute...if her backup failed... No, I couldn't allow it. Wouldn't. Speeding toward her, my head started to throb. *Shit.*

Even if I stayed conscious, I wasn't going to get to her in time. "Now, goddammit!"

The hot pink canopy flared open at the last fucking second.

I gripped my own ripcord, as my heart struggled to recover. I made one more scan of the skies to ensure the other divers were in good shape, because as soon as my chute deployed I'd be less able to assist.

I'd already passed Leo, as he'd pulled his cord almost immediately after leaving the plane. I had to look up to see him hanging below a gold and green chute. Beneath me, nearly parallel to Zee, I could see Nik and Thea both grinning goofily, happily latched together under a rainbow-colored arch, as I imagined they would be their whole lives.

With a tug, I deployed my chute.

The canopy billowed open, yanking me by my rig straps as it dramatically slowed my descent. The sound and sensation of the hurricane force winds buffeting me evaporated into a sudden silence. I lifted the visor on my helmet and glanced around again.

I envied Nik as he peacefully sailed toward paradise, his future bright with Thea next to him. Meanwhile next to me was a hundred-pound dog. And as for a future? Tumor growing in my skull notwithstanding, I could only watch mine from afar as she glided skillfully onto the sand below.

Beautiful, tenacious, reckless...*woman.*

"She's gonna kill me one of these days," I muttered to Titan, who looked like he'd just had the best head-out-the-window car ride ever.

As angry as I was at Zee's irresponsibility, I had to find a way to keep the smile I'd seen on her face as she'd fallen through the air, because *that* smile was most definitely worth living for. And whatever had wiped it from her lips right before she'd pulled her chute was worth killing for.

Aziza

Gritty, warm sand. I grasped it in my raw grip. Clawing at the semi-solidness of it, I pulled my way out of the water as if I were climbing a rock wall. I struggled until my toes were just beyond the reach of waves. Then I lay blissfully still under the heat of the sun, a clump of seaweed washed ashore. My salt-brined skin might never be truly dry again. Being braised by the sun wasn't safe, but it felt so nice to not be fighting for air, to be warm, alive. Still.

Or maybe I had died, because I could hear my mother singing softly in the breeze. Feel the gentle rocking of being in her arms again. She kissed my forehead and called me Aziza, precious, like the gemstones from our emerald mine.

As the heat began to sear my flesh, I knew I wasn't in heaven with my mother. The rocking had been the residual feel of the ocean. The singing? Birds. My mother's kiss? A drop of sea water sliding down my forehead. A memory. I focused on the trees, palms, a line of them. At least this wasn't hell.

Hell was behind me.

I didn't dare turn back. I only looked forward to the shade beneath the palms.

Pearled tears blurred my vision as my tennis shoes imbedded into the sand on the very beach I'd washed up upon twenty-two years ago.

I pulled in a deep breath of late afternoon air as my very first view of the island blinked in the back of my mind. Young palms had lined the beach then. I remembered them well. The survivor who'd escaped this island had been forged under their fronds.

The trees were taller now and mature, while others had been downed from storms over the years. I started forward, drawn toward them just as I'd been all those years ago. A gust caught my chute and jerked my body, snapping my focus back to the present. I turned to corral the billowing pink nylon.

Nik and Thea touched down next. I had to stifle a laugh, now that I had the chance to get a good look at Nik. He was exactly as Coop had described to me one night when he'd been telling me about all of his former teammates. *"Imagine one of the guys in those Christmas in July movies you love. You know the type, from Maplefuck, Vermont or some shit — short dark hair, perfect amount of unshaven stubble, looks good in a flannel shirt and carries around an axe. But Nik has actually chopped wood and you don't want to know what's been in his chipper. He curses, shoots whiskey, and if he takes off his flannel shirt, you'll realize this cat has seen some shit, and not the kind the town busybodies are gossiping about in the back alley between some flower shop and an old inn that needs saving."*

I watched as he unlatched Thea and she immediately spun around, wrapping her arms and legs around him as she kissed him deeply. Thea was hooked, both on skydiving and Nik.

I fought my own longing to run and jump into Coop's arms when he touched down. Even with proof of his actions in the Amazon, turning my feelings off had been impossible. I was still so freaking in love with him.

How many projects had we worked on? How many times had he given me the extra confidence to take bigger chances? Been there when I didn't think anyone in the world was? He was family. *More than.* And the way we had fit together in the war room, the fire between us combusting after just a few kisses... Those intimacies, passions, couldn't be replicated.

My previous sexual experiences had certainly been more physical, but even so, they hardly measured up. Comparing them was laughable. I'd been a curious young woman, exploring. The sex had been enjoyable, but neither my heart nor my mind had been into those men beyond our bodies. Relationships just weren't possible. And I still had my concerns whether one was possible with Coop, but what he and I had went way beyond sizzling chemistry to something even deeper than this ocean.

I couldn't believe I'd almost passed up the opportunity to see if what we had was real. Coop's activities in the Amazon were damning, but I didn't know the reasons.

Like Dr. Walsh had told me more than once, "*we don't base our decisions on reports and numbers, we base them on the individual.*" And if there was one individual on this planet who I knew *always* saw the bigger picture, it was Michael Cooper. No matter what he'd done in the Amazon, he had to have a good reason for it.

In the war room, I'd looked into his eyes and my gut had told me the only purpose for taking this job, for coming to the island, had been *me.* Not for Zaki. Not for the money. Not for some ulterior motive. Only me.

I smiled, watching him safely land and unhook Titan. The German shepherd loped past me, jumping into Thea and knocking her flat as he lapped at her face. I couldn't help but laugh. Embracing the ones you love after an exhilarating experience must be a universal urge that transcended species. Still chuckling, I turned back to Coop. The sharp daggers in his eyes transmitted his eagerness to embrace my neck with both hands.

With hardened jaw and lips stretched in a snarl, he grabbed up his chute as he stalked toward me. When he got close, he hissed in my face, "Don't you ever do that again!"

"Do what?" I backed up a step before his pushed-out chest knocked into me. "What's wrong with you?"

"You! You're what's wrong with me! You waited till the last fucking second to pull your chute! You know how dangerous that is? What if it hadn't opened? There was no way I could get to you in time!"

"Slow down. Yes, I went long. But not to the last second."

"The hell it wasn't! I told you repeatedly to pull your fucking chute and you flat-out ignored me."

I steadied my breath. Coop was hardly the first person to blow up at me. In business I made people, even big blustering men, angry all the time. I'd learned how to keep my cool and de-escalate. In Coop's case, it meant conceding where I could. "I'm sorry for not responding. I had my comms turned down."

He threw his hands up. "Even better!"

"I'm not a novice."

"Then stop acting like one!"

I bit back a curse, but my hackles were twitching and eager to rise. "First off, *if* my chute hadn't opened, my backup would've."

"And by then you would've landed too hard. What about your legs, Zee? You want them both broken? Because I don't!"

I was oddly charmed by the virility of his concern for my legs, for me. He hadn't been angry, he'd been scared. Just as I'd been when he'd disappeared without a trace.

Didn't warrant his being condescending, though.

"If I'd been coming down too hot, I would've steered for a water landing. I can think under pressure, Coop. You *know* I can."

I put my hand on his arm. Despite the spark touching skin to skin gave us both, or perhaps because of it, he tried to step back. I closed my fingers to keep him from leaving. "Just because you kissed me doesn't give you the right to treat me like a child."

His eyes may've narrowed, but not in anger. He studied me as he asked, "Is that what you think, Presh?"

I trailed my hand down his arm to his hand. "It's how your scolding me feels."

He twined his fingers with mine, his thumb stroking the underside of my wrist. "I'm not treating you like a child. I'm treating you like you're the most important thing in my world. And I was fucking afraid I was going to lose you."

My breath stilled. "I'm sorry. I...I didn't...know."

He pushed out a breath. His eyes locked on mine, softer this time. "Please don't do it again."

I swallowed and gave a subtle nod. "Okay."

"Okay." Coop accepted with a chin bob of his own, then he looked down at his feet. "You know, before you should've pulled your chute, you looked beautiful up there. Happy, too. Dancing in the sky."

My memories flickered. "I said the very same thing the first time my aunt showed me a video of her skydiving." There'd been the same awe in my voice that I heard in Coop's, but when I looked up at him he wasn't smiling the way I'd been. His brows were drawn together and his eyes looked more like two hard gemstones.

"Your aunt? You told me you were an orphan and didn't have any family."

The accusation in his voice had me drawing back. "If I made it seem like I never knew any of my biological family, I guess it's because I never really did. How much can a child truly know an adult? Right? My aunt's been gone a long time. They all have."

I looked up to find Coop still unsure of me, or maybe the questioning arrangement of his features was because he wanted to know more. I frowned, not sure how I could tell him everything without him hating me for the extent of my lies.

Deception had been a necessity in my life, and certainly had its place in business, but the relationship I wanted to forge with Coop needed to be built on honesty. My aunt seemed an innocuous enough place to start.

I dropped my gathered chute to the beach and stepped out of my harness. "I called her Am'maty Z. We were very close. We shared a love of animals and she taught me to ride horses. Actually, she taught me a lot of things — to be strong and independent, to survive, to fight. She's why I took up scuba and skydiving. Those were things she did, things she was going to teach me, but she died before I was old enough. She told me skydiving made her feel like she had wings. She'd pretend she could soar across fences and walls and borders. I was young then, I thought she wanted to be able to fly. I understand now that was just semantics. She wanted to fly *away*. She wanted freedom."

Coop's whole body softened with concern. "Are you not free, Zee?"

The hard blue gemstones dissolved and now his eyes were deep as the sea. The kind of ocean depths I could fall into from any height, at any speed, and still never get hurt. I swallowed and glanced away.

"The freedom I seek is a little different."

Maybe once the Ozma Emerald was recovered and the *Esmeralda* scuttled I'd have freedom, at least from the fear of my past catching up with me. Or maybe not. But I knew I'd never have a chance at true freedom until then.

"When I jump, it's like my body is flying faster than my mind can keep up with. I'm able to outrun all the voices, and questions, and thoughts, and noise. That's why I wait as long as *safely* possible to pull my chute. Because when I do, the earth will start spinning again and my mind will catch up and I'll be fighting time again, fearing the fall, trying to prevent the next big wreck. And as you well know, there's always some eminent crash awaiting on the horizon. That's why I turned down the comms and why I held the freefall for as long as I possibly could. To wring out *every* second of peace."

Coop drew me up against his chest, wrapping me in his arms. "You don't have to fight the fall, Presh. I won't let you crash."

Chapter Sixteen

Coop

Somehow I had to find a way to stretch that promise. At least long enough to give her a chance at real freedom.

The sun had begun to descend on the western horizon. Far away, a few clouds had built up high and white on top, dark with rain at the bottom. Typical of the patchy systems that would move over quickly. The ocean was calm and the M/Y *Zamarad* was the only vessel in visual range. At any moment that could change thanks to the half-billion-dollar asset being brought up.

I noticed Nik was also staying situationally aware as he and Titan played an impromptu game of fetch with a chunk of driftwood. Zee and Thea had taken off their shoes to wade into the water as Thea had no memory of ever having been to the ocean. Now the women had returned to sit on the beach while we waited for the tender to come pick us up.

"Fancy diving boat you got us, brother."

I turned to Leo, whose eyes roved the stunning modern lines of the Italian-built *Zamarad.*

"It's not a boat, it's a yacht. A mega one. It's actually the smallest of the three in the Beryl fleet." Both the *Zamarad* and the *Zanjibayl* had been named after Zaki's deceased daughters, while the *Zamirah* bore his granddaughter's name.

Having worked a job off the *Zamarad* in Monaco six months ago with Scott Hayes, I easily recalled the layout of each of her four decks. Like the others, the luxury ocean liner had been exquisitely outfitted. The ship's grand design came complete with all the frills from a topside Jacuzzi, bar, and multiple cushioned lounge spaces all the way down to a teak-paneled, fully stocked tender and toy garage at ocean level.

"So, like, how much would a weekly charter on something like this run?" Leo asked.

Spotting the approaching tender, Aziza stood up and shrugged. "Last season we were getting anywhere between two and three hundred a week. Not including tips, of course."

"Hundred...?"

Zee nodded. "Thousand."

As I watched her brush the sand off her backside, my fingers ached and my cock twitched. "Need help?"

She swatted my offered hand away as she focused on her conversation with Leo. "It stays booked, too."

"A million a month? Dang."

I clapped Leo's shoulder. "Don't worry, bro, we'll likely only be here for three days. With your Outbreak endorsement deal, you should be able to pick up the tab, right?"

Before even giving Leo a chance to do the math, Zee assured him, "Sharky's teasing. No one's getting charged. This is a job, not a charter. But if any of you ever want to take a week's vacation on her, everything will be compliments of Zaki, including handsome tips for the staff."

Leo cocked a brow at me as he flashed a shit-stirring grin. "*Sharky*, is it? That's a new one."

"Seriously?" I rolled my eyes. "Zee just offered you the most amazing week of your life, and you want to ask about that?"

"Yes, I'm very curious, *Sharky*."

I shot my little brother an *I'll-be-killing-you-later* smile, which he returned with an *it-will-so-be-worth-it* one.

"It's actually *mushaeghib* and he earns it. *Often*," Zee added with a chuckle.

"Troublemaker, right?" Thea piped up as she dusted sand from the backs of her calves.

"Yes! You know Arabic?" Zee asked, sounding impressed.

"Apparently. And German. But I couldn't tell you how."

Zee flashed her a sympathetic smile, no doubt aware of Thea's unique lack of memories due to a head injury during a tornado back in Kansas.

"Well, like the troublemaker Coop is" — Zee turned her grin on me — "he's convinced I'm calling him *My-sharky* instead."

"Fits you," Nik said, coming up behind Thea and wrapping his arms around her shoulders. The twinkle in his green eyes as they volleyed between Aziza and me meant the comment wasn't referring to the nickname. "I like it."

He was being a hell of a lot nicer about Zee than I'd been about Thea. Not knowing how long I had before the ticking timebomb in my skull went off, I'd been impatient and on edge. I'd been eager to see Aziza and I'd blamed Thea for delaying us. But what had really gotten my brotherly concern up was how quickly after he'd retired that their relationship had become serious. He still had blood behind his ears from leaving the Teams and he was playing house with new bathmats and a beautiful woman's heart.

Hell, I'd done the same thing with my second wife, Becca. It was only recently that I'd even come to terms with how hard our relationship had been on her — the night terrors, the unreachable days that could stretch into weeks, the alcohol that desperately tried to replace feeling, the anger that came rambling through like an earthquake to my many fault lines.

Some days she'd wondered if I single-fistedly had kept Coronado's spackle business alive, other days she'd cried, "*I love you so much, Coop, but you aren't even here. Not really. Don't you get it? I'm more alone with you here. Go back to your war or your brothers or wherever you are in your mind. That's where you need to be. But don't stay here for me if all you are going to do is go behind your walls while you punch holes in mine.*"

I'd tried the reenlistment route with Lauren, the third Mrs. Cooper. She'd folded like a cheap lawn chair under a fat man when I'd been listed MIA for two weeks. Didn't matter that coming back home to her had given me the motivation to survive. She just couldn't handle the not knowing. She'd loved me too much to go through that again and I hadn't blamed her.

I didn't blame any of them anymore. Not even my first wife, Sarah, who'd cheated on me throughout my first tour. She'd just needed someone she could physically touch. And I was someone who time and again had taken his wedding ring off. Not for the same reason she had, but because having it on had made me vulnerable. I'd never talked about how bad it had been, because then I'd have to justify leaving the best thing in the world for the worst thing time and time again.

Katia had been the only one who'd called me out on it. And she'd done it wearing these lacy red booty shorts and a black push-up bra while cursing me out in Russian. God, she was a firecracker. I'd been so sure she'd only wanted me for a green card until she'd broken down crying when I'd re-upped — she spoke four languages, was brilliant and gorgeous but would rather have gone back to Kyzyl than worry over my sorry ass for one minute longer.

I'd been tough on Thea, because tough was what life with a career operator was. But she'd done more than prove she could handle herself — she'd survived a tornado, thrived despite her childhood, and helped bring down one of the sickest, dirtiest FBI agents in the Bureau all while rescuing one of his victims.

I had a good feeling Zee would be recruiting both her and Nik into the fold. And selfishly, I hoped she'd secure them. Nik could take my role and Thea could give Zee some much-needed help so she could take an actual break from time to time. Get free from the island and out from under Zaki.

"So, um, speaking of sharks...?" Leo asked as he scanned the water's surface for telltale fins. "There aren't any actual ones here, are there?"

I started to answer, but Leo was quick to cut me off. "Not you, Sharky, I want the answer from someone who won't bullshit me. Zee?"

I snorted, but covered it with an awkward cough. Little did Leo know, Zee was the best bullshitter around. Not that this was the kind of thing she would bother lying about. Too easy.

"Of course. I've seen bull, tiger, black- and white-tipped, Caribbean reef, nurse sharks, oh, and hammerhead, of course. There's a wide variety," she said, her love of nature and animals clearly extended to even the scary ones. At least that boded well for me.

"Great," Leo remarked, sarcastically cheery.

"Bullys can be unpredictable, and tigers aren't very selective about what they feed on, so accidents can happen. But we'll stay alert and respectful, so as not to court any danger. No chumming or feeding is ever allowed here."

Leo didn't look convinced of his safety. Feeling benevolent with Aziza near, I offered my little brother a rare reprieve. "Don't worry, you're here for ship-side support, not to dive."

It was just going to be Nik and me below the surface. And as beautiful as the reefs must be in this area, this wasn't a pleasure outing. My goal was to only go down twice, three times at most. One day to prep the area and one to raise the vault. Sticking around to commune with the local wildlife — or enjoying a little R&R on the yacht — was not part of the plan.

For *one*, the location and value of the asset had been identified by an unknown entity, which meant treasure-hunting pirates could come over the horizon at any time. *Two*, the dive dynamics of being inside an unstable wreck at a decent depth required extra vigilance. Multiple dives increased the threat for me.

The sharks didn't concern me the way they did Leo. A lion could walk past a herd of zebras without drawing too much suspicion. He simply needed to act like he belonged there. Granted, in this scenario I'd be a zebra cruising through a pride of lions, but as long as I wasn't flailing or fleeing like prey, they'd leave me alone. The animal world was simpler that way.

In the human world, the truly dangerous predators weren't behavioral, they were cerebral. When they took down their prey or waged territorial wars, the most successful ones did it via methodical chess moves.

Just like in chess, the only way to win was to protect your queen, even if it meant sacrificing the king.

Which brought me to *three*—I popped a gummy to temper the headache I inevitably got when thinking about three—I had no way of knowing the odds of my passing out or having an aneurysm or who fucking knew what. After the small preview from the shallow depths of the Amazon dive, I wasn't looking forward to pushing my luck any more than I had to.

As the tender beached, I recognized Kai at the helm. The ship's bosun was a Hawaiian native with spiky black hair, an easy smile, and an exemplary work ethic. He'd been part of the crew from when I was briefly aboard six months ago. I should be familiar with most of the others as well. Though as I understood it, the ship would only be staffed with essential personnel for this job. Of the nine regular crew members, only the first mate, bosun, chef, chief steward, and captain would be aboard.

Once Nik and I had helped the others load up, I pushed the tender off the beach and leaped onto the bow. Kai reversed the propellers, drawing us away from the tiny island.

I clapped him on the shoulder. "Aloha, brother. How you been?"

"Can't complain. Motley crew you got here," he said with a surfer-boy grin as he took us all in. "Gotta say, I've seen a dog hanging ten before, but never one who skydives. Why didn't you all just have Colton bring you out on the boat?"

I grimaced, putting my finger over my lips, but Leo had already overheard.

"What? You mean we could've taken a boat!"

"This was faster and more fun."

"See why I call him *mushaeghib*?" Zee laughed. "But you have to admit, this was much more fun."

As Kai steered us in closer, I spotted the first mate retrieving our supply container from the sea. Wasn't an easy task as he had to haul the large waterproof box over the side of a heavy-duty inflatable raft. But eventually he managed and turned back to restart the Zodiac RIB's outboard motor. "That Jim? He was with you in the Med, right?"

Kai throttled down. "Yep, that's Jim."

He muttered something under his breath that I'm pretty sure was along the lines of, *Fuckin' ass kisser.* If it wasn't, it should've been, because I'd remembered him being one. Which brought me to Jim's favorite ass to kiss. "Who's captain?"

"Lars Magnussen. You met him in Monaco. He's been on leave, but Hayes flew him back in late last night."

"Why? What happened with Captain Tom?" Aziza asked as the tender approached the aft beach deck.

"Happened overnight, something about Tom's daughter being in the hospital. Car crash, I think. Hayes took care of everything on short notice."

I glanced over at Zee, whose expression made it clear she hadn't been brought into the loop. She cleared the annoyance from her features. "I had no idea. Have we heard a status on Tom's daughter?"

Kai shook his head as he adjusted the tender close enough to the swim deck platform for me to leap across to it. I tied the tender off as Kai cut the engines.

"Head on up and grab a cocktail before the sun sets. Chef Anders has an amazing dinner planned," Kai said. "We did some fishing and trapping while we waited on you guys. Going to be amazing!"

While Leo, Thea, and Titan filed onboard and up the stairs, I took the opportunity to peek in the toy garage and do a quick inventory. Two cases of equipment had been pre-loaded in Miami. As usual, Aziza's planning had provided the very best gear and more of everything than I needed, including plenty of explosives.

"Is it enough?" she asked as she came up behind me.

"I thought you wanted us to kick some doors and walls in, Presh. This is enough to blow up the entire ship."

"Then I have enough," she said with a grin, before heading to the other side of the garage to look in the second storage locker.

Nik laughed, patting me hard on the back as he gawked at the supplies. "I can see why you're in love with her, brother. This one actually gets you."

"If it was only love I was in with her, it'd be easy," I said under my breath.

There was so much I wanted to talk to her about, *do* with her. Remembering her being in my arms, the feel of her in my hands and mouth, only made my body ache for her. I could hardly look at her without craving more of everything, *anything* she was willing to feed me. Even if it were only lies.

I turned to watch her head up the aft stairs, tapping into the Black Hawk Toughbook she'd snagged from the second supply chest. "Back to work," I muttered at her departing form.

As for me, I was in desperate need of a cold shower. I reached back and pulled my T-shirt over my head. Then I stripped off my shoes, emptied my pockets, and dove into the cool ocean. Sharks be damned.

Chapter Seventeen

Aziza

As I headed to the shade of the main outdoor dining area, I shot Vivi a message on my satellite phone authorizing all medical bills and any additional support Captain Tom might require for his daughter's accident and requested an update as to her condition as soon as possible.

I certainly couldn't fault Captain Tom for not contacting me directly, but I hadn't wanted anyone outside of the limited ship's crew to even know a job was taking place. I'd booked the charter as simply a friend-and-family diving excursion for Coop.

Was this why Hayes had been expressing concerns to Zaki about my feelings toward Coop? That he assumed I was going on this charter with Coop as a friend? Or even romantically? I'd been so careful not to let my feelings show during any of our war room meetings. Kept work professional and my desires squelched. And it had worked...until now. Which was why I had to be extra vigilant to not turn this job into some sort of sexcapade. Of course, that didn't mean I had to abstain. I just had to keep it private. Very private. And I needed to focus on my job.

Eager to call Gray, I settled in at the modern dining table, which sat twelve. Fully flanking the table's long sides were a matching pair of slender rectangular fire features. With twilight approaching, the emerald stones would soon be glowing with green flames.

Catching movement, I glanced inside the yacht's spacious living area and recognized Cait, the chief steward, setting up a tray of drinks at the wet bar.

The glass panel doors were folded back, allowing seamless flow from the covered outdoor dining into the creamy, light interior. Hard to imagine a boat, where people splashed salt water and sand, would have such luxurious silk carpets, cool marble, and warm mahogany. But instead of feeling the appropriate awe, it stirred up bittersweet memories of the *Esmeralda*. She'd had exquisite trappings, too. And now they were completely waterlogged and tattered on the seafloor, enjoyed only by schools of fish and various sea life.

"Welcome aboard the *Zamarad*! I'm Caitlin. What can I get you to drink? We have...*everything*," Cait recited as she approached me from behind. Carefully reaching over my shoulder, she set down a drink coaster with the OZ logo and a fruit-infused ice water.

"Water is fine for now, Cait," I replied as I turned to smile at her. "Thank you."

"Aziza!" She stepped back and eyed me in shock. "I had no idea you were coming aboard. You weren't on the manifest."

"I know. I'm so sorry for the lack of communication. It was completely last minute." I stood and gave the elegant lithe brunette a hug. She'd been an elite tennis player up until multiple ACL tears had taken her out about four years ago. "Good to see you! It's been a while!"

"Since the island summit two years ago. I'll make sure your things go into the master." Cait pulled away and her slender hand went to her chest. "Which means Coop will go...where?"

"No. Moving him isn't necessary. I requested for him to have the master. There are plenty of rooms. I'm not picky," I offered, hoping she'd not press the issue.

"The thing is, Captain Magnussen is only briefly filling in for Captain Tom. At Tom's request, I put him in one of the suites, so as not to disturb Tom's things. I've got Nik and Thea in the other suite as they're a couple, and also have Titan. Leo's in the bunk room. I can move him in to share with Coop? But I know OZ will have a field day if I put you in a bunk room. And while you and Coop certainly rank higher in the corporate hierarchy than Captain Magnussen, he *is* the captain of this ship and frankly would be livid to be in a crew bunk. Heck"—she leaned in close to whisper— "he was annoyed about my not putting him in the master. You know how brusque Nordic men can be. I'll move Nik and Thea, I guess?"

I blinked at her, still catching up on the info dump she'd given me. "Nonsense. Nik, Thea, and Titan are our guests. We're not going to treat them like that."

I was also low-key hoping to woo them both onto the Beryl Enterprises team. Besides, if my libido had any say in the matter, Coop and I would be sharing a bed. So the whole room situation was really a non-issue, but I also didn't think it was any of Cait's business.

"You'll be much more comfortable in the master. Whatever you want me to do with Coop, I'll do."

I didn't want her doing *anything* with Coop. But I understood why she was so flummoxed. As Zaki's hand, I was her boss. I was everyone on this yacht's boss. She was simply trying her hardest to make me happy, so Zaki didn't become unhappy. And we all knew how making Zaki unhappy could go. Me, more than anyone.

It was the very reason this job was necessary.

I schooled my breath. "Please, don't worry about it, Cait. Really. I'll look over the rooms after dinner. I'm sure I can fit Coop...somewhere." I shot her an awkward smile, knowing full well after grinding up against him in the war room, he would be a *very* tight fit.

I cracked open the Toughbook to connect to our network, hoping Cait wouldn't see my cheeks heating with what I'm sure was the blush to end all blushes. Besides, I had important things to figure out, and which bed people were assigned but didn't sleep in wasn't even in my top ten.

"I'll put your bags in the master and Coop's in with Leo."

It *was* the most logical arrangement under the circumstances. And would attract the least suspicion. If I hadn't been having lustful thoughts about my employee, I'd have had zero qualms assigning him to share with his brother, and it wasn't like he hadn't had to sleep in worse places for other jobs. This being a job was no different and Coop would be professional about it.

"Perfect," I said, with as much false enthusiasm as I could.

At least Cait looked satisfied. I was glad one of us would be, because clearly getting myself laid was a bigger task than I could navigate.

Hard to believe last quarter I'd pulled off Marakata Cay's annual three-day Meeting of the Minds world summit. Costing over twenty-five million dollars, it had brought in leaders of several countries as well as A-listers and activists who worked tirelessly to fight climate change, human trafficking, and world poverty issues. Thank God they hadn't been horny or it would've been a disaster.

"Shall I unpack for you?" Cait asked.

I started to say sure just to get her moving along, but then I remembered the skimpy clothes, including lingerie, that I'd hastily packed. "No, thank you. I like to handle those types of things myself."

As if I'd ever traveled anywhere, or unpacked, for that matter.

Sensing Cait was *still* standing over me, I glanced up to find her staring, but at least it wasn't at me. Her focus had zoomed in on a soaking-wet Titan bounding up the aft staircase, and proceeding to do a full-body shake that coated Nik and Leo in water.

I barely noticed their curses or Cait darting off, exclaiming, "I'll get some towels!" Because, right behind the rowdy canine, Coop crested the stairs—shirtless and soaking wet from apparently taking a swim and rinsing off. His skin glowed gold in the late-day sun. His chest had just the right amount of dark hair and the kind of broadness that could put younger, harder-bodied men to shame. Not that he wasn't hard—his packed abs rippled with definition and his wet board shorts hung low enough off his hips to show off those channels that made smart girls stupid.

I had to pick my chin off the deck before his navy eyes caught me gawking. He flashed his dimples like he knew. *Of course he did.* As he shook his dark hair out, he sent a sparkling rainbow of drops to scatter on Leo. Titan followed suit with another shake of his own.

"*Mushaeghibs!*" I hollered with a laugh. "Now there are two of you!"

I couldn't help but smile at both Titan's and Coop's wide, naughty grins.

"More like jackasses!" Leo grunted, trying to dry off with the plush emerald-colored, OZ-embroidered towels Cait had rushed to distribute.

As she handed Coop one, she informed him of his bunk arrangements with his brother. Neither he nor Leo looked pleased as Cait hightailed it back into the interior to deliver our various belongings.

Coop cut his eyes to me like this had somehow been my doing. He stalked toward me, barely giving me a chance to admire the parts of him I'd never seen before, like his dark leg hair, slick and straight from his swim. Or his masculine bare feet slapping the deck, which I found oddly sexy.

Before I knew it, his dripping body was looming over me — one hand gripping the back of my chair and one palm pressing into the table. Cool droplets slipped from his hair to my skin as he pressed his hardened lips to my ear. "My brother is *not* who I'm going to be sharing my bed with," he ground out coarsely.

I swallowed. Technically the beds were single bunks and would not be shared, but in a foolish effort to hear that gritted out voice of his, I teased, "Would you rather *I* shared a bed with your brother?"

"You know exactly who I want to share what with." His chest brushed against my bare arm as his wide hand shifted from the table to my thigh and squeezed.

His body blocked the others from witnessing his daring request. Feeling a bit dangerous myself, I opened my knees wider in invitation. His fingers slid between my legs. With a twist to his wrist, he edged the gap wider, allowing him to possessively cup my *kus*.

"Coop, believe me, I want..." I panted out a breath as his fingers gently teased. "You know I've wanted..."

Before I started writhing and moaning, I gripped his forearm with both my hands to stop the pleasure he was giving me. I forced my brain to reboot and tried to explain, "Whatever is going to be shared between us needs to be private."

He took his hand back, dragging his middle finger purposefully across my clit and making my whole body tremble. "You've got a lot of damn secrets, Zee."

"I know," I admitted.

"I'll just have to whet my appetite on something else, I guess." He gave his wrist a shake to readjust the bulky white-gold band of his diving watch, then reached over to snag a peach from the fruit bowl on the table. Opening his mouth wide, he sank his teeth into the fruit.

Mesmerized, I watched him savor it, wishing it was me he was devouring. As the juice dripped over his lips, his spearing tongue swiped the sweet nectar from his chin, proving just how adept he'd be.

"I'll make you a deal, Presh. Every time you make me your secret, you have to tell me one of yours."

Without waiting for a response, he moved to go inside while taking another ravishing chomp out of the peach. A groan of pleasure escaped him, as if it were the sweetest piece he'd ever eaten. The way my body responded, I was confident I'd be the juiciest.

Chapter Eighteen

Aziza

I forced myself to stop imagining Coop eating *my* peach. I needed to focus on work. First I checked in on Zaki's correspondence and responded as necessary. Next I initiated a video conference with Gray to see how her initial deep dive into Olivia and Ophelia Austin had gone. When her screen appeared, all I could see was her cat.

"Say hi to my pussy."

"Gray?" I winced as the orange tabby turned to give me an up close and personal view of his butt. "*That* is most definitely not pussy."

"Oh dear, Mr. McFinkberg! Get down! No one wants to see that!" Gray's disembodied voice rang out from beyond the furry orange butt.

I covered my eyes. "Please, make it stop!"

"Hold up, Zee! I'll be there in two shakes."

"Two shakes of what?" I asked in horror, still holding my hands over my eyes.

"Why, a lamb's tail, of course! Shoo, Mr. McFinkberg!"

The portly orange tabby squalled.

I slowly spread my fingers apart to see Gray had appeared, chestnut hair in a perfect messy top knot and a jumbo sweet tea in hand.

"You named your pussy Mr. McFinkberg?"

"Johnny McFinkberg, to be exact," she said, without missing a beat.

"I'm not even going to ask." I waved Cait off as she rounded up the others for a quick tour of the interior and to show them their rooms. "Were you able to connect any dots?"

"Not exactly, but I did find something out. The twins have historically been close, never fighting, never seen apart. But this last year or so, I cannot find a single public event with them together."

"Well, they are in their what, mid-twenties, now? May just be growing apart, doing their own things."

"Yes. But only Olivia has been seen in public. When paparazzi have questioned her about it, she's remained tight-lipped. But I get the impression she's got something to say."

"Where's Ophelia?"

"Speculation is almost always rehab. She's historically been the more, shall we say, *experimental* of the twins, but substance abuse has never been reported. Ophelia contracted with a new PR firm about the same time she dropped out of the public eye. So far the new PR person has only commented to say Ophelia is happier and healthier than ever, and is pursuing a path of 'ethical enlightenment and feminine empowerment'."

"Whatever that means," I muttered.

"Seriously. Gotta love PR speak. This new lady is pretty flashy, has this gorgeous head of ombre red hair. And get this, a close source to the sisters commented that Ophelia has been *ignited* by the *flame* burning brightly inside of her and will soon rise up and fly. I'm getting…*vibes*, just not sure what for."

"I think the vibes you're looking for are *cult*."

I recalled pulling intel on Thea's situation. Two separate women connected to hunting her down had had orange-red hair. One had been killed during the tornado. The other had given Thea a business card with the name of a women's empowerment organization when she'd tried to poison Thea with some crazy essential oil.

While it seemed unlikely that these situations could be connected, I also knew there were fewer spiders in the underworld than there were webs.

"Ignited by the flame, huh?" I mused.

If I were back at the island, I could pull up multiple screens and drill down into this myself. But I also knew Gray was beyond capable. "Look into a company called Ardent. Their corporate linguistics and branding heavily utilize fire and flame words. I believe they have a master class or leadership series aimed at empowering women as well as an MLM branch for essential oils. While those branches should appear legit, it's not unheard of for organizations like these to court heiress and actress types for funding and publicity. See if the companies you red-flagged under the twins' umbrella have any touchpoints in common with Ardent. Also, while we're being nosy, check to see if the twins have any affiliation to a Clayton Kenyon."

"Who's he?"

"A dirty Bureau guy. Recently deceased, thank God."

Kenyon had been travelling with both of the redheads when Thea had uncovered his involvement with human trafficking. My connection at the Bureau, Todd Coleman, had just started an internal investigation on Kenyon. Unfortunately, it was way too early to expect actionable intel out of the Bureau anytime soon.

"Do what you need to do," I told Gray, "but let's try to keep these searches between us until we know more. We might be stepping on some shined shoes."

"You know me, Zee. Queen of the backdoor!"

"Never would've guessed." I snickered as her hand flew in front of her mouth.

"Oh fiddlesticks, Zee!"

"I heard what I heard." I disconnected the line before Gray could backtrack.

I glanced up, realizing at some point the evening lighting for the ship had turned on, including the green flames in the fire features. I glanced out to where the sun had finished setting, and spotted Thea. She'd be very beneficial in deciphering some of this, if only she could regain her memories. Sensing my focus, she turned from the deck's railing and smiled.

"That was amazing! I've never seen such colors!" Thea exclaimed with the requisite awe of someone who'd never witnessed a ball of fire submerge into the sea before. "Is it always so vibrant?"

"Stunning, isn't it? As are you! Dress looks great," I said, noting she'd changed into a bright turquoise print slip dress, complemented with chartreuse earrings and necklace. Her wavy blonde bob had been pinned back on one side and her cheeks were flushed red from the day's sun.

"Thank you so much for all the clothes and toiletries. I was shocked at all the amazing things! I don't know how you knew what all I'd need. Much less my size."

"Vivi's the fashionista. I'd be in riding attire or sweatpants and T-shirts if she hadn't completely overhauled my closet for me. Did Cait give you the full tour?"

"Oh yes, she even showed me the patch of faux grass for Titan to use as a lavatory."

"Not to be confused with the faux grass putting green or driving tee," I said with a laugh.

"I can't make promises, Mr. T has a mind of his own and is totally my sharky! It's no wonder he and Coop get along so well."

"Yes, I saw that." A warm rush coursed through me as I recalled how Coop had cooed and kissed on Titan while strapping him in to skydive. I imagined the feels were the same kind most women got when seeing a man hold a baby.

Cait made the rounds distributing cocktails for Nik and Leo, a large ice water for Thea, and a cold bottle of Shiner Bock, Coop's favorite beer, on a coaster in front of the chair next to me. She then set what looked to be a mojito down in front of me. "Coop ordered it for you. Captain Magnussen sends his regrets. He and Jim have some work they need to do in the engine room. Dinner will be out very soon."

"Thank you."

I raised my brows as I examined the mojito. Coop knew my favorite, right down to the extra lime. I glanced around, but didn't see him anywhere. *Typical,*

Ghost... Still, I smiled, knowing he'd been thinking of me.

"So what were you working on?" Thea asked. "Looked serious."

"Had to consult on a potential problem which, oddly enough, you may be able to help me with. Any memories coming back yet?"

"No, not memories. But..."

I cocked my head, encouraging her to continue. "But something?"

"Sensations, I guess? I had one when I was in the MRI tube while listening to a country song. Hearing it...I thought I was in a different place and time. It wasn't the first time my experiences didn't reconcile with my expectations. I've had a couple of reactions, or more accurately *overreactions*, that didn't track with the preceding action."

I recognized the almost disconnected way she analyzed her own situation. It wasn't her nature, it was something she had learned. There were a lot of similarities between Thea and me. It was why I was so keen to have her on my team.

"Then there are the dreams," she went on to explain. "When I wake up it all makes sense. Then I reach in to touch the threads—"

"Only to collapse its perfect symmetry?" I asked, recalling how trying to remember the dreams of my mother would go.

She nodded. "All that's left is a tangled mess."

"Like a silky gossamer spider's web, but touching it turns it into a gross, sticky wad."

"Yes, you understand."

All too well.

Chapter Nineteen

Aziza

Just as my phone rang, Coop snatched it from the table and shoved it in his pocket. He dropped into the seat next to me. His body filled the large chair, while his presence overflowed along with warm masculinity and a smell of soap and shampoo.

"Sharky!"

I turned to see the hard set of his jaw, upon which his dark beard was already attempting a shadowed return. My heart thrilled. Both at the fact he'd wanted to impress me by cleaning up to come to the island and that the ruffian I'd fallen for couldn't stay hidden for long.

"No more work tonight," he decreed, as he often did whenever we'd get deep into one of our many late-night conferences. At first the finality of his tone and the insubordination had triggered my stubborn streak, but once I'd started giving in, I was always rewarded.

Just as I was this night, when he proclaimed, "Now it's time for us."

Us.

For the first time, I didn't have to wonder what he meant by that small, perfect word. His muscular arm stretched over the back of my chair. Whether he was protecting me or claiming me or just plain stretching, being under someone else's wing felt warm and safe in a way I hadn't known since I'd been small.

As hard as it was not to obsess on any and all of the unanswered questions, I was determined to stay fully present and enjoy our dinner. Not that it should be difficult, I'd become completely fascinated with Thea from all of the research I'd already done into her life. And through Coop I'd learned bits and pieces about Nik and Leo over the years, and had been eager to meet those closest to him.

But ever since Coop had dropped down into the chair next to me all I could focus on was the way his scent took me right back to the war room table. His knee bumped and brushed mine. The soft hair on his calf tickled my skin. I crossed my legs in a futile attempt to control the sensation between my legs that had awakened with a vengeance.

Coop, Leo, and Nik were discussing one of Leo's recent MMA matchups. I was vaguely aware of Titan drooling on his paws. His big, brown eyes stayed glued on Thea as she slathered butter on a crostini. I tried to find a good place to interject, say *something*, ask a question. *Anything* to show interest in something other than the vibration of heat spooling inside of me.

Trills chased along my spine as Coop's thumb stroked back and forth along the nape of my neck. His thigh brushed mine, and I dropped my hand to the hardened muscle, intending to simply balance and stabilize myself. But soon my hand started sliding back and forth, and not just on his quad.

Dear Lord! I slammed my eyelids together. This wasn't my fantasy world where I could just grab his cock wherever and whenever I pleased. He was my employee! Had I not just had a whole mental breakdown over this very thing and determined that I had to remain professional? *At least in public.*

Yet there my fingers were, freaking stroking his cock under the dinner table as Cait brought out an amazing display of fresh oysters, conch fritters, and jumbo shrimp. Yep, still caressing, petting, fondling. Now squeezing.

I glanced around the table. The abundant seafood platter provided a welcome distraction for the others. I flattened my palm out as I slid my hand over the sharply defined ridge of his head, then curled my fingers as I stroked back down. His length seemed twice as long as any man I'd been with before. Surely that wasn't possible? Maybe it'd just been forever since I even had my hand on a man. Still, who knew he was packing this much heat?

"Presh?" Coop growled against my ear. The low rumbled snarl demanded my full attention. "I've already come in my pants for you once today. The next time I *will* be inside of you and it will be my choice of which orifice. Keep this up and I'll spread you out on this table, slurp you out like one of these oysters, then stuff you like a crab in front of all these people. Or you keep your hand to yourself. My vote is for option one."

The vibration of his voice went straight to my *kus*. My blood thickened, warming my veins. I'd fought the desire to wrap myself around Coop all day, I'd fought my feelings for him for what had felt like an eternity. To be honest, I was tired of fighting and ready to start feeling.

That said, I returned my hand to my own, boring, cockless thigh.

My plan was to feign sudden illness as an excuse to slip off to my room, hoping Coop would take the hint and follow suit, but alarms in my brain had started going off. Something about the variety of appetizers was triggering my brain into action.

My attention zeroed in on Thea's shut eyes and Nik holding a jumbo shrimp dipped in cocktail sauce to her lips.

"Y'all and your food kink," Coop chastised.

Then it hit me. "Stop! She's allergic!"

Thea's eyes popped open as Nik jerked his hand back. The shrimp tail slipped out of his grip, and the fleshy pink comma winged high over his shoulder. Titan scrambled into action, leaping for the flying crustacean and catching it proudly in his snapping jaws.

"How would you know that?" Thea asked, her tone registering both alarm and annoyance.

Confused, I glanced between Coop and Thea. "Your allergy to shellfish was in the dossier I sent. Didn't Coop give it to you?"

"Oh, I gave it to her." Coop shook his head with dismay. "She refuses to look at it."

Thea jutted her chin at him. "My memories will come back when it's time for them to come back."

"Not if you eat shellfish, they won't," Coop groused. "Do you even know if you can swim? I wouldn't wait until you've jumped into the ocean to know for sure."

"You can swim," I assured her, but she didn't look particularly grateful.

"I was making a point," Coop insisted.

A pained look crossed Nik's face at the reality. "I know you wanted to remember things naturally, Tiggs, but maybe one of us *should* read it?"

"I don't want you reading it, either. It's bad enough that other people already know more about me than I do." She turned and asked Coop and me, "How much did I weigh at birth?"

While I knew the answer to the seemingly random question, I also knew she meant to test some theory of hers. I stayed silent.

Coop, however, didn't have the ability to keep his mouth shut. "Just shy of ten pounds. You were a big girl. Born straight up at midnight after a very long labor. It's all in the file."

"Most people don't know how much they weighed at birth. At least, not off the top of their head," I offered.

"Exactly," Thea stated. "None of this is natural. Everything in the file is stats and numbers or some resume of education and employment that explains how or even why I got into the FBI. I don't want to know those things. And I certainly don't want to read one more news article on my sister's kidnapping or how my father being falsely accused had led to his suicide."

"But you do want *something*," I said before I could stop myself. She was desperate to find her sister. Wasn't that what all of the Clay Kenyon fiasco had been about? Wasn't that who she wanted to remember more than her own memories?

"I want to be the one who decides what is relevant and what isn't." Thea's response barely hinted at what she'd tried to talk with me about earlier, but I grimaced, empathizing. My own need to control my past and keep it private had us all here in the first place. Not having any say over what you shared or with who had to be unnerving.

"Can we at least agree that anything that involves you going into anaphylactic shock is relevant?" Nik tried again, as gentle as a Navy SEAL with the muscle in his jaw popping out could.

The former SEALs on my spec ops teams always reminded me of those wind-up toy cars when they'd been wound tight. They looked like all the other toy cars, except the second you put them on ground, off they went.

"You know, there is another option," Coop stated.

We all turned our attention to him. Instead of elaborating, he swiped his beer bottle and took a swig, like he was using it to shut himself up.

Too little, too late, Sharky.

"Don't be shy," Nik grunted. "If it can help Thea, spit it out."

Coop set the bottle down, then smoothed his hand across his jaw, dragging his thumb along his lower lip. "I mean, it's a bit radical, but there's always Ibogaine and 5-MeO-DMT."

"Ibo-five-what?" Thea repeated.

"Wait," Leo interjected, then asked, "Is that the peyote stuff people drink?"

"You're thinking of Ayahuaska tea," Nik answered.

"Ibogaine is a naturally occurring psychedelic dissociate similar to those, yes. You take it as part of a guided psychotherapy. The protocol has had success in curbing drug addiction, PTSD, and even TBI."

"Is this the clinic you told me about a few months back? Down in South America with shamans?" Nik asked. "You never told me how it went."

"How it went?" Leo dropped his oyster with a clatter. "You didn't actually do that shit, did you?"

"Several guys in the community have done it," Coop said, dismissing his brother's obvious upset by skirting his question. But I couldn't help but wonder if this had been the reason Coop had gone to Brazil in the first place.

Directing his attention more to Thea, he continued, "Many have had vivid recollections of their entire lives, especially childhood. It might be worth looking into."

"Yeah, well, people say your life flashes before your eyes when you die, too. Doesn't mean you sign up for it," Leo snapped.

"You think I signed up for this?" Coop muttered under his breath.

My attention volleyed between the two brothers. The tension hung like a thick, heavy fog.

"You've done some messed-up shit, but going off to a third-world jungle to drink drug-laced Kool-Aid so you can trip balls? Really, Coop? Is that how you want to spend this time? You should be — "

"Enough," Coop bit out, cutting him off. "We're not talking about me. We're talking about options for Thea to access her memories."

Leo scraped his chair back, throwing his napkin over his plate. "You're right. I'm done."

Bolting toward the yacht's interior, he nearly collided with Cait as she and Kai brought out the main course.

"No need to get up." Cait recovered balance of the silver-lidded platters in each of her palms. "What can I get for you?"

"Sorry, lost my appetite," Leo grumbled, weaving past her as he headed inside.

"I'll grab it in the crew mess," Coop said to Kai before he could set down his platter. "Keep it warm."

I turned to watch Coop toss his napkin to the table before stalking off the opposite direction. I would've gone after him if Cait hadn't been blocking my escape. She set a tray in front of me, unveiling an artistically plated lobster and striploin combo.

"Tonight Chef Anders has prepared for you prime cuts of A5 Wagyu," Cait recited, as she'd done many times to full tables of upper-echelon business associates, diplomats, and A-listers. Despite the sophistication of our typical clientele, Cait had seen her fair share of drama and knew to power through as if none had occurred.

"In harmony with the three-year-old virgin Matsusaka, we have fresh caught lobster. Unfortunately, no shellfish for you, *of course*," Cait emphasized politely as she set down Thea's platter.

"You too?" Thea huffed, chucking her napkin before leaving the table.

Cait's eyes cut to mine and I shrugged, then smiled to let her know none of this was her fault. Nor was it mine. I refused to feel guilty for having shared Thea's food allergy with the chef and chief stew, but it had made this evening a hell of lot more awkward.

Nik gazed forlornly at the delectable plate Kai had placed in front of him then cursed. He muttered his apologies before tossing his napkin into the ring and chasing after Thea.

Cait scanned the abandoned dinners laid out perfectly upon the elegant table setting. As she realized I was the only one left, we locked eyes. Hers were wide with confusion. I had no idea what mine must've looked like. I just knew the what-the-fuck creases between them had to be deep and I needed another drink.

"I honestly don't know what wine pairs best with a virgin Japanese cow... Wait, is slut-shaming cows really a thing now?"

"Apparently," she said, choking on a laugh. "We can try to keep all this warm, if you want to wait for everybody?"

Cait had gone above and beyond to impress me with the beautiful spread. One which, no doubt, had been upgraded due to my last-minute arrival. As much as I wanted to chase after Coop, I couldn't do that to her. "Not a chance. I'm starving. Let's eat!"

Titan pounced on the opportunity, literally. His front paws slapped down on the tabletop as he set to mauling Nik's slab of Wagyu.

I waved off Cait's attempt to remove him from the table and said, "I'll have a glass of your finest Cab and my date here will have chilled Voss in a bowl of artisan ice, please."

We both looked over at Titan, paws slipping on the table as he leaned in deep, already going for the lobster. "Your date is very...fetching."

I cracked up, laughing way too hard. I schooled my breath enough to declare, "It's been a ruff night."

"Bone appetit!"

Chapter Twenty

Coop

I didn't blame Leo for being pissed, but I wasn't about to get into everything in front of Aziza. She'd call the job off and ship me to the best doctor money could buy. Which on the surface seemed a great solution.

Problem was, taking Zee's money—or OZ's or anybody's—would put me under that person's thumb. Even if I survived the surgery, Zee would coddle and crate-train me, keeping me safe on Marakata Cay and never putting me on any decent job again. Worse, she'd stay by my side, not ever leaving the island, either.

Hell, she had more wild carnivore in her than me. Instead of hunting the great plains with me, she lived in a zoo like some sort of lettuce-eating lion. She didn't need another reason to stay caged. She needed one to break free.

I hadn't jumped at her offer to relocate to the island because I didn't want to be one more excuse for her to continue living imprisoned the way she was. A part of me had hoped when I disappeared she'd chase after me. And while I might not have been motive enough for her to truly get away, I *had* somehow managed to steal her for a night.

And what a craptastic night it had turned out to be. All hell had broken loose. Who knew we had tickets for dinner and a shit show?

After Leo and I bailed, I saw Nik chasing after Thea. I considered going back to the table to try to salvage Aziza's evening, but I wasn't exactly good company and I didn't want to have to explain Leo's reaction.

Nor did I feel like running after my little brother. What could I say that would change the facts? I had a rock in my head and nothing was going to stop me from finishing this job for Zee. I'd leave her with at least that much.

I settled my frustrations by organizing and familiarizing myself with the equipment to bring the Ozma Emerald up. Just like Zaki had briefed us, we had access to both an underwater drone and a side scan sonar to help us map out the wreck site before choosing the best area to insert. Plenty of tanks and rebreather equipment. All top of the line. Aziza was nothing if not meticulous.

I couldn't help but grin as I imagined her in her fuzzy pajama pants, sitting cross-legged on her ebony four-poster bed as she researched shipwrecks. Plucking at her bottom lip as she watched videos of treasure hunters bringing up canons and the like. Jotting little notes on how to fill up lift bags, like balloons, with oxygen from spare tanks. Placing hundred-thousand-dollar orders for equipment as easily as hitting the Buy Now button. All the while that overweight tiger of hers had probably been gnawing on some giant meat bone at the foot of her bed.

Who had a freaking Bengal tiger for a lapdog?

She was a real-life Princess Jasmine waiting for Aladdin to show up with his magic carpet. Little did Zee know, she didn't need Aladdin. She already was her own magic carpet. She just didn't know she could fly.

I, on the other hand, seriously needed that magic genie lamp.

Aziza's freedom.

To live long enough to see it.

For my brother to have the courage to fight for the love of the one who got away.

Those would be my three wishes.

A couple of months ago my wishes would have been different, longer range. I'd envisioned a life with Zee, a true partnership in every sense. But between my TBI and the hang-ups I had from failed relationships, I needed mental clarity.

I'd always tried not to bury the awful things that happened in field. But the home front had been a whole different story. And perhaps not surprisingly, my past relationships had created more trauma than field ops had. The last thing I'd wanted to do was repeat my past mistakes with Zee.

I'd heard talk within the SEAL community of a therapy that had worked for both TBI and PTSD. The protocol was a psychological journey in which you unpacked your emotional baggage through guided psychotherapy.

Some of my trusted teammates spoke of a place in the Amazon that had jumped on the medical tourism trend. Nestled in the heart of the rainforests of Brazil, this world-class facility combined local tribal healing practices and Eastern medicine alongside experimental Western ones. In addition to cutting-edge surgeries and experimental therapies, they offered various protocols with the local shamans.

When I'd first heard about Ibogaine therapy, it had seemed desperate, insane, dangerous even. All the things I, myself, had felt. It had been my only hope. Yet, I'd known it would work. Once it had, I'd planned to suggest Aziza move to Dubai or anywhere with me. I just wanted her free of the island. Free of OZ.

But that was all before the clinic had discovered that my issues weren't entirely from TBI. I had a ticking time bomb in my skull, a tumor that doctors in the US likely wouldn't touch. But the clinic had had a surgeon they'd wanted to bring in.

Trouble was, Alvarez had become increasingly greedy and ruthless in targeting the financially successful medical facility. The cartel had become so entrenched in the region, the clinic had major issues getting specialized surgical teams and the medical supplies they required.

"We have the surgeon and all the medical supplies we need, but in order to get them here, we must pay, and it's not just hundreds of thousands of dollars anymore. We don't have this kind of money."

I didn't either. I'd given most of my earnings away over the years, not believing I needed it. My salary was icing on an already delicious cake, thanks to Aziza assuring all employees had access to whatever they needed. But just because I didn't have the funds to pay off Alvarez didn't mean I couldn't solve the problem. An opportunity had come along, a job. And against my better judgment, I'd taken it.

Eradicating Alvarez had major drawbacks. The cartel weren't good guys, by any means, but they also had connections, allies, who would see my going after Alvarez as a declaration of war on a tenuous battlefield. The bullseye wouldn't be drawn on me or the clinic. It would be on OZ, and especially on his cherished emerald mine in the Bahia region of Brazil. The mines didn't just hold gemstones either, they actually bunkered all of the hyper-secure databases of intel. The mecca of meta. But Beryl had the resources to protect itself, the clinic did not.

This wasn't just about me and my surgical needs. My fellow military personnel as well as those who lived in the region and their future generations all benefited from the clinic's impressive work. More inspiring, they'd found ways to retain their cultural traditions and practices while bringing in modern medical solutions as well. My plan was meant to ensure that not only the clinic, but the whole region, would no longer be under Alvarez's gun.

Like all best laid plans, mine had gone pretty fucking astray. Alvarez may've been weakened, but he'd hardly been stopped. In fact, the past few weeks he'd been in a heavy recruitment phase to bolster his power. Now, not only did he have the clinic on lockdown from receiving any new shipments, but by not being successful in taking Marco out, I'd put a target on Beryl Enterprises. What was that saying about no good deed? Because I was pretty sure I was being punished.

I finished prepping for tomorrow's dive then went up to the bridge to double-check on the radar for any other boats in the area. As Zaki had briefed, Island I&A was keeping a close eye on all ships in the area, not only for our job but because of the music video shoot for DV8 and Lil' BayBay. Still, I wanted to see for myself as well as touch base with the captain.

The vacant bridge stretched the width of the yacht with large, full windows to allow for maximum visibility. The whole room was illuminated with nightclub-worthy undermount lighting, and the controls were backlit in red for easy night visibility. A wall of high-tech instrumentation panels ran along the rear wall. In the middle of the room a curved, plush seating area and table that sat on a raised platform beckoned one to have coffee, lunch, or even a cocktail. In the front, sophisticated instrumentation panels and touch displays as well as black box electronics promised a most exquisite driving experience. In short, the bridge was a cross between a NASA-esque control center, a swank club lounge, and a very large cockpit.

I ran my fingers over the dual chrome throttles and smirked, recalling a time two years or so ago when Captain Tom had let me take the controls and open her up to her top speed of nineteen knots in the Arabian Sea. Too bad we were at anchor now. I checked the radar for nearby vessels and followed with a manual scan with the binos. No pirates on the horizon, which was a good thing.

Heading out, I bumped into the captain and Jim in the hallway outside the captain's quarters.

"Just coming to find you. Good to see you again," I said as I shot my hand out toward Magnussen.

The meaty captain shook it. His strawberry-blond hair kicked out in waves just like the seas he sailed on as he said in a deep Norske timbre, "You as well."

"Jim," I said, nodding toward the Midwestern American. He was rather vanilla-looking with his medium brown hair and basic blue eyes, average build, and borderline shorter stature. Had that Boy Scout quality about him, like he'd gotten his badge in gentle lovemaking.

I returned my attention to Magnussen. "Cait told me you all had an issue in the engine room. Everything okay?"

"Nothing major. We were just slipping a note under Tom's door so he'd be aware."

"Aren't you supposed to be at dinner?" Jim asked. He liked a strict regimen and in Monaco he'd been squirrelly anytime I went off schedule.

Clapping him on the shoulder hard enough to make him wince, I said, "Headed to the crew mess now. Want to join me?"

"Nonsense," Magnussen practically bellowed. "Have dinner with me on the bridge. Jim, tell Cait to bring it up. Then be sure to clean up our mess in the engine room."

"Of course, sir," Jim said and quickly headed off.

Magnussen turned back to usher me toward the bridge. "Kid's a hard worker, but I swear he'd wipe my ass if I'd let him. I have to make things up for him to do just to get some privacy."

I laughed as Lars poured us each a Scotch on the rocks. "Yeah, I noticed."

"Speaking of people who are up my ass, Scott Hayes just called again. He's hyper-concerned about pirating activity on this charter. Wants me to post someone round the clock to watch the radar for ships approaching."

As far as I knew, the crew had not been privy to the details of the job. They knew we were diving and bringing something up, but they had no idea of its value and certainly not that it was worth a half-billion dollars. "Interesting. Has there been an uptick in pirating in the Caribbean?"

"Not that I've heard. He's saying the Alvarez Cartel has been making threats. Know anything about that?"

I dropped down into one of the captain's chairs and took a sip of my drink. "About as much as you, I assume."

Chapter Twenty-One

Aziza

Sleep proved too lofty a goal. I hadn't spent a single night off the island since the *Esmeralda's* wreck. The gentle rocking of the yacht at anchor came too close to those first moments I'd washed up on the beach. The feeling of being in my mother's arms too sweet, reality too bitter. Each time I'd close my eyes to sleep the motion away, I would be taken back to the night the *Esmeralda* went down. I hadn't been able to sleep then either.

The electricity flickered back to life, reassuring me more than my father's kiss had. "See, Princess, I told you everything would be fine."

"It's not fine," I cried as Baba sat on the edge of my bed. "I want to go home!"

"Mira," he pleaded. "When you wake up tomorrow, you'll be on the most magical island. Beautiful beaches. Horses to ride. There is even a zoo full of animals."

"Zoo animals don't live on islands, Baba!"

"On this island they do! There is every animal your heart desires. And whatever it doesn't have, we'll get!"

"I want Mama and Am'maty Z."

"I know, love. But they are in heaven, remember?"

I nodded. But I didn't remember. Not really. Baba stroked a hand through my shorn hair. The kidnappers had done it to disguise me by making me look like a boy, or at least that's what I'd been told. The way I remembered it, Am'maty Z had been the one who'd shaved my head. Trouble was, everything was foggy between the sleep and the medication. The long days at sea and so many foreign countries. Too many hours since I'd seen my mom or Am'maty Z.

"I want to talk to Zanji,"

Baba stiffened and squeezed his brows. "Where'd you hear that name? Who told you about Zanjibayl?"

"Am'maty Z. She said Zanji was my am'maty too. She said she lived on an island."

"Zamarad told you Zanji was alive and living on an island?"

"Yes, we were going to get her."

"No, Mira. Zanji is in heaven. She's been there a very long time, since before you were even born. Mama is with her now, I hope."

"No, I talked to her."

"That's impossible, Princess. Even if she were alive, Zanji didn't speak. Noises maybe, but never words."

"She didn't speak words aloud, Baba. There are other ways to talk," I said with a roll of my eyes. Sometimes Baba didn't understand the most obvious things. "She typed them. I talked to her on the computer."

"You talked to Zanji on the computer?"

"Yes, Baba, but online her username is Jingur."

"Ginger?"

I laughed at him repeating me again. "Don't you know, Baba? Ginger is the English word for Zanjibayl."

"It is, isn't it? You're such a smart girl."

"But Zanji spells ginger different from the English version." I spelled it out for him the way she had in her username. "People do that, spell things in unique ways. Online, I mean. Are you listening? Anyway, she's really nice and very funny. Smart. I was looking forward to meeting her. Is this the island where she is?"

"I'm not sure who you were talking to online, but you must be mistaken. Zanji wasn't... She had something which made her...unique. Special. I don't think you would've found her nice and funny. Smart, yes, I believe she was very smart and maybe nice and funny in her own way. But she wasn't easy to connect to. Not the way your Am'maty Z is. Was."

"I know. Mama told me all about it. She said Zanji is on the rainbow."

"Spectrum, yes."

"Zanji prefers the term rainbow, Baba. She uses the computer to speak for her. With it, she communicates really well. It wasn't hard at all to connect with her. She told us where the island was and how to get to her. That's why we left."

"Left where?"

"Home. On the ship."

"Princess, I want you to think very carefully. Where were you when the kidnappers came? In the hotel?"

"No, we were never at a hotel. We were on a ship, but not like this one. One with tall masts and sails. Several men came over the railing with guns. I was scared. So was Mama. She and Am'maty Z tried to stop them, but..." The words caught in my throat as my mind spun back through the memories.

"It's okay, baby." Baba kissed away the tears ripping down my cheeks. "You don't have to remember the rest. Just sleep. Close your eyes."

I obediently flitted my eyes closed, but Baba didn't wait for me to fall asleep. A few minutes after he left, the sounds of voices kept me from drifting off. I strained to hear, but couldn't quite follow all the curses and shouts volleying between the deep, masculine voices. The fighting reminded me of the kidnapping. But that night I'd hid, too scared to help Mama and Am'maty Z.

Fearing the worst, I snuck out of my room, edging along the short hallway until I was close enough to make out the voices. The men fighting weren't strangers who had boarded our yacht to kill and kidnap us, they were my father and grandfather.

"Where did you get such a preposterous idea, Malik?" Jadd asked Baba.

"Mira said Zamarad told her. Is it true?"

"Mira's confused. She's an imaginative, rebellious child who's just survived an extraordinary trauma. The drugs and medications are making her say such crazy things."

"I don't think it's crazy. I think you wanted Zanji hidden away. You were always ashamed of her. Did you lock my sister up on the island like some kind of animal? That's why you bought Marakata Cay, isn't it? To hide her away."

"Where'd you get these ideas? Your blasphemous sister?"

"You wanted Z shut away too."

"I wanted Zamarad calm and happy. How dare you claim I didn't love her or treat her fairly. Did I not give her everything she could ever dream of? Did she not do all the things you did – skydiving, scuba, horses?"

"You wouldn't let her speak her mind!"

"I wouldn't let her be sinful!" Jadd bellowed.

"She wanted to leave, but you wouldn't let her go. Are you going to shut me away, too?"

"You're my son."

"Exactly. I'm male. You vilified her for the very things you praised me for."

"Why are you talking to me like this? Vilify? Do you think I'm some sort of monster?"

"Honestly? I'm not sure anymore."

"Tread careful, Malik. Where would you be without me? What would you have?"

"My wife! My sisters!"

"Do you even hear yourself? You should be ashamed of these thoughts! These crazy ideas, are they yours or your white wife's?"

Baba scoffed. "My wife's skin color is to blame now? And Coptic Christianity is what made Zanji unique, isn't that right?"

"Unique," Jadd sneered. "Your mother was punished for her beliefs. As the head of this family, I was punished for allowing her sins. We all were."

"Zanji wasn't a fucking punishment! She was a gift. And Mira wasn't kidnapped at all, was she?"

"Silence! You will not speak to me this way. Accuse me of such horrible acts. It is your guilt making you say such awful things."

"My guilt?"

"You couldn't control or protect your wife and daughter... I could. I did what needed to be done."

"Did what needed to be done? What does that mean? What did you do, Father?"

"I found them."

"From the kidnappers?"

"Yes! What has gotten into you?"

"Hmm. Your men were the kidnappers. That is what I think."

"You think I kidnapped my own family? Drugged them and dragged them out on some ship in the Arabian Sea? Sent ransom demands to myself? Why would I do such things?"

"No, I think Zamarad was escaping you and you stopped her. Your men boarded that ship, your men killed my wife, my sister. They didn't rescue Mira, they were the ones who traumatized her. Put a bag over her head, drugged her! Your men, under your orders!"

"You're in shock and saying these sinful things. You're ungrateful, Mal, always have been. I've given you everything, just like I gave my girls everything. Are you really going to accuse me of kidnapping?"

"Your actions killed them. You killed them!"

"I'm a murderer now? What else? If you'd done your job as a father and husband your wife would be alive today."

I charged into the room, wedging between my father and grandfather. "Stop! Stop fighting!"

Jadd grabbed my wrist. "What lies have you been telling your father?"

I wrenched my arm, but he yanked it so hard I felt the pain all the way up into my shoulder. "You're hurting me! Let me go! Let me go, Jadd!"

He lifted me until I flailed in the air. I struggled to kick, but I might as well have been a desert mouse being dangled by its tail.

"Let her go!" my father demanded.

"You're not able to protect your child."

"Like you've protected yours? By putting one in a cage and another in a grave? I will not stand by and let it happen to Mira, too."

Panting, I scrambled out of bed before my trip down nightmare lane came to its inevitable conclusion. I should've known the Ozma Emerald wouldn't be the only thing brought up from the depths on this job.

I had to get out of this room, breathe in some fresh air. But as soon as I threw back the covers, I felt naked. Thinking Coop might steal into my bed once he'd cooled down from his fight with Leo, I'd worn a silk cami and matching sleep shorts. Shorts? The way they were slit up the sides they fit more like a loin cloth.

What had I been think— Okay, scratch that, I knew exactly the erotic thoughts ripping through my mind when I'd chosen to wear the overly revealing, pathetic excuse for pajamas. No wonder I couldn't sleep. With every movement the exquisite fabric teased across my skin, titillating all the places that burned for Coop's touch.

I snagged a kimono-style robe made from the finest silk from the closet and slipped it on. The covering was emblazoned with the OZ logo, which helped to snuff some of my arousal and remind me again of the flashbacks and why I was really here. It wasn't to get laid. The fire and ice waring within my thoughts only served to confuse me.

Still breathless from my hurried movements, I padded, barefoot, topside for fresh air and to clear my head. We were expecting scattered storms, but directly over the ship the sky was cloudless, like a path up to the stars and clear to heaven.

"*Mira, you're going to love it here,*" Zanji had told me when she'd learned I was coming with Am'maty Z. "*The night sky from Marakata is even more beautiful than in the desert. You'll think black velvet had been laid out and all the diamonds in the world scattered upon it.*"

Little had I known Zanji had never even seen the night sky, not directly anyway. She'd only viewed the island from her computer screens. Now that I'd escaped, even for just a day, I realized how similar Zanji and I had become. But I didn't want our fates to be the same.

I drew in a long breath of ocean air. Tonight it was infused with the sharp aroma of chlorine from the hot tub and the wet, cool scent of approaching rain. To the east, a cluster of puffed-up clouds sporadically glowed and flickered. The lightning hovered too far away to worry about for now.

Leaning on the rail, I tried to let the rhythmic splash of waves against the yacht's hull and the rippling play of silvery moonlight soothe my anxiety down and center me in the present.

On Marakata, I had things like work and riding horses and skydiving to help distract me. And for a time, I'd even used sex. Keeping it impersonal, the men never even knew my name. I'd wear wigs, outfits, pretend to be someone, *anyone* else. Whoever I thought the man of the hour's fantasy woman would be. It was easy, and fun, but eventually I'd realized fulfilling their fantasies had done nothing to fulfill mine. The trysts were merely a series of illusions. Mirages. Lies.

I'd been chasing false freedom, same as *Am'maty Z.*

As time moved on, my desires had become clear and focused, and tonight I needed nothing more than to disappear into the only real thing I had—Michael Cooper.

He'd been on the deck with me the whole time. My guardian. My ghost.

I kept my focus on the water, the surface of the sea, glazed in moonlight. My nerves sizzled, as alive and charged as the distant lightning.

For a long time now, sex had been solely me and my very active imagination. I'd been able to predict exactly what would happen to my body, because like everything else in my world, I regulated it. But I'd never been adept at controlling Coop, nor could I predict what he would do to me next.

My heartbeat sped in wicked anticipation as I invited him over. "Are you just going to look or do you want to touch?"

His gritty voice came from the shadows. "You owe me a secret first, Presh."

Chapter Twenty-Two

Coop

"After," Aziza whispered. The word barely cut through the thickened air. "I'll tell you anything you want to know...after."

The heat of the air between us rose with each step closer. My breaths came deep and fast as I stood behind her. Aziza didn't turn. She wasn't in the frame of mind for conversation. Neither was I, really.

We'd spent four years talking, and while there still was so much we had to say to each other, right now we both wanted and needed each other on a physical level. Proof that everything we'd imagined between us was tangible, real.

With my right hand, I skimmed my fingertips purposefully forward along the curve of her waist. Sliding them across the delicate fabric of her robe, I palmed her stomach, pressing her body back flush with mine. Unable to resist the intimacy of her against me, I lingered long enough to breathe her in. But before either of us got too comfortable in the embrace, I fisted the sash of her robe and yanked. The covering snapped open, catching the ocean wind like a sail. She gasped, but followed it with an encouraging, ground out, "*Yes.*"

I clenched my teeth and rasped, "My sweet girl doesn't want it sweet, does she?" I gathered her hair, spiraling the silken strands into a rope before methodically wrapping my fist like a boxer.

"Not tonight," she conceded.

"Good. I have no intention or ability to take it easy on you."

She gulped. Then, so tentative it bordered on cute, she asked, "Will I need a safe word?"

I schooled the smile from my lips. With a taut pull, I brought her head slowly back, until her chin jutted up. "Do you want one, precious girl?"

"No," she admitted, pushing the word out like it was a plea.

She attempted to turn her head enough to make eye contact, perhaps to assess the seriousness in my eyes, but I kept hold of her hair and snarled, "Hands on the rail. Look forward."

She did as told, while a trill of excitement scattered goosebumps across her bare arms. I swallowed, stunned to have confirmation that she felt the same intensity for me. She was the first woman who brought out this need to possess. Maybe because the *only* thing Aziza had ever submitted to was her feelings for me. And that made me the luckiest son of a bitch in the whole fucking world.

I'd long suspected she'd tired herself out on being in control. As strong a woman as I knew her to be, I also caught the signs that she didn't relish delegating — or being in charge of others. She'd resigned herself to the role simply because nine times out of ten she had no choice. OZ controlled her and secrets had to be kept. But the task of making her body insanely happy was one job I was more than eager to take the lead on.

I released the tension on her hair, flipping the rope of black over her shoulder. Gripping the neck of her robe, I stripped the covering from her as if it disgusted me and tossed it aside.

"All these years of watching you..."

Edging my booted foot between her legs, I nudged one of her bare feet out.

"...wanting you..."

I gave her other foot more of a bump to ensure her stance was nice and wide.

"...planning all the things I wanted to do to you..."

Her sleep shorts hung loose off her hips, the silk billowing like laundry on a line. The wide leg holes slashed so high on the sides they flashed her ass cheeks. I stepped back, appreciating the way the thin crotch fluttered between her thighs.

"...and I never even knew what you looked like under all those clothes."

I drew my finger up her spine, then wrapped the nape of her neck in a firm clasp. "Down," I instructed, bending her at the waist.

She took her chin to the railing, like a pirate locked in a pillory.

"Show me." I kept my voice gruff, as if nothing about this pleased me. One look at my raging hard-on would tell a whole different story. Making sure my voice threatened discipline, I growled, "Now, precious girl. If you don't show me, how will I know where it's okay to touch you?"

After her initial hesitation, she realized what I was asking and thrust her ass up and back, giving me proper visual access.

I stepped back to admire the view of her pretty pussy. The breeze kept teasing the thin slip of silk back and forth across her shiny slit. My cock throbbed as it leaked pre-cum, but I held back from ripping my fly open and burying myself in her.

"We've had a lot of late-night conferences, but I don't think I've ever seen these clothes on you, Presh." My taciturn tone implied I was coldly inspecting her and finding her wanting. In actuality, it took everything I had to hold back from declaring my undying love and begging her for just a kind look in response. "Did you buy them for me?"

"I didn't know if I'd ever see you," she gasped, panting for air enough to form the words, even though she'd done nothing exerting.

"That's not what I asked. Let's try again. When you bought these, were you thinking about me? About how your sweet body would tease me? Tonight when you slipped them on, did you imagine my hand having easy access?" To demonstrate, I ran the thin silk crotch through my fingers, purposefully grazing her slit with my rough knuckles. A shudder went through her.

"Truth," I warned, palming the orb of her ass. I circled her cheek with a pressured stroke that promised a spanking if she didn't answer honestly.

"Yes."

"Good girl," I whispered, a little dismayed that I wouldn't get to swat that delectable butt of hers. I grasped it, unable to disguise my need, then reached between her spread legs. My mouth watered and my cock pulsed as the silk barely restricted my hand. I drew the heel of my palm back across her velvet-soft skin. "Like this?"

"Yessss."

The way she'd drawn the short word out in a long, quivering moan made my dick twitch. I bit down on my own groan while gripping the deck rail with my free hand. I reached through her legs again, this time letting my fingers course over her slit, my middle finger slipping between her heated flesh, so silky and slick with arousal. "And like this?"

"Yes." The jagged edge of distress in her whispered confession set a desperate fire inside of me. As I repeated the stroke, she pushed back, trying to catch my finger so it would drive in deeper. I flexed my arm tight to hold back from plunging all my fingers into her.

"Tell me what else you imagined me doing, Presh?"

"Sliding…" Her voice shattered as I kept running my finger between her honeyed flesh. I was dying for a taste, but like hell was I going to relieve her agony by pausing for even a few seconds.

I swallowed, my own voice threatening to crack. "Sliding what?"

"…y-your f-fingers," she stuttered needily, "…inside of me."

"Like this?" I drew my index finger in teasing, slippery circles before barely dipping in.

"Deeper," she begged on a moan.

I tested her, taking her only a knuckle deeper. Her body milked my fingertip and I almost shot my load off in my pants again.

She growled, "Deeper," like she was cursing me.

A smile hinted at the corners of my lips. I flexed my jaw and thrust two fingers deep. I had to gnash my teeth together to keep my own control as Zee keened in ecstasy.

Sliding my fingertips along the wonderous, smooth sheath her body made, I rhythmically drove in and almost out. Every few strokes I cocked my knuckle and brushed it across the spot I knew would send her into orbit. I didn't focus on it, because I wanted her begging, and the angle would be better in a minute. I worked her over until my hand was soaked and she was squirming and pleading for release. Then I slipped my fingers from her and penetrated her with my thumb, using the rough pad to massage her G-spot. I should've turned her around so I could see her face as she came, but instead I clamped my wet fingers over her clit to play with it as well.

Her wails of pleasure were a fucking siren song. Thank God the approaching thunder covered them, because they were fully capable of luring the most skilled of pirates to wreck upon her treasured shores.

Her body fought the waves of pleasure like even she was afraid of their intensity, but she was driving her hips into my hand and coming hard, and harder still. She tensed as I lifted her off the ground so my thumb could rasp with even more pressure. That was when she collapsed, her body clenching as she cried out.

Spent, she draped her head against my shoulder as she caught her breath, trusting me to fully hold her. I marveled at how right it felt to have her satiated weight on my forearm, her pussy still pulsing around my thumb in waves.

She didn't have one thought in her spectacular mind or a single fear in her beautiful heart. I wanted it to last forever. Angels or devils, Zee and I were the same. And *this*…this was the moment I'd take to heaven with me, or hell.

The misting rain began sprinkling in earnest as I reluctantly lowered her. Using two fingers, I dipped back inside of her before bringing the stolen honey into my mouth. I moaned blissfully before I sucked my thumb for more of her sweetness. "Damn, I knew you'd taste good."

Falling steadier now, the rain shower roused Zee back to her senses. But instead of turning her free to run for cover, I drew my hand along her jawline. Capturing her chin with my fingers, I brought her face around to mine, our lips meeting with a desperate force. The water streaming down our faces made it feel like we were drinking each other in gulps, never quite quenching the thirst.

Chapter Twenty-Three

Aziza

Coop ran his hands around my hips, pausing to knead the flesh of my buttocks. With a growl, he squatted, dragging his grip down the backs of my thighs. My skin was slick with rain, but still he scooped me easily up and flush against him.

I wrapped my arms and legs around his stout body as our kissing increased with desperation. I had no idea where he was carrying me, but I'd go with him anywhere.

Vaguely aware we were descending, perhaps down steps, I figured he was taking me to the master suite. Then suddenly my cold, wet body became emersed in liquid heat. *The hot tub.*

"Your shoes! Your clothes!" I realized in shock. *"Mushaeghib."*

"They were already pretty wet," he chuckled.

We both looked up as the sky continued to rain cold down from above while the tub warmed from below.

"Street clothes aren't allowed in the hot tub!"

"*Street clothes*?" he laughed again.

I lifted my eyebrows in challenge as I shot him a devilish grin. "Let me see you or I won't know where it's okay to touch you."

Coop threw his head back and laughed. "Yes, ma'am."

He set me down and quickly stripped every stitch away. I watched, enjoying the rigid contours of his flesh as he stood in the hot tub naked and flashed those devilish dimples of his. Curling his lip in a toothy snarl, he nipped the spaghetti strap on my cami top, plucking it with his teeth and letting it snap back. "And what is the policy on sexy lingerie?"

A low growl of gratitude sounded as I lifted my arms. His navy eyes sparked with sin as he peeled my wet cami up over my head. Without haste, his mouth descended on my breasts like they were his favorite dessert — sucking and lapping, nipping and licking. In a rush, he hoisted me into a sitting position on the surrounding deck and stripped my shorts off.

The rain tickled as it washed over my fully naked flesh, but all I could think about was Coop. His hands stroked down my legs, encircling my calves. Heat tingled everywhere he touched. I sucked in a shocked breath as he swung my legs over his wide shoulders. I went with the momentum, dropping my back to the deck so his hot, hungry mouth could ravish me into another round of orgasms.

I'd been wrong. *This*…this was his favorite dessert.

The more he enthusiastically explored and savored, the more ravenous and wanting I became. "Cock. Now," was all I could manage as I writhed in need.

Angling my body toward the object of my desperation, I vainly tried to edge closer as I imagined impaling myself upon it.

"Condoms are in my pants," he murmured against my clit, showing little interest in abandoning the pearl he was intent on plundering. "I threw them...somewhere. Overboard. Who knows?"

He nipped and teased. Licked and sucked. Did he expect me to go get them? Because I was completely powerless to pull away from my descent into mad oblivion.

Cock...tongue. Tongue...cock. I wanted them both. Desperately. Equally. Why couldn't I have them both? Was this what that saying about not being able to have his cock and him eat you too was all about?

I panted until I could form a sentence. "Maybe they aren't necessary. I'm on birth control for my fibroids—" *Seriously, Zee! Fibroids? Way to bring the sex talk!* "I just mean... I wasn't on them because I was worried about getting pregnant. I haven't been with anyone in..." I hesitated, not eager to admit I'd pined for only him for years now. *Sheesh*, I was going to talk him right out of a sure thing! "In a long, long time. You?"

He lifted his eyes to look up. His pirate's smile was further punctuated by his swollen, flushed lips. He swiped the tip of his tongue across them like he was cleaning the blood of a kill off. "Truth?"

I really didn't want to know he'd been with others. But I also needed his cock inside me, filling me to the hilt. Now. "Truth."

"I already told you. It's been four years of foreplay."

"What?" I scrambled to fully sit up. "How is that possible?"

I mean, I knew it had been possible for me. But for him?

"You've kept me super busy with work, which hasn't left much time for relationships. It's not like I didn't have opportunities. Several, actually. And I tried, not to start a relationship or anything, but to take the edge off."

"And?" I used my hand to swipe my rain-drenched hair from my eyes, so I could see his clearly.

"And nothing. *Not. A. Thing.* I legit thought the big guy was broke. I went to the doctor and got a prescription and everything."

"Oh? You wanted to be with someone and..." I recalled how earlier he'd had no erectile issues. "It worked, right? The medication. I mean, obviously, the 'big guy' is working now."

He slid his palms back and forth over the tops of my thighs. "I mean, *shit.* Okay, this *does not* leave this hot tub. Yes, I filled the prescription and I'd planned to take it, but not because I intended on being with anyone. At least, not anyone specific. I was on my own."

I held back a laugh. "Are you saying you took Viagra to masturbate?"

"Let's call it a shoot-house run through."

"Is that what you Team guys call it?" We both snorted at his comparing his alone time to the live-fire, close-quarters mock-ups Ops teams used to train for missions.

"I was worried I'd get one of those raging eight-hour boner things they warn you about. *Anyway,* you called right before I took it, and well, turned out I didn't need the little blue pills after all."

I widened my eyes at the awkward admission, but he didn't look the least bit embarrassed. "You got a raging boner? From taking my call?"

"Presh, it's hardly a novelty occurrence. More like an occupational hazard of having you for a boss."

"It must be torture," I replied coyly, enjoying this story way too much. Though I fully understood just how agonizing this particular ailment was, since I'd suffered from the same exact symptoms.

"I wouldn't waste your time feeling sorry for me."

"No? And why is that?"

"Oh, *Presh*, the things I got to imagine you doing... *Mmm-hmm*. My Rolex runs a good ten minutes fast most days."

When I looked at him, confused, he shook his wrist as he explained, "Perpetual motion. You should be ashamed. Moral of the story — my problem wasn't physical. My problem was the big guy likes you, and *only* you."

I widened my eyes at him and he started laughing.

"You don't have to smile so big, you know?" he groused. "It's not like it means anything."

We both dropped our gazes to his cock, which was straining so hard the head had popped above the steaming waterline like Nessie making an appearance at Loch Ness.

"Oh, I think it means something. Unless...?" I leaned in to wrap my hand around his shaft.

As I stroked, he pushed out a barely controlled breath. "Unless?"

I took my time answering, enjoying the feel of him in my hands as he started to look like he might lose consciousness. "Unless my new best warrior here wants another few rounds in the shoot-house?"

Coop's lulled eyes flared back to life. "No, no, he's ready to serve, ma'am. More than ready to infil downrange and in country, in *your* country."

My grin was smothered as Coop scooped me off the hot tub's ledge and kissed me deeply. I wrapped my legs around his hips as he spun me around and drove into me with a thrust. The forward momentum surged our bodies through the water to the opposite edge of the tub. My back flattened against the wall and he took advantage of the stability to enter me fully. Shocked, my moan of pleasure was captured in his mouth. He smiled against my lips as he rocked, pushing inside of me, penetrating me deeper and wider than I'd ever known. Filling. Stretching.

I ground my hips, meeting his intensity. He surged again, sending my head back in ecstasy. Another thrust and heave and another and another until I lost count. He adeptly flipped me around and set the same grueling pace from behind, this time taking one hand to grasp my hair and the other to cup my breast. His strong fingers clamped my hardened nipple between them, scissoring until I was begging for release. Then he buried his hand down south over my *kus*.

His fingers expertly stroked and swirled, teasing my flesh and setting me on fire. Just when I was about to fly off the edge into oblivion, he spun me around again. "Not yet. I need to see you," he said through panting breaths.

He positioned my hands behind his neck as his arms looped under my knees. Watching me intently, he scooped me tight against him and plunged his cock deep again. The embrace felt awkward and tight at first. The water in the hot tub made things tricky — between buoyancy and lack of lubrication — but I fell mesmerized into his eyes. So bright with life as his thrusts became shallow and slowed to a grind as he rubbed against my G-spot.

"Oh, shit, Sharky," I exclaimed as the maneuver sent my body out of control. "I...I..." I had nowhere to move, no way to ease back from the brink. All I could do was explode around him as he did the same inside of me.

Keeping us joined, Coop lowered until he was sitting in the tub with me straddling his lap. I clung to him, holding tight as aftershocks pulsated through me. He slipped his arms out from under my knees and banded them around me, turning our exhilarating lovemaking into an intimate and caring embrace.

The rain must've moved on, as the dark expanse above us was full of stars again. One blazed a bright streak across the sky, but I didn't waste any wishes upon it. Right now, I had everything I could dream of wanting.

Chapter Twenty-Four

Coop

"Time to wake up, Precious." I trailed my index finger along her naked spine.

With a girlish sigh, she grappled for the rumpled white sheets. The king-sized bed swallowed her small frame now that she was alone in it. "It's still dark out," she groaned.

My response was an ominous click of the bedside sconce and allowing the sudden bright light to hit her eyes.

"It's too early," she bemoaned.

"It's *after*."

She rubbed at her eyes and blinked a few times.

"You owe me that secret." The sternness of my tone had her furrowing her brow or perhaps it was the fact I was fully dressed and sitting on the vanity chair I'd pulled in from the master bathroom.

"What are you doing?"

"I'm going to ask you a few questions and you're going to be honest with me, *Princess*."

She clenched her teeth, though I wouldn't have blamed her if she'd bared them at me. "I've asked you repeatedly to stop calling me that."

"Question one. Why do you hate it when I call you a princess?" I took a sip of the black coffee I'd snagged from the crew mess after I'd snuck out and changed clothes. "Truth."

Pushing herself more upright, she snagged the corner of the sheet and covered herself with it. "If we're going to do this, could you hand me a shirt or something? Please."

As much as I wanted her off-balance and vulnerable, I didn't want her to ever look back at this moment and mistakenly believe I took any pleasure in doing it. I found a T-shirt for her, handed it over, and resumed my interrogation pose.

"There are actually two reasons," she said, pulling the shirt over her head.

I couldn't help but notice she managed to shield her breasts from my view with her bedsheet as she did so. *Good.* I liked that I had her backed on her heels a bit.

"First, I love it when you call me Presh. It makes my day every time you say it, because I know you went out of your way to research my name's meaning just so you could call me something special that was all yours. Second, the nickname Princess is bittersweet for me, because my father used to call me that."

I slowly clapped my hands. "Nice evasion tactic with the personal details, the compliment, and the sentimentality. I appreciate the sprinkle of honesty as well. But let's try this again, why did your father call you a princess?"

"Don't many fathers think of their daughters as princesses?"

"What's your real name?"

She pursed her lips, which were beautifully flushed and darkened from our hours of ravishing each other's bodies. Her eyes flicked to mine like she was not amused by any of this. "I could tell you, but then I'd have to kill you."

"I'm serious, Zee," I assured before taking another slow drink. Though from the set of her chin, I suspected she was serious, too. I didn't doubt for a second Zee would put me down if I didn't handle this properly.

"It's too bad you can't shine that sconce right in my eyes or waterboard me in the bathtub. You know we have a CIA-grade lie detector machine back on the island, if you prefer?"

I flashed my dimples. "I trust you'll answer my questions honestly. It's how much you'll try to omit that concerns me."

She treated me to an airy, mocking laugh of the '*I've got nothing to hide*' variety. "My real name *is* Aziza. My legal name is not."

I sipped my coffee and flagged my hand to encourage her to keep going.

"Just like your real name is Coop, but your legal name is not."

"Presh, let's not go there. You're better than these basal evasions. Besides, this isn't a game or an interrogation. This is *us* putting everything on the table so that we can have a real chance. Isn't that what you want, too?"

She was slow to answer. Zee didn't trust me, and from my activity in the Amazon, I didn't blame her.

Still, she relented. "Yes, I want us to have a real chance."

"Good. I'll make this easy then — I call you a princess because you are one. Perhaps sheikha would be the more appropriate term, though, yes?" I reached out and took her hand, clasping my fingers around hers to stifle their tremble. "You see, I already know who you really are. *I know.* So please, just come clean with me."

Her fingers clenched and I returned the grip, letting her know it would be okay, I had her.

"I was named Ozma when I was born. My mother always called me Aziza, though. My father called me Mira, which means female leader or queen, hence he often used the endearment. My father was a sheikh, yes. But I'm not a princess nor a sheikha. Not anymore. Not for a long time."

I was impressed she'd revealed so much without really telling me a thing. "Ozma what? Tell me your full name."

"Ozma Zamirah..." She paused, her deep brown eyes pleading with me to understand. Little did she know I'd understood and forgiven her the lie a long time ago. "Zaki."

I lifted her knuckles to my lips and pressed a kiss on them. "It's nice to finally meet you, Ozma Zamirah Zaki."

The tension dropped from her body, her relief to have the monstrous lie off her back obvious. She studied me, questions swirling in her eyes — *How did I know? How much did I know? Was this going to change anything? Would she ever have the upper hand with me again?* Her eyes narrowed, but not enough to hide the spark in them or her lip twitching into a mischievous smile. "Nice to meet you, too, Michel—"

I flared my eyes wide and pulled my lips in a snarl. "Oh, no you didn't."

Her impish smile grew confident enough I knew she wasn't bluffing. She'd tracked back through my name changes. Hell, she probably had an original copy of my birth certificate. The woman was the best tracker and sparring partner I'd ever had.

"*Ohhhh*, I did, Michelangelo Amadeus Cooper."

Like a lion, I pounced. Springing from the chair and onto the bed, I captured her in a full-body tackle as she burst out laughing. We wrestled with each other until we were limp with exhaustion and gasping for air from laughing too hard.

Then she straddled my midsection and said, "My turn. You owe me an explanation. What were you doing in the Amazon?"

"After," I agreed huskily as I rocked my hips, ready for round three. "I'll tell you everything, after."

"After what? After we take care of this?" she asked as she ground against the hard bulge in my pants.

"After we finish this job."

Aziza

The reminder of the real reason we were on this ship in the first place sobered me up. Not only were we bringing the Ozma Emerald to the surface, but Coop knew my birth name. Knew I was Omar Zaki's granddaughter, the one everyone believed had gone down with the *Esmeralda*. If there was one thing I'd learned as Zaki's hand, it was that just because someone has the answers doesn't mean they know the question. And the questions are invariably more useful in revealing a secret than the answers.

Depending on where in the depths of the wreck site Coop looked, I knew those questions would be coming up with him.

Coop smoothed his palms over my thighs. His eyes studied my face as he peered up. But I couldn't bring mine to make contact with them.

"You've got the thousand-yard stare."

I shifted my gaze then closed my eyes completely. I didn't want him to read the apprehension I felt. The fear.

"You were on the ship when it went down, weren't you, Presh?"

He rolled to his side, taking me with him. Cradling the whole of my body, he embraced me in a way no one had since my mom had been murdered.

I didn't *have* to tell him about the night the ship had gone down. Knowing who I really was gave him plenty of ammunition. With it he could prove Zaki had been fraudulent, which could ruin the credibility of everything we'd done. Beryl Enterprises would be reduced to no more than a lucrative emerald mine and several defunct businesses. All the good we'd done would be overshadowed.

But even with the risk of losing everything, I desperately wanted the ideal he presented to me. I wanted everything on the table. I wanted us to have a real chance.

"There was the most horrible, shuddering vibration. The sound was...a screaming squall of death, a monster's claws scraping down a chalkboard. But the *Esmeralda* actually being damaged hadn't occurred to the ten-year-old me, not right then. Because for a minute, even the storm seemed to go silent and still. We must've been in the eye, but I just thought whatever had happened was over. I had an inside cabin, so I didn't have portholes, just a nightlight. The darkness hit with a punch as the electricity cut out. Even though it could only have been off for a few seconds, the air had turned thick and suffocating. I didn't think about logistics of electricity and air-conditioning though. I just thought a pillowcase had been dropped over my head again. I started thrashing and screaming, believing the kidnappers had come back for me."

Coop's arms tightened as his lips pressed against my temple. Just as my father had done when he'd come in to comfort me that night.

As an adult I understood my reaction to the electricity going out had been a flashback. But when I was a child, my reality had been distorted due to the drugs the so-called rescuers had used on me and the medication the doctors had given me to ease the shock of my 'ordeal'. *My ordeal.* I never knew if the term referred to my having had a hood thrown over my head and being crammed into a trunk or losing my mother and aunt.

But just because I understood everything now didn't mean it wasn't still traumatizing. I steadied my breath before another wave of panic rolled through me.

I explained how my father had come in and what we'd talked about, about how he had confronted my grandfather. How their fighting had turned physical. Soon I was right back in the moment.

My ears rang as the gun fired and my eyes slammed shut. When I dared to open them, I saw both Baba and Jadd frozen in shock, no longer struggling against each other, but holding each other in an awkward hug. For just a sliver of a second I thought they'd come to their senses. Blood pooled between them, both of their robes turning red. Slowly my father's body sank. He sagged to the floor in a heap and Jadd dropped to his knees still trying to hold him.

Tears sprang to my eyes as I raced to my father's side. I expected Jadd to try to help or cry, but instead he wheeled at me.

"This is your fault, Mira! Your lies have caused this!"

He scooped his arms under Baba's, lifting his upper body as he dragged him. "Get your father's feet," he barked.

Fearing Jadd's wrath, I scurried to help him move my father. My uncontrollable sniveling and shaking made it impossible for me to keep hold of Baba's heavy feet and my dropping them only served to annoy Jadd further. "Just forget it, Mira. You're useless and lazy. You want to make this better? Go clean up the rug. And bring me my gun."

Eager to get away, I ran back to the living room. In that short time, the water had begun seeping through the carpet and the bloodstain had spread. The captain slogged across the room, paying no attention to the stain or me. I begged him for help, but I couldn't form the words to explain what had happened.

"We all need help, Mira," he grunted.

"Where are you going?"

"The ship's sinking," he said, matter-of-fact. There was no invitation to follow.

"What about us?"

"Find your father and grandfather and tell them to hurry to the deck. Once I release the rafts, I won't be able to wait long."

"My...my father..."

"Now, kid! Did you hear me? I'm not going to go down with the ship. This ain't like the movies."

I scrambled to go find Jadd, quickly grabbing up the gun he'd shot my father with. My steps splashed as I ran toward the galley. When I turned the corner the sight paralyzed me.

I watched as Jadd dragged the son he'd murdered, my father, into the deep freeze.

I no longer saw my distant, but generous grandfather. I saw cold eyes. I saw evil and hate. Any doubts I'd had about Jadd being capable of the things Am'maty Z and Zanji had said he was had vanished.

He glanced up, no longer looking at me like I was his ten-year-old granddaughter. "You, Mira, you did this. This is all your fault!"

"It wasn't your fault. You aren't his scapegoat," Coop whispered, encouraging me back to the present with his lips against the back of my head. "You've been living in this cage of his for far too long. You know that, right?"

I started to agree, but the truth came out instead, because that was all Coop and I had anymore. "He looked like I was already dead to him. He wanted to kill me."

"Kill you? But you're his granddaughter? You were just a child."

"Yes, he said that as well."

"And who in the world would believe a child's lies?"

Chapter Twenty-Five

Coop

Nik and I spent the morning running the underwater drone over the wreckage site. We'd propped the computer on the padded captain's chair of the tender as it was the only way to shade the screen for decent viewing. Evaluating the findings, we'd be able to identify any debris paths and determine the yacht's final position. The technology wasn't sophisticated enough to get a full internal layout of the ship, but Zee had spared no expense and the imagery and mapping we were getting back on the laptop was better than expected and more than adequate for our needs.

"I don't like this," Nik said as he rapped the display with his knuckle. "Looks like it's ready to cave in right here, and that's if this section doesn't slide right off into an abyss."

I agreed. The bulk of the yacht's starboard aft leaned perilously off a ledge along the reef wall, beyond which the seafloor dropped completely away. It was a perfect day for diving, though. The waters were calm with no major currents, so risks were mitigated. While below the surface things were perfect, the way the sun had started to beat down from above, I wouldn't have minded a nice stiff breeze.

"Let's insert here." I pointed to the ship's bow, which appeared to have lodged itself into the coral, making it slightly more stable. "The *Esmeralda* was a luxury vessel, not a cargo ship. Between the favela gangs, the Commando Vermelho, and the corrupt police, it wouldn't have been safe to transport the emerald to any cargo port or marina in Brazil. So I'm guessing they conducted the transfer at a private dock or canal, most likely used the yacht's toy cranes to load the safe. The ones on the bow make the most sense."

"Agreed." Nik swiped his forehead and resettled his ballcap. "And it's not likely they relocated it once it was onboard."

"On our way back to the ship, let's drag the sonar over this area in case the safe detached when the ship capsized."

"Roger that." Nik whipped the boat around as I prepared to redeploy the sonar.

We silently trolled westward, letting the draft our movement created cool us off.

Before I could reminisce on last night with Zee, Nik asked, "How are you and Leo doing? Is he okay?"

"He's..." I couldn't in good conscience say Leo was fine. I couldn't even say he *would be* fine. This situation was only going to get worse, and now I'd selfishly dragged Zee deeper into it with me.

"I thought I heard him crying last night."

"That was me. I always cry after sex," I joked. Then I tamped down the guilt of making light. My brother was scared for me.

"Yeah, I heard that too, asshole. Seriously, I've never seen Leo like this." Nik wasn't going to let me play it off. If he was, he'd have at least tried to mine my sex comment for more details.

Not that I was about to share those amazing memories with him. *Shit.* Zee and I both should be ashamed...*and proud* of ourselves. Definitely worth the wait. But now that I knew what I'd been missing, I was eager to get back to her.

"Leo's been edgy about this whole trip." Nik flipped his baseball cap backward and popped the top on the Outbreak energy drink he'd fished from the small cooler Kai had loaded for us. "Something is off between you."

I took a page from Aziza's playbook and went with as much honesty and information as I could, without giving him anything he didn't already know.

"Leo's all weirded out about the Bermuda Triangle stuff...and sharks. But mostly he's concerned about my diving given the number of concussions I've had. A couple months ago, I told him I was taking part in a TBI study. I didn't think he'd understand about the Ibogaine protocol. And I get it, I thought it sounded like some hippie excuse to get fucked-up while hiking through the rainforest, too. But there's something to it."

"Is there? Something to it? Did it help?"

"With some things...yes." After going through the guided process of tapping into my past relationships, it had felt like the bullets had been removed, the infection purged, and the wounds healed. I no longer feared I'd make the same mistakes with Zee, nor did I feel I was doomed to make new ones. Truth was, Zee and I had already had the friendship and the partnership, the attraction and the respect, the love and the bond. All we'd waited on was the physical, and if last night was any indication, we certainly didn't have issues there.

"And other things?"

"Not so much." But my having a tumor wasn't the fault of the therapy. "I will say this, there was a part of the experience where I felt like I was in a movie of my life. It was so vivid. I wasn't just watching the past, I was reliving it."

"Reliving it?"

"You know how in dreams, you're you, but sometimes you're also watching you? Under the psychedelic, I saw past events as they really were, like without the bias remembering has. And I'll say, it was not all fun. But it helped unpack the memories and resolve things, which is why I brought it up for Thea. Given everything we know about her childhood, a triggered recollection of any of those events may be overwhelming. Ibogaine and 5-MeO-DMT might lessen the trauma of her going home again."

My mind flashed back to Zee's recounting of the shipwreck. I was grateful I'd been with her and that she'd trusted me to hold her through it. I was also thankful to help her complete this job, which would have more emotional impact on her than I'd realized.

"If it wasn't a scam and you think it helped, why didn't you tell Leo after the fact?"

I grimaced. "You saw his reaction. Actually, it was worse than I'd expected."

"Tell me about it. I had no idea Thea felt so strongly, either."

"She okay now?" I asked, nabbing the opportunity to move the conversation away from Leo.

"Yeah. She cooled off quickly. We talked through her concerns and she wants to try the Ibogaine if you think it'd help."

"Wow, she actually trusts my opinion on something?"

"Let's not get carried away. I pushed it. The near miss with the shrimp and then your comment about swimming convinced me we need to do something. I'll feel better after going over the finer points with you, but yeah, she agreed. She's been having some weird dreams. Reactions to things that don't make sense, so she thinks they might be triggered memories. It's freaking her out. We both want to plan a trip ASAP. She'll need a fake passport to get into South America."

Theadora Gale was still considered deceased, to give Agent Coleman time to determine who could be trusted at the Bureau. Besides, if Thea used her own credentials it would make her an easy target for the woman who'd come after her back in Colorado, Seraphina Westin. Too big a risk in my opinion. "It's illegal in the States, but I bet Aziza could arrange for her to do it on Marakata."

Shit. I realized my mistake the second the words left my mouth. It didn't take much longer for Nik.

"Why didn't you do it there?"

I had a few motives. For one, didn't seem logical or fair to try to resolve my hang-ups from past relationships while simultaneously attempting to get another off the ground. And while I'd wanted to keep my issues under wraps until I knew how the therapy worked, I'd also secretly hoped my disappearing act might get Aziza off the island to give chase. At the time,

I hadn't quite understood just how hard it had been for her to even hold her heart out to me.

But there was only one motive Nik would understand. "Same reason we didn't report every injury or talk about concussions when we were deployed. I'm not ready to be sidelined."

I'd come up in the Teams when TBI wasn't even on the radar. Nik hadn't been far behind. Not sure it would've changed things considering we took self-diagnoses to the extreme, often performing medical procedures on one another. Hell, some of my biggest scars looked more like I'd been sewn together with jute twine.

Nik slowed the throttle until the boat stopped. I relaunched the sonar off the back of the tender. As we slowly started trolling again, Nik eyed me with concern. "What are your symptoms?"

"Dude, you put that penlight in my eyes, I swear I'll snap your wrist off."

"You can't exactly slap some mud on your brain and move on this time. Besides, if we're diving deep together, I need to have your six. What are your symptoms?"

Nik had left the door ajar, keeping the option of diving with me open. I decided to be forthcoming, to an extent. "Aural migraines, mostly. Headaches that come on sharp and fast. I've passed out a couple of times."

"Coop, this doesn't sound like something you should ignore and override."

I grimaced at the familiar mantra that had gotten me through many a deployment. But I also realized I needed to confront and overcome this time around.

"I've got an appointment already set up. Trust me, I'm taking this seriously. I just need to do it my way."

"You and Thea both," he muttered. He had to drop his concerned stare in order to angle the bow of the boat into a round of heavy waves. It didn't distract him long. "What happened before you passed out each time?"

"First couple of times was on a job in Europe about six months ago. Each time was after I'd gotten up out of a dead sleep. Chalked it up to sleeping pills and standing up too fast. Once was after puking up the Ibogaine. Last one was after an RPG shot me out of a tree. Guessing the noise and exertion played a role there."

"That's more than a couple. Want to tell me about the RPG one?"

"There's not much to tell."

"Not-much-to-tell stories usually end up being the best ones around a campfire in about three years."

Three years. A sliver of a lifetime I didn't have.

"Leo's right," Nik conceded. "I don't think you should be diving."

"This isn't up for negotiation, Steele. The job needs to get done. I need to make it out. Will you watch my back or not?"

"Why? Why is *this* job so important? If it's the money—"

"It's not." The money *was* integral. I wasn't going to ask Aziza or OZ or whoever the fuck for a loan or a handout. And since the Alvarez hit job had been a bust, the clinic would still need money in order to get everything they needed. I had no other means of making that kind of cash, certainly not quickly. But the job, the money, the procedure, the ticking time clock were all driven by the same 'why'. "I need more time with Zee."

Nik scoffed, "All the shit you gave me and *look at you*. A couple weeks ago I'd have told you love's not worth losing your life. But now, with Thea, I get it. Your life isn't worth much if you lose the one you love. I gotta say though, I've been your best man enough times — shit, how many *has* it been? Four?"

I clamped my teeth together, expecting a nice ball-bashing about how many other women I've claimed to be in love with and how those relationships had ended in heartache. "Three."

"Are you sure? I remember two brunettes, the blonde, and a redhead."

"Am I sure?" I cocked a brow. "If I didn't remember the marriages, I certainly remember the divorces. Of which, there were three — Sarah, Becca, and Lauren. Katia and I never got to the altar, so the second brunette doesn't count."

"Oh, Katia fucking counts!" Nik whooped. "I had to learn a poem in Russian *and* go with you on your honeymoon, where you told everyone I was your better half."

"I wanted the free champagne and chocolate strawberries. And you loved the couple's massage and the private beach dinner. Get to the point."

"The point is, I've been your best man three times and your better half once. I know you loved — and still love — them all. You've never been heartless. Where was I going with this shit?"

"Who the fuck knows? Can we just get back to the yacht?"

"*That's right*, I remember now... I've seen you in love more than a few times, but this is, legit, the first time

I've ever seen you look at a woman like she's your only source of oxygen."

I wasn't going to deny it. Zee was my air, my food, my water, my shelter. But she was also something much more. She was my 'why' I desperately needed to survive this brain tumor.

Chapter Twenty-Six

Aziza

It was a good thing Coop had prep work off-ship to do this morning, because my addiction to his body consumed each and every one of my senses. My past sexual experiences had never left me like this—raw, yet healed. Full, yet craving. Consumed, yet worshipped. I drew in the smell of his skin on mine. My *kus* hummed and pulsed if I so much as thought about how gloriously he filled me. In fact, thinking about sex with Coop had so thoroughly distracted me while I checked Zaki's correspondence, I'd sent the prime minster of Canada an order for stallion semen. Thankfully, he had a good sense of humor and simply responded with, *"My price is twice that and I prefer the term stud."*

"Morning, Zee."

I jotted down some notes while my focus was momentarily sharp. Beryl had three ops going that I needed sitreps on, the Alvarez Cartel had been in a heavy recruitment phase so I wanted to beef up security at the emerald mine, and there was something going on in Kenya that I was forgetting. I drummed my fingers on the table, trying to remember.

"Zee?"

I blinked at Titan licking my leg, and realized he and Thea had been standing in front of me.

"Morning." She flashed me a sheepish smile.

"Oh, sorry, I was lost in thought." I closed the Toughbook, to give her my attention. "Good morning."

I started to ask if she'd slept well, but was too worried Coop and I had kept everyone up. So much for keeping our relationship secret!

Thea gripped the back of the chair across from me. "I just wanted to apologize for last night."

At first I had no clue what she had to apologize about, because all I could recall about last night was how freaking amazing it had been. Then I remembered the dinner fiasco. "No need. Sit. Cait's bringing breakfast now."

"I'm starving." Thea grimaced as she pulled a chair out and sat. "I can't believe I passed up such an amazing dinner."

"We had a great time, didn't we, boy?" I leaned over and patted Titan's head. Then I met Thea's worried eyes with empathy. "I should be the one to apologize. I just assumed you'd want all that information in the dossier, and didn't even realize I'd been insensitive. I spend ninety percent of my day sifting through bits of data on people. I tend to forget the information isn't an accurate indicator of a soul."

I started to explain how I'd grown up with someone whose social patterns were so black and white that my own responses often came off robotic and without empathy. I knew Thea's father had been on the spectrum, or rainbow, as Zanji had preferred. But if Thea hadn't read her dossier, then she probably didn't know that yet. Still I knew it shaped her, in ways she would come to understand and hopefully appreciate.

"It wasn't just the information. I've been struggling with who I *was* versus who I am now," Thea said as she tucked a wavy blonde strand of hair behind her ear. The rest continued to be tousled by the light breeze off the sea. "I thought I had control over it."

"Yeah," I murmured, understanding the feeling. I so wanted to tell her all the ways we were similar. But I hadn't even told half of those things to Coop. Or Vivi, who'd I known and trusted forever. "Control is a funny thing, especially when it comes to our brains, our bodies."

"Exactly. In the plane, after we landed, I had this weird moment where I was actually scared of Nik. I flinched from his touch. I'm really worried about resurrecting old fears and not having any control over them."

"What does Nik think?"

She let loose a smile. "He doesn't want me to die from peanut butter."

"Oh, you're not allergic to pean — sorry. Doing it again."

Thankfully, Cait had started bringing out family-style breakfast platters and Thea dove head-first into the bacon pile.

"If it's any consolation, we vet everyone who comes to the island. We know things about people they don't know about themselves all the time." Though given Thea's history, and frankly my own interest in her, I'd delved deeper than I typically would've. Still, I smirked. "You're hardly special where that's concerned, at least."

"Why? Why do you do it?"

I grimaced and lifted a shoulder. "We don't want to accidently kill someone with a crustacean?"

From the look on her face, I guessed she wasn't ready to laugh about this. I actually wanted to bring Thea and Nik into Beryl Enterprises, so I stopped trying to sugarcoat it. "Typically, I throw Zaki under the bus and say it's because OZ is so paranoid. But in reality, Intel is a lucrative commodity—HUMINT, SIGINT, CYBINT, FININT, U-NAME-INT. We track so much information because we supply several governments with the software to do the same. For one, we have to test it. And two, our products and services wouldn't be worth much if we couldn't protect one man or one little island."

"What exactly are your services?"

"We're quite diversified. We strive to meet whatever our clients need. Some needs are bigger than others. Some are humanitarian in nature. Some are for profit, while others are pro bono. Few are simple. Many are straight-up miracles."

"What if a client needed to get her memories back? Would that be the kind of miracle you could make happen?"

I considered what I knew about Ibogaine and weighed it with Thea's memory dynamics. While the tornado had been the inciting event physically, she'd also had emotional trauma. I wasn't a brain doctor, but I suspected she *could* recover her memories, given there was no actual damage done to her brain. Plus, Coop wasn't a throw-spaghetti-on-the-wall-to-see-if-it-stuck kind of person. He wouldn't have brought it up if he didn't think it would help. "If you're wanting to try the Ibogaine, we could arrange it."

"For a cost, though. You don't have yachts like this because you give things away. What would we be talking about?"

"Nothing." I held up my hand to ward off any protest. "The pro bono isn't so all altruistic. For one, you're important to Coop, which makes you important to me. And two, I've actually already approached Zaki about courting you and Nik to work with us. You'd be under no commitment of course, so please don't feel the help obligates you or that you need to make any decisions soon. But who you were before the tornado is just as important to us as who you are now. In fact, I think the combination will be an extremely powerful one."

I could sense Thea was getting uncomfortable with the focus on her. I wasn't surprised when she snagged another round of bacon and changed the subject. "You know, Coop makes sense now."

I chuckled. It wasn't an anomaly for Coop to rub someone wrong at first. "How's that?"

"He blamed me for delaying this trip and didn't make his irritability with me a secret. Now I know why he was so eager. He couldn't wait to get back to you."

I didn't correct her about the *get back* part, just smiled down at my buttered toast. Then I remembered it was well past my normal breakfast time. Back on Marakata there would've been toast waiting for me and a steak for El Hambre. I knew I'd forgotten something. I held back from calling the island. What was one steak in the grand scheme of things? And it wasn't like El Hambre would waste away without his breakfast snack. Nor would Zaki's empire crumble if I took a little time just to enjoy the ocean breeze and a nice breakfast with a new friend.

The phone started ringing. *Gray.* So much for abstaining from work. "Sorry, I better take this."

Thankfully my rudeness was diluted as Leo, all lean muscles and rumpled bedhead, ambled toward the table like a young cub waking up from a nap. I greeted him, grabbing up the fruit smoothie Cait had made for me. Then I excused myself and headed up to the sundeck.

"Okay, what have you found out?" I asked.

"A couple of things. First the Austin twins. You were right. There've been several large donations, like *account-draining* donations, to a handful of charities that are under the Ardent umbrella. The two which the twins have contributed significantly to are the self-help series you told me about and a mountain refuge for human trafficking victims called the Sanctuary. I didn't see any other connections between the twins and Clayton Kenyon, though."

"Well, not publicly. But he was connected with Ardent somehow, and I wouldn't be at all shocked if he had his thumb in the Sanctuary. It's gotta be a cover for something." It always intrigued me the way some people publicly condemned the very thing which they privately engaged in. Happened a lot with protest-too-much types like Kenyon. But the Austin twins came as a bit of a surprise, and I wondered if they, or maybe it was only Ophelia, even knew the real workings of these supposedly good, wholesome endeavors.

"Very possible. You want me to get Scott's opinion on any of this? Or should we still keep this quiet?"

"Let's wait to bring in Hayes. He won't be interested until it's more actionable anyway." He valued intel over hunches, which was why it had taken him so much longer to bring up the activity in South America or to name Coop. Right now we had nothing conclusive. Just some loose connections that I still hadn't even been able to solidly link to the so-called production company. Besides, Hayes' questioning my focus to Zaki still rubbed me wrong.

Gray added, "It's just, Hayes was with the Bureau around the same time as Kenyon."

So was Thea. And Thea had been the one who'd actually had enough on him to bring him down. What if she had more? An ace up her sleeve still?

Now I really wanted Thea to regain her memories. Her knowledge of Kenyon, and possibly any associates, was more current than anything Hayes could provide anyway.

I shot off a text through OZ to our medical team requesting an indigenous tribal doctor and some Schedule I psychedelics be put on a plane to Marakata as soon as possible. No one ever questioned Zaki, but it probably should've been concerning that an order for a shaman and toad venom didn't even warrant a repeat back for accuracy.

As I headed down to get ready for the dive, I got a call from Vivi. I'd been expecting an update on Captain Tom's daughter, so I answered with, "How's Natalie?"

"Natalie is perfectly fine," Vivi said. "As are Tom's wife and son. He's not been home. No plane tickets were ever made in his name out of the islands. No charges to his cards or transactions in his bank accounts. No calls made from his cell phone or internet activity of any sort."

Fear crept up the back of my neck. "Where the hell is he?"

Coop

I'd never gotten nervous before an op before. I really didn't want to start now. This dive needed to go easy-peasy, so the Ozma Emerald could be brought up without a hitch and its namesake and I could spend the night rolling around naked in celebration.

Kai helped me load the last set of tanks as Nik kissed Thea goodbye. They both hopped into the tender as I glanced around. I was a little miffed that the only one waiting for a goodbye kiss from me was Titan.

Even if the sex hadn't been off-the-charts amazing last night, I still would've expected Zee to be on hand to see us off on such a big job. Of course, she didn't realize the risks I was taking, nor did I want her to. Truth was, I needed to see her, even if it was just one last time. My nerves were getting the best of me.

"Could be worse, I guess," I muttered before crouching and giving Titan's snout a smooch. The scamp took complete advantage and went for the full French version. "Okay, big mistake... Way too much tongue, fella!"

As I swabbed my face with my forearm, my eyes widened. Zee was here *and* wearing a full-body wetsuit. She strode toward me with determination and confidence as the sleek, black neoprene clung to her curves like a second skin. Saddle me up and call me Seabiscuit, because I suddenly understood people with dominatrix and latex fantasies. My brain snapped back into action when instead of a fringed whip, she grabbed up a rebreather and backup tanks.

"Whoa! What are you doing, Presh?"

"What does it look like, Sharky?" She oh-so casually pulled her wetsuit zipper down as if her breasts could use a little air. "Playing tennis, obviously."

God, I wanted to plant my face right in that sweet canyon of cleavage. Boobs or not... I was not going to let Zee distract me. "No, no, absolutely not. You're staying on the boat."

Hands on the luscious curves of her hips, she squared off with me in the yacht's toy garage. "You say you won't live in a cage, but you seem to want to keep me in one."

"The hell I don't. I want your freedom as much as you do. Maybe more. But this isn't a pleasure dive. Nik and I have enough to focus on without adding the safety of a third party." Not to mention I had plenty to worry over with my own damn self.

"I'm a skilled diver, Coop. Scuba, sky —"

"I'm well aware. But we're going to be tearing into an already unstable wreck site, setting explosive ordinance. I can't be worrying about your safety *and* do the job you've brought me here to do."

Zee wrapped her hand around my biceps. "I'll worry about my own safety."

I really wished she wouldn't look at me with those big round eyes when she was touching me. It worked too well. Especially when her lower lip, darkened and full from a long night of loving, was suddenly shiny and beckoning for me to plunder it. *No, no, no!* I just had to fight fire with fire.

"That's not how this works," I said softly.

"How what works?"

I stroked a strand of silky black hair off her forehead with my pinkie as I cocked my chin and looked down at her. "How *we* work, Presh."

Yep, that did the trick. The hard resolve in her chocolate eyes melted like marshmallows in cocoa. Which was a damn good thing, because my own doggedness when it came to giving in to Zee was mushy at best.

She set down the equipment and narrowed her eyes as her lip jutted out. "You fight dirty."

The way she drawled that last word out made my dick twitch.

"You had no problem with dirty last night," I growled in her ear.

"*Mmm*, no, I sure didn't." She popped up on her tiptoes, a slight pout on her lips opened in invitation. "Promise to hurry back to me?"

I stepped into her and wrapped my fingers around the back of her neck. Hauling her body against mine, I kissed the shit out of those sweet-tasting, dirty-deed-doing lips. Then in place of any promise, which would've been just another lie, I gave her my heart instead. "I love you, Zee. No matter what happens, know that."

Chapter Twenty-Seven

Aziza

Michael freaking Cooper told me he *loved* me! Me!

He may love you, but he's totally going to kill you! That man... Damn. He fought, *and loved*, dirty. Then again, so did I. I throttled the Zodiac from the yacht to where Kai had anchored the tender.

"*Aziza...*" Kai's voice was drenched with caution and dripping with concern as I tied up alongside of him. "What are you doing?"

Why did men always ask the obvious? I was in a wetsuit with a raft full of diving equipment. What did he think was going on?

"Well, I didn't bring the boys sandwiches, if that's what you were thinking," I muttered. Then I spelled it out, because his forehead was still scrunched in confusion. "I'm diving the wreck."

"But..."

"Don't even try to fight me on this," I warned as I quickly prepped my gear.

"Oh, I wouldn't dare fight you on anything, but I'm going to have to tell Coop and Nik. They'll be setting off charges."

"Safety first, of course," I acknowledged with a nod. Then I added, "Just wait until I'm in the water."

Otherwise Coop might talk me out of it again.

I finished my prep and rolled back off the side of the heavy-duty rubber boat with a splash. As I'd promised Coop after the skydiving situation, I kept my comms on and heard each and every one of his curses when Kai alerted him to my approach.

"Please, Coop. You have a job to do. So do I."

"Keep alert on your way down," Nik interjected. "We spotted two large bull sharks."

"Roger that."

My nerves fluttered as I controlled my descent. I was going farther down than I typically went and using equipment I wasn't as familiar with. The rebreather would allow me to stay deep for a longer time than a traditional open system. The closed system also didn't emit air bubbles, which meant it was much quieter, both to the surrounding sea life as well as for me. Too quiet. Voices from the past, no longer drowned out, now flooded my ears and surged through my mind.

Soon the wreck came into view. Despite my best intentions, I had trouble keeping my focus on anything else. The shell of the *Esmeralda* had been taken over with coral and sea life, but in my mind the grand yacht would forever be exactly as she'd been when I was a child. Elegant. Strong.

She'd been my home for months as I'd sailed with my father and grandfather. So many countries, and even more days at sea. It all had become a blur after she'd gone down. But now, as I swam along the topside, I remembered the days with clarity. Playing games with whomever I could guilt into spending time with me, having tea with my stuffed animals. It hadn't been all bad. But I wasn't here to resurrect those memories. I was here to bury the one I'd never forget.

A school of fish crowded the captain's bridge as I approached. Toward the bow I had minimal visibility of Coop and Nik working an underwater torch as they cleared the debris surrounding the vault. The large, inclined windows of the bridge had been busted out, allowing me to pass through them.

"I'm at the bridge. Going in," I stated over the comms, then braced for another litany of curses or a diatribe on how insane I was being. But none came.

"Be safe," Coop said in a tone of voice I knew well. I couldn't help but smile, knowing I had his full support, now that he'd resigned himself to the fact that I wasn't going to be swayed or stopped. "Please."

"I will. I promise." I swam toward the opening leading to the hall. Beyond that would be the stairwell. Thanks to all the games of hide and seek I'd played with the staff, I knew each and every room and corridor.

"I'm here if you need me," Coop added.

Warmth rushed through my veins. "I wouldn't be doing this if I thought for one second you wouldn't have my back."

Navigating passageways as a ten-year-old had been effortless, but swimming them with the rebreather and backup tank was awkward and clunky. The depth of the wreck didn't allow natural light to filter down through the portholes and windows. I swam with a flashlight poised in front of me like I was clearing the rooms with a weapon.

My equipment snagged on hall sconces, buckled walls, furniture remnants. The stairwell curled down dark and tight like a coiled snake. I steeled my nerves as I descended into its dark throat. The narrow space closed around me, constricting.

I reached out, grasping the edge of the banister and pulling myself through, eager to get to the openness of the salon. It had functioned as a living room and had been huge when filled with air and light, but submerged with murky water, I could scarcely move through it.

I edged through the place where I'd watched Jadd kill my father, memories flooding me. A pelt of algae had replaced the carpet, which had dissolved away, blood and all. But the ghosts still hovered, good ones and bad. Circling me like sharks, their shadows floated amidst tatters of furniture and movement of fish.

I scanned my flashlight toward the galley, catching the light on the counter where Chef Jess had started leaving me two fresh chocolate chip cookies every night, knowing I would sneak down to rummage for a snack. Tamping down a sudden wave of grief, I tried not to think of all the crew members I'd come to love who had perished the night of the wreck.

Swimming to the galley, I felt ten years old again, with the *Esmeralda* threatening to go down. Hovering in the water above the counter in the utilitarian kitchen, I was in another world. And as I stared at the deep freeze, I was definitely in another time. The past waited, still fully intact and locked, just as I'd left it. But in my mind the door to all my secrets was wide open.

"*Come, Mira.*" *Jadd motioned me closer.*

His body language reminded me of the men who supposedly had rescued me. How they'd tried too hard to seem safe, even after what they'd done to me. I knew better. I knew he was luring me to a trap. Looking in his cold eyes, I knew he'd already buried me in that freezer with my father.

"*I'm not coming in there,*" *I asserted, as much to myself as to him.* "*I've got your gun.*"

I didn't hold it out for him to take. I held it the way Am'maty Z had taught me, warning him I wasn't a child who had to do as told ever again.

"*Put that down, Mira. You don't know how to use it,*" *he said, still standing behind my father's slumped body.* "*It's not safe for you, child. You could get hurt.*"

I gave him one more chance. "*The captain said we have to go now.*"

"*Then you must stop wasting time, Mira. Come kiss your father and tell him goodbye. You don't want to live with having never told him you're sorry.*"

I didn't expect the deep freeze door to open, but I clasped the handle and tried to lift it anyway. Stuck. It had been sealed all these years, meaning the pressure was too great to open it. It also meant that desiccation and no marine life to slowly consume the bodies would've preserved them, much like mummifying. Just as I'd feared. I braced the crowbar I'd brought into the jamb and pried the door.

The bar budged just enough for me to be able wedge the width of the steel in the crack. Water started to seep in, but it would take a while for the deep freeze to fill and the pressure to equalize enough for me to get the door open.

As I waited, the ocean flowed, shifting and changing against me. But it wasn't coming from the deep freeze sucking in water. The motion had come from something higher up. Something swimming.

I wasn't alone.

Chapter Twenty-Eight

Aziza

Don't panic. I grasped my flashlight and pivoted my body, putting my back toward the deep freeze, where the skeletons of the past had remained untouched. Their ghosts, however, were very much disturbed.

And that's all this was...this feeling of not being alone. I was just spooking myself.

Methodically, I shined my flashlight around the metal cabinets. Debris floated in the water. Pans, a stool, and various utensils which had survived over the years bobbed against the ceiling with the residual motion of whatever had displaced the water.

Or maybe just from my own movements.

No one could possibly be down here besides Coop, Nik, and me. Unless...Kai?

I continued scanning the room, my flashlight putting out a small glow over the surfaces. Scanning toward the main room, I shined my light into the dark opening I'd just come from. Floating in the murky water, I caught a glimpse of something nodding, like a head. Of course, it couldn't be.

I shined my light directly at the strange object, which appeared human. Maybe a tattered life jacket covered in seaweed of some sort?

Transfixed, I waited for the entity to reveal itself. It appeared to rotate. Seaweed or hair? I couldn't tell. Another stirring in the water shifted and turned it again. Cold fear trailed down my spine like a sharpened fingernail, and a deep body tremble followed behind it as an eyeless face stared back at me. I screamed, losing my rebreather mouthpiece and dropping my flashlight.

I scrambled to get the mouthpiece back in before losing too much oxygen from the closed-circuit system. Sinking down, I felt along the floor for my flashlight.

My fingertips brushed various debris as I searched blindly. I kept my eyes toward the galley where it opened to the great room. *Not a body. No way it was a body.* Unlike the protection the deep freeze offered, between the water erosion and the marine life, it wouldn't take but a few days for a submerged body to disintegrate to the bones. They would've sunk to the floor and been gone by now too. Fearing my secrets would one day come up, I'd researched every scenario. No, the face had looked too pristine to even be someone who might've been down at the wreck weeks ago. Which ruled out anyone who'd been scouting the wreck last month before the storm hit.

It had probably been nothing. My own guilt spooking me. A trick of the mind. Some seaweed, a fish, or something which looked like hair and a face. Ears and nose.

Okay. Breathe. Think.

Whatever it was, might not have looked like Coop or Nik. But logic prevailed. It was dark, really dark, and there was a lot of debris in the water. One of them had to have come to check up on me and maybe I'd just panicked and my imagination had gotten the better of me. I pressed my comms. "Coop, Nik—are either of you inside the ship, by chance?"

"Negative, Presh. We're still on the bow, cutting one of those circles Wile E. Coyote-style. You need anything?"

"Kai? You still up top? Alone?"

"Yes, ma'am. What's going on?"

"Probably nothing. I'll be headed out soon."

My fingers brushed against the flashlight and I scrambled with both hands to grab it. Sharp pain sliced through my left hand just as my right clasped the handle.

Shit. The cut immediately caught fire with the sting and singe of saltwater. I blinked the piercing tears away as I toggled the flashlight back on and pointed it down at the burning pain in my palm. Sure enough the skin was slit wide and leaking a river of red. I pressed my hand tight to my side, attempting to hold pressure as I scanned the room with the flashlight.

I didn't imagine strange human body parts this time, just the tail fin of a large shark. And it definitely wasn't my imagination.

I schooled my fear. Then used my comms.

"Coop, Nik—be advised, it appears that nothing was a whole lotta female bull shark. I'm in the galley, port-side, mid-ship, deck two." I flashed my light, scanning toward the main room and catching the gills on the shark's side. "She's making a few laps of the main room. I think I better hang here for a bit, see if she moves on."

"Copy that," Coop said. "Let us know if you need us."

While I appreciated Coop not thinking my alert meant he needed to drop everything and rush to my rescue, I wouldn't have hated on some good ol' fashioned save the day heroics, either.

You've got this. I settled my thoughts and scanned for something to wrap my hand with to control the bleeding. All I could find was the deteriorated chef's knife which had cut me in the first place. It gave me an idea.

I braced my back against a solid portion of the metal cabinetry and shoved my heels into the galley island to keep my buoyancy locked. Then I took out my own diving knife and carefully cut sections off the ankles of my wetsuit. Pausing every few seconds, I scanned the water above me and to my sides. The bull shark was nowhere to be seen, but cutting the makeshift wraps had sent streams of my blood into the water.

As quickly as I could, I coiled the neoprene around my palm. Then I twisted it into a knot tight enough to hold pressure on the wound and hopefully stem anymore blood loss. Flagging my good hand through the water, I tried to disperse the blood trails, or at least get them to flow away from me.

I needed to hurry and get back to the surface. I'd already compromised my oxygen levels thanks to losing my mouthpiece and now this. Focusing, I fished out a satchel charge similar to the explosives Coop and Nik had for clearing debris.

Originally my plan had been for Coop to scuttle the whole ship once the Ozma Emerald was up. But since I was here and could do it, blowing just the deep freeze would have much less impact on the local marine life.

The waterflow shifted around me again. I scanned with my flashlight, catching the shark disappearing along the opposite side of the galley island. Without waiting for her to round the bend seeking me out, I wrenched the crowbar to pry the door to the deep freeze open wider. I wasn't able to budge it far and had to stay braced to hold it beyond the width of the crowbar itself. More water seeped in through the narrow breach as I kept prying. *Fill. Damnit!* I struggled against the crowbar, breathing too hard between exertion and panic. My focus held on the shark as she rounded the corner. *Shit.*

The door jumped open, the sudden give knocked my grip loose and sending me scrambling to grab the dislodged crowbar from the floor. The shark spotted my erratic movements, heard the clang of the metal, and smelled blood in the water. I didn't have time to hit my comms and call anyone to my aid. I barely had time to crab crawl backward into the now-flooded deep freeze. Hooking the door with the crowbar, I pulled it shut.

Catching my breath, I waited. Safe. For now. How long I'd have to wait, I had no idea. I'd started to call in for the calvary, when something brushed against my now-bare ankle.

My heart skittered. I bit down on the mouthpiece to keep the scream I so badly wanted to make at bay. Nothing living could possibly be in the deep freeze all these years. Only ghosts come back to haunt me.

"I'm not sorry! I didn't do anything wrong. This wasn't my fault."

"Wasn't it?" Jadd mocked. "You were playing with my gun and accidently shot your father."

"I didn't kill Baba."

"Don't worry, child. You will be forgiven."

I leveled the pistol at him. "I won't need it."

He laughed. "Who is going to believe you? Your prints are on the gun. You're a child. No one in the world will believe your lies, little girl."

When I still hadn't budged, Jadd moved to grab me. I fired.

Keeping hold of the door, I turned and my flashlight lit up the mummified body of the man I'd murdered, Omar Zaki.

You'd be surprised, I mentally communed with his spirit. *Seems the whole world believed this little girl's lies after all.*

All but one person. Coop knew the truth of who I really was and loved me anyway. Still, I had to make sure the rest of the world kept believing the illusion that I was dead and Zaki was alive. The stability of Beryl Enterprises depended on it.

There was also the very real issue of Zaki's brothers and their extensive lineage, who would try to take away everything I'd built and worked so hard for. People who wouldn't value and protect the technology we'd created nor the data we'd mined. People who would sell it to the highest bidder. The repercussions of which would be disastrous, personally and globally.

Which was why I did my best to ignore the very creepy DNA evidence clawing at me as I secured the explosive charge.

Coop

I'd reached my limit of patience. Not that I had much to begin with. My head was throbbing, I was tired, hungry...and for fuck's sake, what was Zee doing down here? Putting herself at risk for who knows what? A lost teddy bear? More emeralds? Playing petting zoo with yet another jagged-toothed people-eater? For my own sanity and focus, I needed her back on the yacht, safe and sound.

It was taking everything I had to concentrate on the job at hand and not swim down into the wreckage to fish her out.

Nik cut off his torch and signaled that he was ready to set the charges. I pressed my comms button.

"Hey, Presh, gonna need you to wrap up whatever you've got going on. We're about to detach from the bow. It's going to make the rest of this rust bucket very unstable. How ya lookin'?"

"Still having trouble with the locals. I...um...I've been holding out in the deep freeze. Just a sec, I'll take a peek."

After a few seconds Zee came back on, "Yeah, shark's still here. And um...I think she's feeding on...something. I don't think I can get past her without help."

She sounded more spooked than before. "Hang tight, we're on our way."

I signaled Nik and he nodded, then followed as I swam to the bridge and slipped through the busted-out windows. Between our head lamps and flashlights we were able to see our way through the ship. She'd told us her position inside, so I knew we had to go down the midship stairwell to the second deck. I slowed at the base of the stairs to clear the main room, and spotted the glow of Zee's flashlight as she waited in the opening to the galley.

She waggled her flashlight, flagging me to follow it as she silently guided my attention. The glow traveled the room, coming to abrupt stop. *Jesus, fuck...is that a floating arm?* Then she lit the way farther, to the detached midsection of a man. *Captain Tom!*

He'd never left the *Zamarad*. Which meant...*what?* He'd been murdered and disposed of?

I scanned back to Zee. She put her finger up to her mouthpiece and shook her head, then pointed up, indicating Kai could hear all our transmissions. Did she suspect him of being a part of this? *Shit.* Everyone on the ship could be a potential suspect.

Over the comms her voice was steady and calm, belaying the fear I easily read in her wide eyes. "She just circled past the stairwell. Problem is, I've got a cut on my hand. I can't swim and keep pressure on it."

"Copy. I'll run interference. When I get close, start heading this way and go immediately up the stairs. Nik, get ready to block off the passage at the top."

"Copy," Nik replied as he whipped around and disappeared back up the staircase.

I swam to Tom's body and clasped the back of his neck, bringing what was left of him to my chest like a shield. I kept eyes on the shark as she looped to head back toward the galley, and motioned for Zee to make a swim for it.

The shark was good-sized, maybe as much as nine feet, probably five hundred pounds or so. Her movements had been slow, lazy. Despite the dead look in her round eyes, she'd alerted to the scent of Zee's blood and the thrash of her movements. Her massive body curled, her tail flicked to change speed. I had to prevent her from intersecting with Zee's escape.

Using Tom's torso as a blocker, I rammed her blunt, snubbed snout to knock her off Zee's path. The shark's jaws flashed wide. Jagged rows of serrated teeth glinted under my headlamp as they sank into Tom's dead flesh. Pushing off, I power kicked to the stairwell, hot on Zee's fins as she coiled up to the third deck.

Nik was already moving large debris to block the shark should she try to pursue us. I helped him finish the job as Zee popped out of the bridge windows. Once we were in the open water above the bow, we slowed our pace and visually checked one another over to ensure we were in fact intact.

"Shit, that was crazy. Everyone okay?" Nik said over the comms. "Was that a —"

"Bull shark! Yes!" Zee jammed her finger to her lips, her eyes begging him not to verbally mention Tom. "One of the biggest I've seen."

Behind his diving mask, Nik's green eyes went dark as it dawned on him that the pirates we'd been so worried about had already come over the horizon. They'd been aboard our ship the whole time.

Chapter Twenty-Nine

Coop

Kai held his hand for Aziza, helping her from the water. I scowled at the fucker, not wanting him to touch her. Nik jabbed an elbow into my ribs, reminding me to play it cool. Unable to, I edged Nik out of the way and rushed to haul myself onto the dive platform then to my feet right behind Zee. If Kai tried to so much as sniff her hair, I was prepared to throttle him.

Once onboard, we wordlessly began stripping our gear. After the heavy work of securing any loose tanks was done, Kai leaned back against the captain's chair. With his dark skin, white T-shirt, board shorts, and Maui Jim shades hanging from a neck strap, he looked every bit the part of a young bosun on a billionaire's private yacht. And nothing like a pirate out to abscond with Zee's treasure. But no one had expected Judas or Iago, either.

Taking chances on who to trust when it came to Zee wasn't going to happen on my watch. As much as I got along with Kai, I'd put the fucker down if he was involved in anything that aimed to hurt her.

"Guess everyone's pretty shell-shocked, huh?" Kai glanced around, his easy smile faltering at our cold awkwardness. "Big bully, eh?"

"Biggest I've seen yet," Zee said. Her fingers quivered as she dragged the zipper of her wetsuit down.

I couldn't help but notice her breasts curving out from the red bikini top. So did Kai. I faked a smile and suggested, "Next time, you should come down and run interference."

Showing signs of intelligence, he turned his attention from Zee's cleavage to me. "No thanks, brah, my sister's already been nipped once. She doesn't recommend it. Besides, now that the shark world has had a taste of the sweet Kekoa blood, word is out and they all want some."

"Oh really?" Zee said with a laugh that rang genuine. If she thought Kai was guilty of anything, she sure as hell wasn't showing it. "Must be all that pineapple you eat."

"You know, I've heard pineapple makes other things sweet —"

I slapped him on the back, cutting him off before he regaled us about his high-fructose porn-syrup. I tried my best to keep the warning shot from knocking too much oxygen from his lungs.

"Speaking of blood," I said, "let me see your hand, Presh."

Zee held her left hand out to me. She'd cleverly tied it off with a strip of her wetsuit. Given her flinches, I suspected my clumsy attempts to gently untie the knot were failing.

Distracting herself, she looked away from the cut and started to wring the salt water from her dark hair with her free hand. "How is Kilikina doing in the ranks? I haven't been able to keep up. Is she still kicking ass?"

I cocked my lip, admiring Zee's ability to shift gears. Somehow she was managing to appear as if we hadn't just seen the dead body of a friend, while also re-establishing her personal connection with someone who quite possibly was hell-bent on fucking her over. Perhaps she was reminding him of their friendship in case he was on the fence.

"Yeah, she — shit, Zee, here." Kai tossed me a bottle of water before hustling to get the first-aid kit out.

I winced at the sight of her hurt, but she was doing her best not to let it show. I rinsed the gash out, then dabbed it with alcohol before wrapping it tight with gauze.

Looking on, Nik *hmphed*. "You sure weren't that tender with me, Nurse Ratched. Zee, you might take a look at some of my scars before you let him keep working on you."

I huffed out a small laugh as Nik folded the top half of his wetsuit down. He proceeded to turn his back to us, showing off his muscles along with my not-so symmetrical handiwork. "Tell you what, Steele, I'll let you do the honors of stitching her up if the bleeding doesn't stop."

"I'm sure it'll be fine," she muttered. "It's not that deep."

"Next time, promise me, you'll let me know you need help, Presh." I didn't care if this was a job. I leaned over and kissed her, then whispered, "You're not alone in any of this anymore."

She flicked her eyes up, and I'd swear I saw a tear of gratitude form in them. But just as quickly it was gone and she'd turned them back on Kai. "Where is your sister this week?"

"Killa's in Rottnest." His voice sounded a bit jealous while his wide, white-toothed smile beamed pride.

"Australia! How wonderful! It was her dream to surf there, I remember. Please tell her how excited we are about her comeback and making the tour."

"Oh, she's not just on it, she's in striking distance of the lead. '*Kilikina Kekoa, World Champion Surfer*' has a nice ring to it."

"Yes, it does! You and your family have to go watch her in the finals at Trestles! I'll have Travel arrange it all. If you all need anything, Zaki will make it happen."

I met Zee's soft brown eyes. She wasn't lying, nor was she subtly reminding Kai not to screw over a friend, a *really good* friend. She truly didn't know if Kai was involved in whatever was happening here. Until she knew for sure, he was still her family and she genuinely cared about him. Not just him, every employee and anyone they cared about fell under her protective bubble. She'd always been that way, taking care of us behind the guise of doing Zaki's bidding.

Zaki. What a fucker.

My jaw tensed. Zee had trembled when she'd told me how he'd treated her the night the *Esmeralda* went down. Why she gave him credit for anything now was a mystery to me.

"My sister would've never gotten back on her surfboard, much less the tour, if it hadn't been for OZ's help. We're eternally grateful."

"It's his sincere pleasure. She is such an inspiration." Aziza turned to me and placed her hand on my shoulder. "You know, I think I've lost more blood than I thought. Maybe you should drive the Zodiac back with me?"

Her eyes held mine, and I knew she wasn't really feeling faint. She wanted us to be alone so we could do what we did second best, strategize.

"I can take her back and drag the Zodiac," Kai interjected, jumping up and adjusting the tie off rope for towing. "Save gas."

I practically growled. *So much for getting to talk privately.* "Maybe we should all head back for now, go down again this afternoon."

Zee nodded.

"Already?" Kai asked as he turned the engine over. "Not bringing anything up?"

Was he disappointed? Eager? Trying to get information? I couldn't get a read on him.

"Not this round. Making good progress, though," Zee assured, intentionally vague while sounding positive.

She realized, like I did, that whoever was involved with Tom's death intended for us to do the hard work of bringing the emerald up. Once we had, our services would no longer be beneficial. And neither would we.

Aziza

In the wrong hands, my secrets were worth more than the Ozma Emerald. But I wasn't about to let anyone take either from me.

Especially whoever had murdered Tom.

He'd had family. Just thinking of him made me want to break down and cry. Demand justice. Repent my sins. Hell, I would've traded places with him if it had been possible.

If I could've gone back in time and somehow prevented all of this... But I couldn't. The only way to erase the hold the past had was to blow it up. And I'd only managed to set the charge. I'd have to remote detonate it after the vault had been safely raised.

Trouble was, bringing up the emerald put us in a vulnerable spot. Some, if not all, of the crew must've been involved in Tom's murder. Which meant also gone was the option of safely transporting the emerald to Marakata via the *Zamarad*.

My mind had started activating a Plan B the second I'd realized the body had belonged to Captain Tom. One thing was for certain—we needed to get the emerald up and back on Marakata as soon as possible. Today.

First, we needed to confirm Thea, Leo, and Titan were safe. We found them topside, engrossed in some sort of exercise or training session. In a boxer's stance, Leo shifted his weight, bopping side to side on the balls of his feet. He threw mock punches at Thea while Titan barked out referee calls.

"Put 'em up! Put 'em up," he taunted as Thea successfully blocked a series of punches. Spotting us, Leo broke his stance just as Thea landed a kick into his tattooed side. I barely had time to appreciate the gorgeous ink of a crowned lion, which looked like the kind of old-school drawing you'd see on a flag or crest, before she followed up with a sideswipe that landed him on his ass.

Leo's hands went to his face. "Is my nose broken?"

"Of course not. Such drama. I didn't even touch your face."

Coop shook his head at his brother, who was still on his back. Then he asked Thea, "Where'd you learn that?"

"Muscle memory, I guess." Thea shrugged a shoulder. Then, proudly smiling, she jogged over to Nik for a kiss. "Did you see? I knocked him flat!"

Coop reached out and helped Leo to his feet. "Some king of the beasts you are."

I realized then those were the words tattooed along with the heavily pawed lion rearing up on his haunches from Leo's hip to just below his armpit.

"Yeah, well, that's why I don't fight in the women's league," Leo retorted graciously.

"You okay?" Coop asked. The gentleness in his tone seemed to imply he was asking less about physical injuries and more about the tension between them from last night.

"Yeah. How'd the dive go?"

"Not too bad," Coop said, which made my eyebrows rise, because um...sharks, dead men? "Zee got cut, so we better go take a look at it. Steele, want to help?"

Nik gave Thea another kiss and a swatted her butt as she proudly resumed bouncing on the balls of her feet, eager to take Leo on again. Then we headed to the main deck dining table under the pretense of checking my wound. I kept an eye out for any crew members hovering or lingering close by. Only Cait had come around with basil-infused ice water and a charcuterie board of light hors d'oeuvres.

"I've been running scenarios in my head," I commented to Coop, though he'd been through enough last-second plan changes with me to know I'd already begun repositioning us. "Vivi's got the helicopter on call. Wolfe and Colt have teams readying to come via boat as well."

Nik's eyes widened as he asked, "We just got off the tender. How did you arrange all that?"

I flashed my wrist. The sleek personal computer prototype from Beryl called the Facet went way beyond smartwatch technology. And apparently passed the waterproof and pressure tests to consider it for diving.

"I never saw you use it!"

"Sleight-of-hand wizardry, right, Presh?" Coop mocked before growing serious. Beryl Enterprises had never had this big of an internal breech in security before.

Except when he went rogue on Alvarez.

Could I really trust he wasn't somehow a part of this too?

I had to.

Nik settled into his chair. "Look, whatever goes down, I want Thea and Titan off this yacht as soon as possible. I assume you want Leo off too?"

Cooped nodded.

"Totally agree," I said. "And actually, I was thinking they would be part of our excuse for the helicopter, which should be leaving Marakata right now."

"Shit, you plan for this or something?" Nik asked.

"I planned to bring up an asset worth half a billion dollars. I prepared for everything."

Everything except my own team betraying me.

My eyes flicked to Coop's, but I couldn't read them. Turning back to Nik, I said, "Feigning some excuse that they need to return to Marakata, the helo can come pick up Leo, Thea, and Titan. At the same time, we'll bring the emerald up and attach it to the helo for extraction. Then we'll secure the ship."

"We?" Coop asked, eyeing me like I was insane. "No, that's not going to work."

"You're right, we should really have someone with ops experience in the helo in case they've already planned for that contingency. Nik, you should go with Thea and the others."

"Whoa whoa whoa. *You* should go with the helo, Zee."

"But I don't have ops experience."

"Exactly. Which is why you shouldn't be on the ops part."

Did Coop want me offsite so I couldn't stop him or because he didn't want me hurt? I still had so many questions for him about Alvarez, but my gut was telling me I could trust him. Of course, my gut had told me the same about Cait and Kai and...*Magnussen*.

I barely knew Lars Magnussen. He'd only been with Beryl a few months, not even a year. And he'd replaced Captain Tom. *By killing him?* Who would be next? No, I wasn't going to leave *anything* of value where I couldn't protect it. Not ever again.

"I'm not evacuating in the helicopter, Coop. This is my job."

Coop huffed. "One you weren't even going to show up on until I *'strong-armed'* you. We still don't know who *they* are or even how many of them there are. It'd be stupid for you to be in the line of fire. Who would take Zaki's calls and respond to his emails?"

I narrowed my eyes at the subtle dig. "I'm more than an administrative assistant."

"Exactly. You run this organization and are the most integral cog in the machine. He's just the figurehead."

"*Careful...*" I warned.

Coop quirked his lip. "Why? Is he listening? Because there are a few things he should hear."

I sighed. I'd known telling Coop about the way Zaki had treated me as a child would make things problematic, but now was not the time. "Let's just focus on the job, *please*. I'm going back down. I have unfinished business. End of discussion."

Coop's only response was a resigned grimace and subtle shake of his head.

"Nik should be in the helo," I continued. "To ensure it's secure, not just because of the emerald but because Thea, Leo, and Titan will be on board. Colt and Wolfe have teams en route now to secure and clear the ship. They'll be here in a few hours. We have another team waiting on Marakata to protect the Ozma Emerald."

"Sounds like a solid plan," he agreed, though Coop shot daggers at him for it. Then Nik hustled to stand, grabbing a couple panini bites and a macaron. "*Okay...* Well, I guess I'd better let Thea and Leo know to get ready."

"What is this unfinished business anyway?" Coop groused as he turned back to me. Then he tacked on for good measure, "Truth."

"I'll tell you, *after*," I said with a tight smile. "Unless?"

I arched a brow to suggest we could have a *quid pro quo* regarding South America.

He growled as he got up to leave. "After it is."

Chapter Thirty

Coop

Having survived the first dive with minimal repercussions, my hopes were bolstered that I'd make it through the second one. Realistically, though, I knew my chances had gotten increasingly worse. But sitting alongside me I had every reason I needed to fight to stay alive.

Not liking the guy didn't make Jim guilty of anything, but I was actually glad it ended up being him taking Zee and I back to the dive site. Breaking his scrawny neck would be quicker and more pleasurable than snapping Kai's. Not that I was looking forward to the task, but it'd be easier.

I couldn't help but glare at the back of the Midwesterner's close-cropped head. Zee elbowed me in the ribs and made wide, beautiful eyes at me as those perfect lips mouthed a growly, *Stop!*

Oh, I'd stopped. But just looking at her started something altogether different stirring inside me. Clearly seeing the change in my mood and my focus, her eyes twinkled and her lips curled in a shy smile as she mouthed a flirty, *Stop!*

She grabbed up a coil of webbing and carabiners and shoved them into my flexed abs, but her fingertips lingered, her eyes perused. She wetted her lips. I wetted mine. God, if we'd been alone on this boat right now, the things I would've done to that sweet body. Stepping into her touch, I rumbled, "*You* stop."

"Stop?" Jim asked, turning his head and sending Zee jumping back about a foot. "But the marker buoy is still up a ways."

"My bad, dude," I said with a chuckle as I zipped up my wetsuit. Then to Zee, "You owe me another secret."

Once we were back to the red bobber, Zee's game face was back on. She'd quickly secured her injured hand in a full neoprene glove, which would help protect it as well as keep the pressure of my wrap job on it. Jim helped me drop supplies down via the marker line.

After noting the helo was making its landing approach on the stern helipad of the *Zamarad*, Zee and I rolled into the water and began our own descent.

I concentrated on my breathing, trying to stay calm and alert despite the intense pressure building at my temples. Once at the vault I was able to ignore and override as I concentrated on strapping up the safe. Zee and I fell into a smooth, ops-mode rhythm of working in silence, communicating easily with our eye contact and hand gestures. We'd always had a good flow hashing out logistics and planning together, but having our partnership play out physically came just as natural. I might as well have been working with Nik, or any other of my Team buddies.

Soon we had the vault cradled in a makeshift web sling and were ready to start prepping the lifting balloons. Raising the vault in a balanced, uniform way by each filling our lifts at the same slow rate was critical. At well over a thousand pounds, if the straps didn't hold, the vault could easily plummet to the ocean floor, destroying it and the Ozma Emerald.

About halfway to the surface, we got the call over our comms from the helo notifying us that everyone had been picked up and that they were safely in the air. Zee came over the comms next. "Coop? I need to...um...make an adjustment. Be ready for it."

I glanced up and noted the remote detonator in her hand. I shook my head in disbelief. "*Unfinished business,*" indeed.

I'd noticed significantly fewer explosive charges than had come with the crates. There had been enough missing to take down a full ship. God, I hoped she hadn't gone overboard on the ordinance. But nothing I could do now. She held her hand up and used her fingers to count down. *Three, two, one...*

Aziza

I closed my eyes and said goodbye to the past as I pressed the button. I didn't expect the blast to knock through me so hard or for the vault to start thrashing. I opened my eyes just as the corner of the vault shifted hard and slammed right into Coop's head.

I watched in helpless fear as his eyelids dropped and the strength seeped from his bones. Limply, his body sank, drifting away from the vault.

Shit shit shit… No!

I scrambled to swim, not caring about the fate of the vault, or the emerald, or even the empire. All I cared about was Coop. I propelled myself against the current, my legs kicking out as hard as I could. The water slowed me, like I was in a dream where I was trying to run but couldn't.

As I grabbed at his arm he shook me off, spooked. Luckily the water leeched the strength and velocity of his elbows or I'd have found myself knocked out too.

"It's Zee, Coop," I pleaded over the comms. "It's just me."

Faded and far-off, I heard Nik checking in on us over the comms. But it scarcely registered as something I needed to respond to. My narrow field of attention centered on one thing — keep Coop alive.

It was only once I'd managed to spin him around and he could see me fully that he stopped fighting my help. His eyes widened dramatically then returned to normal. "What the hell happened?"

"The corner of the vault hit you. Knocked you out cold."

"Everything okay down there?" Nik asked over the comms.

Coop panted through another coughing fit, then hoarsely responded, "Just trying to figure out why Tweety Birds are circling my head underwater. Zee was on it."

"Copy that," Nik confirmed.

How could they both be so calm? The air in my closed-circuit system felt more like I was heaving a strip of sandpaper up and down the back of my throat. And my heart pounded way too hard. The blood in my temples surged through my veins with a heavy pulse and my ears were ringing as if I had been the one whose head had been hit.

Coop looked toward the vault, which dangled lopsided above us as it drifted away with the current. The lifting balloons were basically upside-down buckets that had continued to suspend and slowly lift the oversized load, but Coop's bucket had lost air when he'd dropped.

I followed his gaze as he looked to where the wreck had been. Below us the water was cloudy from the explosion and the Esmeralda was gone. What hadn't been decimated had dislodged from the coral ledge to plummet another hundred meters down.

My heart collapsed like it'd been kicked in. My chest went from heaving to deflated as tears pearled in the corners of my eyes. Had the sudden rush of emotions come from nearly seeing Coop die or knowing the *Esmeralda* was finally gone? Anything left of Omar Zaki would erode away, but so would all that remained of my father.

Coop gently curled his fingers over my hand, his fingers entwining with mine. I turned my attention back to him.

"Ignore and override," he told me. "Let's finish this."

Keeping our fingers intwined, we strong kicked our way back to the cockeyed vault as it crept its way unmanned to the surface. With a squeeze to my hand, he let go and resumed his post on one side of the vault while I took the other. He added additional air to his side until the vault balanced, then we began to add air simultaneously to the balloons until both sides ascended in unison.

The helicopter hovered above us as we broke the surface. The rotating blades were too high above to do more than stir up a heavy mist, but the thin, wet shears added to the challenge. Coop used hand gestures to request the line be dropped. I glanced over to Jim at the tender to gauge his reaction, as this would be the first sign of our original plans going astray. It was hard to tell from the distance, but my stomach churned seeing he was on the radio to someone who must've being using a different comms channel than we were.

I returned my attention to balancing the vault as Coop worked quickly to clasp all the straps to the wench hook. I had to be mindful of my finger placement, or they would get crushed as the webbing slackened and snapped tight from the motion of the surface waves. Coop motioned me back, then flashed a hand signal up to Nik. The helo lifted. Squealing, the web belts stretched taunt. I feared they'd snap as the vault slowly breached through the surface, but like something out of a dream, up into the sky it went.

I wanted to breathe a sigh of relief. After twenty-two years the world's largest emerald, and the biggest threat to uncovering my secrets, had become airborne and headed home. But just as the treasure hung in limbo, so did so much more.

Jim gunned the tender, aiming it our direction.

As he flagged Jim in closer, Coop removed his mouthpiece to talk privately with me. "We're just going to play it cool. We don't know who's involved in this. Just trust me, okay."

I nodded.

After cutting the engine, Jim came to the swim deck to help me aboard. I handed him my fins first, then took his help as he hoisted me out of the water. I'd started stripping off my gear when I heard the shot. Before I could even comprehend what had happened, Jim jumped back to the controls and fired the engines to life.

I screamed, trying to rush to Coop's aid, but Jim grabbed my arm with bruising force.

"You're safe now," Jim assured.

I stared at him in horror. "Safe from who? We have to go back! Coop needs help! He's going to drown!" I struggled to free myself, but my body was exhausted from the dives and Jim's fingers were like claws digging into my flesh.

"Ma'am, you need to calm down and listen to me. Chief Hayes just notified me that Coop and his team have targeted you and the emerald. You were in danger. We all were."

"No!" I repeatedly wailed as I kept my eye on Coop's lifeless body drifting on the ocean surface until it was a blur. This was all wrong. There was no way it was true. All my doubts about Coop had vanished, I didn't even care what had happened with Alvarez. Alvarez deserved it and we'd figure out how to handle the repercussions together. *Wait.* How did Jim know about the emerald?

I wheeled back to him, wrenching my arm from his grip. "Hayes? Scott Hayes told you Coop was trying to take what?"

"The Ozma Emerald."

How did Hayes even know about the emerald? I'd purposefully been vague with the details of what was to be brought up.

"The helicopter extraction was all part of Coop's plan to transport the emerald away from Marakata. You're safe now."

Safe? Oh, I was so far from safe. And from the dopey explanations Jim was throwing my way, so was he. Hayes had played him for a pawn.

"We're to go back to the *Zamarad* and wait. You're going to be fine. I'm going to take good care of you."

My fingers trembled and tapped. I gazed back, but it was too far to jump in and swim to Coop. I forced myself not to think the worst.

Over the comms I heard Hayes calling the shots with Colt and Wolfe. Taking a deep breath, I grabbed up a sat phone and called him privately. "Scott, it's me, I'm on the tender with Jim, heading back to the *Zamarad*."

"Zee, thank God. I've been so worried Jim would be too late. I know you trusted Coop, I know you were aware of his involvement in the Alvarez sitch down in South America, but he orchestrated all of this just to get the Ozma Emerald."

My gut felt kicked in. Hayes' betrayal coursed through my veins like a dark, staining ink. But I steeled myself. I'd break down, fall apart, mourn my loss of *everything* later. "Give me the SITREP."

"We've got it under control. I have all hands on deck for this. Just sit tight and we'll get you home safe."

"Thank you, Scott, I don't know how I'll make this up to you. I don't know how I could've been so foolish..." The words burned like poison in my mouth. I just couldn't believe Hayes had been behind this. I'd seen the signs...I just hadn't wanted to believe that someone I'd trusted for so long could do this.

"Don't beat yourself up, Zee. Michael Cooper was one of the best. He used you. Played on your emotions. But neither he, nor his team, will get away with this. I assure you, I have everything under control."

Nothing was in control. Not my breathing, not my heartbeat, and not my mind. But I dared one last question, needing to know just how far Hayes was willing to go. "And Zaki? They haven't gotten to him, have they?"

"No. OZ is fine. In fact, I just touched based with him."

"And what did he say?"

"He's given me full authority to pursue this with whatever means necessary."

Of course he has. My breath stuttered out as I fought to stay standing. "Whatever means necessary..." *Like killing Coop.* Killing whoever threatened the empire. The realization iced over my heart so fast, it felt like every vein in my chest had expanded and cracked. "Then that is exactly what we have to do."

Chapter Thirty-One

Aziza

As the swim deck of the *Zamarad* came into view, so did three armed men awaiting our arrival. A shockwave of recognition rocked through me. I'd seen these men before, their likenesses sketched out on paper. They were the crew members who'd abandoned the reality show kids. I turned to Jim. "Pirates! Go!"

"It's fine," he grunted, waving me off. "Hayes said he'd be sending reinforcements."

I grabbed for the wheel, but Jim fought me for it. Too late anyway. We were well-within firing range, and for whatever reason they weren't shooting at us. Didn't make them safe, though. I hissed, "These aren't our guys, Jim. We need to get the hell out of here."

"Hayes said the first guys to get here would be local."

"Do you even see a boat? How the hell did they get here?"

"If they were bad guys, they'd be shooting at us. You need to stay calm and just know we're taking good care of you."

Yeah, fuck that.

The men greeting us must've been aware I was valuable to Zaki. With the Ozma Emerald gone I was their only leverage, or they would've killed us already. We were too close to escape. At this distance, with their ARs, they'd have decent shooting accuracy, if not to kill, then for sure to injure into submission.

If I had any chance at all of surviving, I needed better odds. One of them would have to take his hand off his weapon to tie us off. If I could get another one to drop his, that would give me a fifty-fifty shot.

I scrambled to the edge of the tender, smiling like I was thankful to see them and eager to jump aboard. As I balanced on the step, I kept jutting my hand out like I needed help. I used my weight to rock the tender a little harder than the waves, feigning having trouble with my balance.

"*Ayudame*," I pleaded. Again I held out my hand. "Help."

Finally, the asshole across from me let his grip on his AR slide as he swung the weapon to his back. Just as Jim tossed the tie-off rope to the pirate nearest the bow, I stepped across the gap. Before the man's fingers could grasp mine, I retracted my hand and took a deep breath. Crossing my arms over my chest, I dropped into the water. Ducking under the dock-like platform, I shot as fast as I could below the yacht. Grappling for one of the propellers to hang onto, I watched a flurry of gunshots pierce the sea. Seconds later, Jim's body tumbled down with a splash before floating back to the surface.

Lungs burning, I half-swam, half-edged my way under the *Zamarad's* hull to the port side at midship, hoping the gunmen wouldn't be able to get a decent angle. Maybe if I was really lucky I could get the Zodiac. Kicking through the pain, I surfaced, desperate to catch my breath. But before I could get a lungful, I heard one of the men saying, "Don't be stupid, lady. We don't want to kill you. But we will hurt you if you don't come out."

When I didn't take his bait, a sharp report of machine gun fire rang out. Several bullets punctured the Zodiac before I darted back under. *Shit.* I headed toward the bow to steal a second gasp, but this wasn't a game I could win against three gunmen. We were in the middle of the ocean. Even if I could swim to the island, I would be a sitting duck there too. I had nowhere to go.

With a pang in my heart, I realized no one would be coming to my rescue. Certainly not Michael Cooper. If I thought about the loss of him too long, I'd just stop kicking. It would be so easy. My muscles were fatigued to the point I couldn't feel pain anymore. My buoyant body would be trapped under water, under the boat, and I'd be gone. Free of the need of my lungs, of air. I would just stop. So easy. But I still had work to do.

I clamored for the anchor chain, grasping it to give my legs a break. This spot provided a much better shield for me, but all it would take would be one of them jumping in. Between struggling against the belligerent waves, breathlessly swimming, and my emotions on full tilt, I was way too fatigued to combat a fresh enemy.

Where had these fuckers come from anyway?

They'd have had to have been on board this whole time. *How?* I tried to access my brain. Between my exhaustion and the adrenaline of survival all I could process was a heavy pounding throb, suggesting my pulse was stronger and steadier than it felt.

I needed to know what I was up against, but I was skimming just barely at the surface physically and mentally.

Focus. Focus.

Hayes had arranged for Magnussen to come aboard, which meant he had to have known about Captain Tom. *The locked captain's quarters.* The men had been holed up in there the whole time. For what, a couple of days maybe? Just waiting for the opportunity to take the ship, the emerald, and our lives.

There'd been three men on the swim deck when Jim had pulled alongside of them. That room couldn't have held more without anyone knowing.

Was Magnussen in on it? Jim? Whatever his involvement, Jim was dead now. My heart sank as I realized the gunmen had to have disabled and probably killed anyone on the crew who wasn't involved. Cait...Kai...Chef Anders?

Above me, on the bow, I could hear two men arguing in a foreign language. Spanish or Portuguese. Then in English, one said, "We don't have time for this horseshit. The charges have been set. We have less than an hour."

Charges? Like explosives?

I briefly thought about surrendering myself, getting away from this yacht before it blew, buying time to come up with a Hail Mary play. But fuck 'em.

This was war.

I pulled my dive knife from my thigh strap and swam aft. If at least two of them were arguing on the bow, that left one to keep watch on the tender. Pausing midship, I ducked out to grab a quick but deep breath. Then I swam. With an eye out above me for where the hull of the *Zamarad* ended and the tender began, I caught sight of Jim's body floating. Two red punctures seeped blood from his chest.

His handsome, lifeless face stared back at me. He didn't look apologetic—he looked surprised. I wasn't. The kind of trash we were dealing with sacrificed people. Tossed them away when they'd finished using them.

It was why I couldn't surrender.

I surfaced again on the opposite side of the tender. The current pulled at me toward the open water between the ship and the island. The slick sides of the speedboat's hull gave me nothing to hold on to, which meant more treading water, more kicking, more everything. But I was so amped to exact my revenge, I suddenly had energy to spare.

Was this what Coop felt on his missions? Like he was hearing in color and seeing smells? Like he was a fucking super God?

I could hear Coop's husky voice in my ear. *"Doubts are just things in your head, Presh. Wrecks in your mind. They're not real, they're not like you and me."*

I glimpsed the lone sentinel. He was young, and not a seafarer. He looked pale and uncomfortable with the rocking, which was strong at the swim deck. He also kept pacing over the ropes, which had been tied off improperly.

I maneuvered quietly into position, and as the man bent over to dry heave through his seasickness, I reached up and cut the taut line holding the tender to the yacht. The bow swung wide with the current. A *zing* rang out as the loose rope the man had been standing in cinched tight. His legs were swept out from under him and he fell. I surged to cut his throat while he was too stunned to fight or even know he'd drawn his last breath.

Panting, I scrambled up the swim ladder and went straight to the lockers, where I outfitted myself with weapons. I didn't have time to cherry-pick, so I just grabbed what was handy. Padding barefoot, I made my way up the back steps.

My path to the bow was not a straightforward one. In fact, from sitting in on several after-action meetings, I knew I'd be strongest coming from above. Moving in spurts, I found an internal access ladder and scaled it all the way up past the bridge and the sun and sky decks to the comms platform housing the satellite domes and nav equipment. Belly crawling, I swung the speargun I'd grabbed and aimed it for one of the pirates. Above me the Garmin Fantom radars swung as if all was normal.

After drawing the bands into place, I aimed at the larger of the two men as he leaned over the railing trying to locate me in the water. "I'm not down there, asshole, but I'll give you a hint where you can find me," I whispered as I pulled the trigger.

He turned just as the spear sailed through the air and pierced his shoulder. The momentum flipped him over the railing, heels over his head, and down with a splash.

A flurry of gunshots rang out and I rolled behind one of the domes. *Come and get me, motherfucker.*

I was sitting at a dead end, and there was only one way for him to come. He must not have thought much of me, because he charged right up the stairs and the ladder. I waited until he got to the top before popping out from behind the dome and opened up the fire extinguisher on him. He fell to the deck below with a loud thud, but I turned the Ruger on him and put a couple of rounds in him, just to be sure.

So far so good. Now, to see if there were any crew left on board I could trust. I found Magnussen next. He was tied to the bolted-in table post, bleeding from his forehead. I ripped the rag stuffed in his mouth out and cut the plastic zip ties from his wrists. "You okay?"

His voice was hoarse. "I might need stitches, but I'll survive. There's three of them, I think."

"*Were* three. Head down to the tender. I'll go see if anyone else is okay."

Chef Anders had a broken leg, but was otherwise okay. He and Cait were bound together. She helped Anders to get to the tender while I searched for Kai. His family had already endured so much with Kilikina losing her arm from the shark bite and her subsequent depression. I scrambled through the ship, finding him in the engine room, unconscious, bruised, but breathing.

I ran back to get help. Magnussen and I were able to carry Kai to the tender. "We'll get back to Marakata and get him a doctor."

"No, Princess," a masculine voice, hoarse with exhaustion, called out. "You're not going anywhere. You're my payday now."

Chapter Thirty-Two

Aziza

Princess. The word punched my heart, while the voice split the back of my skull like a sharp knife. I turned to face the man I'd thought was dead. He stood there, having hauled himself up from the water in the tender garage, drenched and angry. Which made sense given I'd ruined his chances with the Ozma Emerald, shot him with a speargun, dropped him four flights into the ocean, and killed his two buddies.

Behind my back, I tossed the last rope securing the tender. "Go, you have to hurry. Save Kai. I'll be okay."

"Listen to her if you want to live. She's going to be just fine here with me."

I didn't hear the tender fire up, but I wasn't about to turn my eyes off of the asshole with the gun. He hadn't moved, either, if the blood pooling at his feet from the spear wound was any indication. He might be alive, but he was wounded. On his dominant shoulder no less. His shots would be shit.

"He needs me alive," I assured the crew. Though at this point I doubted I was much value to anyone anymore. "Hurry! Kai doesn't have much time if there's internal bleeding."

"We'll send help, Zee," Lars promised before turning the engine over and speeding off.

"Now, Princess, why don't you ease on over here and get comfortable."

I fixed my eyes on the Ruger semiauto trained on my forehead, not my heart. If he raised at all with the kick, the 9mm bullet would sail over my head. And considering I'd harpooned his right shoulder, chances were solid he'd flinch. He should've been aiming for my chest. Bigger target, bigger chances. Still, I held my hands up in surrender as I plotted my escape. From the corner of my eye, a ways out still, I spotted something swimming toward us in the water. *My Sharky...*

Without a single doubt, I stepped backward off the deck, shouting, "You want me, come and get me!"

A couple of shots rang out and I ducked under the waves and swam, this time away from the yacht and toward the open water. When I resurfaced, the man was stripping off his boots and anything else that would weigh him down. Then he dove toward me.

That's right, come and get what you deserve.

I swam a frolicking circle, feeling like a mermaid. I enticed him like a siren out away from the boat, staying just close enough to him to give him false hope of catching me. I ducked and surfaced a few times, laughing as he struggled to find me. The adrenaline coating my exhaustion made me loopy, but this wasn't a game to me. This was survival.

He bobbed, treading water. So tired already. So pissed. "Get your ass over here!" he screamed.

But I was exactly where I'd always been, swimming with the sharks. *My* shark. I reached out to stroke my gloved palm across his back as he passed beside me, just below the surface.

Blood was in the water. The current around me thrashed with the excitement of the kill. And I laughed as the man's eyes went white and wide with the realization that we weren't alone in the big, blue sea.

In truth, I'd never been alone. Dead or alive, Coop had always been with me. And now was no exception.

The man scrambled to swim, but his body jerked back. He screamed as the sea swallowed him whole. Then his head bounded back up. I didn't stay to watch and didn't listen for his pleas. I only swam hard and fast for the yacht.

Once on the swim platform, I scrambled to grab the Ruger he'd left behind. Then I darted, slipping up the stairs, up and up and up, until my legs finally gave out. I crumpled into a corner on the sun deck. As I waited for death to come, I summoned Coop's spirit to stay with me. Imagining him as I used to do.

"Hey, Presh."

I let my head drop against his shoulder and closed my eyes.

"Just you and me now."

Coop

As I came to, I stared at a clear blue sky. My lips were salty. My whole body ached, dry and wet all at once. I bobbed, floating on the waves. For minute peace surrounded me. We'd made the dives, the emerald was up, and I'd survived.

Then I remembered fucking Jim had tried to kill me with a goddamned flare gun and left me for dead. He must've taken off with Zee. I heaved my body over and coughed up salt and water. With long strokes and wide kicks, I propelled my body forward. My purpose hardened me. Churning my arms, I paddled through what remained of the speedboat's wake with only one goal in mind. Aziza.

I couldn't use the comms to let her know I was alive, or to tell Nik to watch his back. I wasn't sure who might be listening and I'd need the element of surprise. I also needed every precious second to get to the *Zamarad* before it started moving. Then I remembered the missing explosives.

Grunting, I hauled ass, fighting my way through the chop without a single thought to sharks, bullet wounds, brain tumors, or anything else that dared to stop me. Getting to Zee before the yacht exploded was the only thing.

The aural migraines nearly blocked out the vision in my left eye, but slowly the yacht grew bigger. As I got near, I shrugged out of the rebreather, fins, mask, everything that would only get in my way of boarding the *Zamarad* and getting to Zee before it was too late.

The tender was gone. Blood smeared over the white swim deck and in the water a body slapped against the ship with the waves. Jim. Another man was tied off by his leg with one of the boat's ropes. He wasn't anyone I recognized, not crew or staff. Where the hell had he come from and who had slashed his throat?

After hauling myself aboard I grabbed up a pair of binos and tried to determine who had been in the tender, but it was already too far away for me to find out if Zee was aboard it. Nor did I know who else might be on the yacht. I only knew that I wasn't leaving until I was certain Zee wasn't here.

I quickly rummaged in the storage lockers, looking for what I could use as well as what had been taken. Just as the pit in my stomach predicted, several of the firearms and explosive charges were gone. If there were any survivors on the yacht they wouldn't be alive for long.

I grabbed up an M4 and a couple 9mms, then cased the area for a getaway vehicle. The Zodiac had taken a round of fire and wouldn't be seaworthy for long. The Sea-Doo wouldn't get us far, but it was better than swimming. I launched it from the toy garage. With any luck it would get far enough from the yacht to survive whatever might happen.

Entering the engine room, I found the charges, set and counting down. I had less than ten minutes. I took the stairs two at a time and began clearing the ship, looking for Zee.

Evidence of struggles and bloodshed remained in several rooms, but no bodies. *Fuck.* I kept moving, not knowing if Zee had been taken hostage for collateral or killed. I just knew that if she was still on this yacht, I was going to find her before it was blown to bits.

Flinging doors open, I called out for her. Then moved with speed up to the next deck and the next. The bridge had sustained the worst damage. Blood was smeared over the consoles and broken glass glinted from the floor, but I didn't stop to investigate. Catching my focus was the sound of the door to the captain's quarters banging open as the *Zamarad* rocked from a larger set of waves. I smelled the scene of too many men sleeping in too tight of a space before I pushed the door wide. Littering the floor was three days' worth of empty MRE wrappers and a dozen or so plastic water bottles recycled into piss containers. The waste suggested multiple men had quietly sequestered themselves right under our noses the whole time.

Whoever they were, they'd come aboard most likely via fast-rope from a helo during the night, a day or two before we'd arrived. Whether Captain Tom had stumbled upon them at the wrong place and time, or his sacrifice had been part of their plan, they'd hunkered down in his room waiting for the emerald to come aboard. At least we'd thwarted their plans to kill us and take the ship with the emerald. But still, I was pissed I'd failed to clear his room.

Why had I trusted the story about Captain Tom's daughter so much that I hadn't bothered to even look in his quarters?

Because Scott Hayes had arranged the transfer.

Which meant Hayes had to have known something, been involved. I thought back to the Monaco job, trying to figure out what I'd missed. We'd talked about the South American clinic, he knew I'd taken vacation—had he put two and two together? Known I was going to be out of pocket and planned to pull this shit while he thought I was down periscope?

Even though his original plan had been blown, Hayes would have backups for his backup. Thank God Nik had gone with the helo as Zee had suggested. Hopefully he wouldn't trust Hayes. I prayed Zee was safe and that she'd gotten away from Hayes' goon squad. If she hadn't, she'd be dead as soon as they no longer needed her.

"Where are you, Presh!" I growled. Mere seconds were left before the whole ship was going to explode.

I pushed myself up the last flight of steps to the sun deck. Swinging around the corner, I slipped on fire extinguisher foam and tripped over another dead body. As I scrambled forward, I saw yet another body huddled in the corner. "Zee!"

I nearly fell back to my knees in relief, but we didn't have time for that. And besides, Zee didn't look all right. Her eyes regarded me, but her gun remained in her hand.

"You're not really here," she seemed to say more to herself as she stared blindly at me. Exhaustion cloaked her folded body. Wet hair stuck to her face and shoulders. Her skin was streaked with blood and her eyes were wide and spooked. "You're just a ghost."

"We're both alive, Zee," I assured her as I slowly lowered my weapons to the deck.

She kept her Ruger trained on me. "Are we?"

"Yes, Presh, but we won't be for long."

"No. Not for long," she agreed. Her voice, faded and resigned, shattered me.

"We've got to go."

"You don't understand. *We* can't go. I promised Zaki I'd personally put down anyone who betrayed us."

"I've never betrayed you, Zee, not intentionally. I'll explain about the Amazon and Alvarez, I swear, but we have to get off this yacht. *Now.* There are explosive charges set in the engine room. We don't have time. Seconds, if any."

Her lip quivered and her chin trembled as she tilted her head. The wall in her eyes dropped away and she studied me. "Did you hear what I just said?"

"I heard you. You can kill me, if you need to. Just, please, we gotta jump." I held my hand out to her.

"I'm so *so* sorry." Tears streamed down her cheeks, but instead of pulling the trigger, she handed me her gun. "Please don't hate me."

I took the Ruger in one hand and her hand in the other. Pulling her to her feet, I brought her flush against me. "I know you and you *know* me. You'd never have had to go through with it. I will always have your back. Which is why we've got to fly." I shoved open the railing gate. "You remember how to fly, don't you, Presh?"

She nodded. With her hand still gripped in mine, we backed up several steps before running and leaping from the ship. Airborne, I hollered at her to cross her legs, before our bodies torpedoed back into the ocean. Then I kept swimming, propelling us farther away, while above us a giant fireball exploded across the surface.

My lungs cramped in pain as we kicked and pushed our way toward air. By some miracle, I'd managed to stay conscious through all of that. Gasping to breathe, we breached as the last remnants of flaming debris splashed down around us.

"I can't do it... I can't...I can't swim anymore," she cried as she clung to me.

"Can you drive?" I pointed toward the Sea-Doo bobbing opposite of us with the swells. "I would, but I can barely see out of this eye."

"I *can* do that," she said a grateful chuckle. "Just get me out of this water."

After swimming the short distance, I held the Sea-Doo steady as she climbed up on it. Then I pulled myself up behind her, coiling my arms and hugging her from behind. She turned her cheek and huddled against me for a moment before saying, "Not enough gas or daylight to make it home."

I pointed to the island. "I've booked a private getaway. Gotta warn you though, the accommodations might be a little rustic."

"You know, I've actually stayed there before, it's not so bad. I know a great place for coconut milk."

"So you'll go with me?"

She turned the personal watercraft toward the island we'd originally landed on. "Sharky, I'd go anywhere with you."

"Promises, promises," I teased.

She gunned the Sea-Doo so hard, I had to grab hold of her or fall off the back. I couldn't help but smile, knowing that was exactly how life with Zee was going to be.

Chapter Thirty-Three

Coop

As soon as Zee ran the Sea-Doo up on the shore, she bailed and flat-backed it on the sand. I went to my knees next her and frantically searched her for injuries. I couldn't see any obvious ones, but her wetsuit covered most of her. My fingers quaked as I pushed the wet black strands from her face. "You okay?"

"Yeah, I just need..." Talking made her cough, so I held her up and helped her through it. "Solid ground."

Even thoroughly worn down and in the midst of a hacking fit, she was the most beautiful woman in the world. Her fingers reached to feel my face as she finally opened her eyes and looked at me.

"Your eye, it's bleeding." She winced as she studied it. Then she checked me over for more injuries. "I thought Jim shot you. I thought you'd been killed."

"He tried. Knocked me out pretty good and I'm lucky I didn't drown. But how would it look if, after all these years, a tough Navy SEAL let himself be taken down by a cheesehead from Weyauwaga with a flare gun?"

That made her smile. And Zee's smile fed life into me every time. But it was short lived. "He was following Hayes' directives. They killed Jim right after I escaped."

"Hayes?" He'd been my top suspect, too, but I had no proof. "And you're sure?"

"A thousand percent. He tried to throw you under the bus and make me doubt you."

"*Tried*," I said, turning on my side to smile at her. "See, you knew."

"He tried to call me out to Zaki, too."

Now that made me laugh. "And how did that work out for him?"

"I gave him the shovel and let him dig his own grave. But this is bad. Hayes has access and information we can't let out."

"We have to alert Wolfe, Colt."

She lifted up her wrist. "Already did. Zaki has let Wolfe, Colt, Vivi, Nik, and Gray all know Hayes can't be trusted and must be brought down."

"Wizardry to the rescue again. And what happened with the rest of the crew — Cait, Kai?"

"When the stowaways got word the transport plan for the Ozma Emerald had changed, they came out and tried to take over the yacht. Some of the crew had injuries, mostly flesh wounds and such from trying to fight the pirates off, but everyone is alive. Nothing too serious, except for Kai. He must've taken quite a beating and was unconscious. I'm worried he might have internal bleeding. They're all on the tender heading to Marakata."

I traced her jawline with my fingers. "You should've gone with them, Presh."

"I was going to. I thought I'd killed all the pirates. But the one I'd harpooned and sent over the railing, he managed to get back on board and pull a gun on me."

"Harpooned? Damn, I would've loved to see that."

"Yeah." She chuckled. "It was pretty epic. You met him. He was the guy, the one you killed in the water. He'd kept me from getting on the tender. He was going to use me as leverage since Hayes had no use for him without the emerald being on the *Zamarad*. Didn't work out so well."

Confused, I squeezed my brows together. "Presh, I didn't kill anyone in the water."

"Sharky, I *saw* you...I lured him to you. I touched you!"

"Touched? That wasn't me, Presh."

"Yes! You were swimming next to me and I ran my hand across the back of your wetsuit."

"No, babe." I laughed at the insanity of it. She had to have swum to the sharks. It was incredulous but it had to be true. "Between the guy with the slit throat and Jim, there was a lot of blood in the water. Sharks were in the area, I spotted them when I was swimming toward the *Zamarad*. Tiger, I think. But I wasn't one of them."

Her dark eyes went wide. "Are you saying I pet a tiger shark?"

"Sounds like it."

Her hands went to her face as a wide smile spread. "That's freaking awesome!"

I fell back against the sand laughing. "God, I love you, Zee. But you're going to get mauled petting an animal you shouldn't!"

"Careful, Sharky, I shouldn't have petted you either."

"If you're lucky, I'll let you do it again."

She curled into me for a delicious kiss and against my lips, she said, "Oh, I'm feeling very lucky indeed."

Aziza

The sun sank down into the sea as we headed inland from the beach. I led Coop to where I knew there was shelter and a freshwater spring. Our first order of business after rehydrating was to build a fire. We worked on that until we had a decent blaze. Coop flashed his dimples. "What next?"

I slowly zipped my wetsuit down, rolling the top half off my shoulders till it hung at my waist. "I think I misspoke when I said I didn't want to swim anymore."

"Oh?"

"Care to join me?" I asked as I peeled off the rest of my wetsuit.

"Are we really going for another swim?"

I grinned as I tugged the strings from my bikini top and let it fall away. "I think the technical term for it is skinny-dipping. You coming?"

He started pulling off his own wetsuit and trunks. "Right behind you, of course!"

Fully naked, I rushed to toward the clearwater spring as Coop chased after me. I led him past the small bonfire and across the large flat rock I used to lay on and dove into pond. The cold refreshing water stripped the salt and sweat from our skin and hair in a flash. We surfaced in unison and our bodies immediately tangled, sleek and slippery, as we kissed. For a long while, we just held on to each other. Thankful to be alive and together.

Coop scooped me against him as he carried me from the spring. We settled in on the smooth rock next to fire, ostensibly to dry our bodies and warm back up. But we both grinned like fools as we started kissing and tangling our bodies together again. As long and tiring as our day had been, we didn't go hard for each other. Our touches were caresses, or kissing, exploring and languid.

We were Adam and Eve, naked on our island of Eden, alone. Whether we had all the time in the world or it was our last night on earth, this was just how we wanted to spend it.

His wide palm smoothed up my back. His fingers skimmed over my skin with soft intimacy. The pads of his fingertips swirled along the edge of my hairline, sending waves and rushes of pleasure cascading through me. He whispered how beautiful I was as his lips teased my earlobe, and his breath warmed my shoulder. His cheek, rough with stumble, felt like sandpaper, but I nuzzled against it anyway.

Threading my fingers through his hair, I brought him to my lips and he rolled me to my back. I parted my legs, making room for his body to settle over mine. With no pretense, no hesitation, he pushed fully inside of me. Breaking our kiss, he threw his head back as we both gasped. Him inside of me...sheer, deep, filling perfection.

The rock was cool and hard against my back, while Coop's chest pressed warm and solid against my breasts. The soft hair over his pecs teased my hardened nipples as he started a slow, rhythmic thrust. His thighs brushed against my mine as our bodies shifted and rocked, ground and thrust. Our lips collided again, tongues wrapping with each other as we panted and groaned with every feeling, the small ones, the big ones, the painful ones, and the relieving ones.

The fire crackled as a breeze picked up. But between us, the heat only increased as our arms and feet tangled. Unable to maneuver much, I threw my arms up over my head in an effort to stave off the intensity of my building orgasm.

Looking down into my eyes, Coop drove his body harder and faster into me. The sound of our skin slapping carried over the spring. Our scent smoldered between us. With one hand, he clasped my wrists together, gripping them hard. At his sudden possession of me, everything in my body tightened with the same force. I dug my nails into my palms, wincing as the cut on my left hand protested. Even though I was causing myself pain, I couldn't release. The pressure inside had built too high, too strong. Like a singular rogue wave that threatened the shore.

"I…I can't…I," I stuttered.

"Give it to me, Presh." Coop's navy-blue eyes bored down. "Give me everything."

A tsunami of feelings, thoughts, emotions crashed as I bucked, digging my heels into the rock beneath us, then the backs of his thighs, his hard ass, the rock again. I torqued against him as the cresting wave broke. The intensity forced a cry from my throat. Coop pushed in harder with his hips as my now pliant legs wrapped him. His arm flexed, his fist gripping my wrists, his chest rearing up. And I smiled watching it all, blissfully spent as he roared with his own relief. Warmth overflowed between us as we collapsed in the aftermath.

We snuggled, spooning until our energy came back. Well, his. I could've lain there purely sated through the night. But he scooped me into his arms and carried me back to the spring to wash off again. I protested and pounded his back and called him Sharky, but as I clung to him, I was happier than I'd ever been.

Coop spun me slowly around as he took in our surroundings with a laugh. "So, you've stayed here before," he said, as if it were a swank hotel or trendy B&B instead of a small cave next to a spring-fed pond.

"Once upon a time, yes. When the *Esmeralda* went down, this is where I landed. I was here alone for several days. No morning breakfast buffet, I'm afraid. We'll have to settle for the coconut milk and berries we collected for tonight."

"Is it official? We're staying the night?"

I flashed my wrist. "The helo, crew, and emerald all made it safely to Marakata. Hayes has been led to believe his plan worked." That part had been easy, with Hayes always playing the boys-club angle to impress Zaki. A little praise from the great and powerful one was all it took to have Hayes to come running like a lapdog. "He's en route now to Marakata, where he'll be taken into our custody. The helo will be back to pick us up first thing in the morning."

"It's over then," Coop said quietly as he brought me against his chest and dropped a kiss on my forehead.

The emerald was safe, the wreckage of the *Esmeralda* gone. Scott Hayes would be heavily interrogated and handled as needed. So if Coop was right and it was really over, why did it feel like it wasn't?

Chapter Thirty-Four

Coop

Now that it was over, I owed Zee the truth.

"Hey, Presh, that fancy watch of yours wouldn't happen to be able to make a financial transaction on it, would it?"

"Of course. Why?"

My grin pulled at the corners of my mouth, tight and serious. "The job is over."

"You want to get paid?" She scrambled out of my arms to stare at me. "Like, now?"

"I know you're not going to stiff me. But it's time for this job to be over. I want to quit, and I want to tell you what happened in the Amazon."

"You want to quit?"

"Yes."

After a few quiet seconds, Zee flashed her wrist to me. "There, the money's been wired."

"And you accept my resignation?"

"I...if you don't want to work with me I'm not going to force you to. But I'm very confused right now. I thought we'd be together?"

"Part of us having everything on table is that we are both coming to the table equally. That's why I can't work for you anymore."

"You work for Zaki, not me."

"Semantics, Presh. And I certainly won't let you dumb down your role in Beryl to make me feel more important."

"I thought we worked well together? I thought you enjoyed it?"

"I do. I want to work *with* you. I want to *be* with you for as long as you'll have me. More than you know. But after I tell you what I've done and why, I'm going to need a little time."

"Time off? Or do you mean time away? To do what? Take out another cartel? We're already scrambling assets to protect ourselves in Brazil. Are you going to tell me what that was all about now?"

I scrubbed my hands through my wet hair, shaking it out. "Yes, it was me in the Amazon. Yes, I killed several of Alvarez's top men. I didn't do it to put a target on Beryl or Zaki or even myself. And I certainly didn't do it to put you in harm's way. I did it to help the clinic I went to. Alvarez's men had been siphoning off their profits and keeping them from being able to effectively bring in revenue, supplies. They weren't able to treat the natives in the area."

"Why didn't you just tell Zaki? He could've helped."

Zaki. I broke eye contact as I rolled to my back. "I couldn't explain why I was there and I didn't have time."

"You went for Ibogaine treatment. Why was that such a secret?"

"My head wasn't right, Zee. I went to treat my PTSD. Any TBI. I wanted to be whole—for you. I had fought my feelings for so long, but I couldn't anymore. And I have a lot of trauma surrounding my past relationships. I was scared of it affecting us. I didn't know how to explain, and if it didn't work, I didn't want to drag you into that."

"You recommended it for Thea, so it worked. Your head is...?"

I pushed out a slow breath. "The Ibogaine helped me, yes. It put my whole life in perspective and I don't have fears about us becoming a repeat of my past anymore. I know you're the woman for me, the *only* woman." I hated the stutter in my voice, the cracking. "I just wish I was the man for you."

"Of course you are!" Her hands went my cheeks as she pleaded with her eyes. "Why would you even question that? Is this because I told Zaki I'd...?"

"Zaki," I muttered. "No. This is about what the doctors there told me." I took a deep breath and willed myself to just bite the bullet and get it out. "I have a brain tumor."

"What?" Zee jerked back, her eyes imploring as they became watery. "Why aren't you in a hospital right now getting it removed? Why on earth would you go scuba diving? I'll get a surgeon on the next flight to Marakata. We'll get a medical flight here tonight."

I grabbed her wrist before she ordered an entire surgical unit be set up on the beach. "Presh, I know you would move heaven and earth and all the fucking stars in the sky for me. And I love you so much because you'd do it for anyone. You *have* done it for so many." I twisted my grip, intertwining our fingers. "But the surgery is experimental at best. The clinic is willing to arrange for a surgeon, a good one, but I needed the money. And the job to take out Alvarez was like killing two birds with one stone."

"That's a horrible expression." Zee sniffed back her tears, then she shrugged the Facet wrist computer off and handed it to me. "Arrange for the surgery. You have the money, Beryl can deal with Alvarez, and when you come out of surgery, hopefully a little smarter, we'll figure out who exactly hired you to take him out."

I grimaced at her jab, but turned the device over in my hand, realizing I could use some extra smarts about now. "How do I even operate this thing?"

"Here," she said, holding her hand out to take it back. "It's a hybrid Morse Code. Tell me who I need to talk to."

After Zee sent the orders and assured me everything would be a go, she explained, "I learned Morse Code from one the crew members on the *Esmeralda*. I taught it to my aunt."

"I thought you said she'd died?"

"My other aunt."

"It's truth time. Tell me what happened, tell me it all."

Aziza

After I explained about the confrontation in the deep freeze that had led to me to killing Zaki, I expected Coop to flinch or recoil. Certainly to question me about who the hell he'd been talking to all these years if it wasn't Omar Zaki. But instead he encouraged me to continue with the night of the wreck. "You and the captain were in the life raft, but he didn't survive?"

"The waves were huge. He fell out and he struggled to get back in. I tried to help him, but I was just a kid.

His hands kept slipping out of mine. When he did get a good hold he was heavier than me and was pulling me over and into the sea with him. A wave knocked him off me or I would've drowned too."

Coop nodded understanding. "I had a hold of this man off the roof of a building, but he couldn't keep his grip on mine and he was panicking and pulling me with him. He wasn't listening to my direction and he fell. It bothered me for a long time. But you did everything you could."

"I don't even know how I stayed in the raft as long as I did. Or how I survived after the raft ejected me. Somehow I made it to this island. It was like the ocean spit me up. I was here for what seemed like forever, but then a boat came along. A security sweep from Marakata after reports had gone out about the disappearance of the *Esmeralda*. I didn't know who I could trust, or who would even believe me about what had happened. So I didn't tell them who I was. They kept calling me boy, because my head had been shaved, so I went with it. With my skin tone, I'd become quite tan by then, and looked like any other Caribbean kid. The security team took me back to the island to decide what they were going to do with me, and I escaped."

I'd known exactly where to go thanks to my many conversations with Zanji about the island. But after living off berries and coconut milk for a week I'd scarcely had energy for the hike and Zaki's palace was at the top of the mountain. My fear of being sent back to the desert had kept me motivated. Who else would have taken me in? Zaki's brothers? They were worse than he.

After finding the palace came the task of sneaking inside past the guards, but after many days at sea playing hide and seek with the crew, I'd gotten pretty stealthy. I knew from our conversations that Zanji was deep inside the palace, so I'd just kept working my way down.

I hadn't been prepared to find Zanji locked away in what was essentially a cave-like prison. Nor had I been prepared for her to know I was coming. "*Nice move back in the dining room,*" she'd said in her specialized computer voice. "*Don't look so shocked. I have access to all the cameras. I've been watching you since they got you ashore.*"

I'd huddled against the rock wall, terrified of what I would find. What must she be like if they had to lock her away?

"*You've come all this way,*" she'd said. "*Don't chicken out now, kiddo.*"

I'd reminded myself of the things my mother had assured me. When I'd dared to peek around the corner and saw my aunt Zanji for the first time, my eyes had widened in shock. She was just a woman. She'd gotten up and came to the barred door. And it was only then that I saw the unique way she moved her face and body, but it was hardly anything scary, in fact she was actually quite beautiful. But suddenly she had become overcome with distress, she'd made groaning noises that startled me and began flailing her arms. As soon as she was back at her computer she'd merely said, "*I forgot. The code to the door. You need to enter the code.*" She'd rattled off a long series of numbers and it had taken me five times to enter it correctly.

She hadn't rushed to hug me or even smile, but she'd quickly started typing and telling me she was happy to see me. Her corresponding facial gestures hadn't correlated, and at first it had been disconcerting, but soon I'd stopped even noticing.

"I saw the news story about OZ's yacht going missing. What happened?"

I'd told her everything and within an hour, she'd had a plan concocted. One that would ensure both she and I would be safe from Zaki's brothers and no one would ever know what I'd done on the *Esmeralda*.

She'd said the only way for it to work was to keep Zaki alive and well. She'd known all of his habits and schedules and the fact that he tended to be a recluse, especially when on the island, had made it even more likely for our plan to work. Zanji had been the one to program all of the holographic systems, because while he'd locked her away, he'd made sure to put her talents to good use for him.

"Zanji had been the brains behind it all. With Zaki gone, she knew no one would respect her to run the empire. Zaki's brothers would take it and make things worse for us both. She reformed his emerald empire and turned it into something better."

"What happened with you?"

"I pretended to be an orphaned island boy for a long time. People called me Tip and I served as Zaki's personal assistant, the only one he'd allow to care for him. While I wasn't doing that, Zanji trained me on all the systems. But obviously pretending to be a boy wasn't something I could do forever. Besides which, my role with Zaki had the undesirable side effect of starting a round of rumors about him. Obviously we couldn't allow them to perpetuate. So we killed Tip off and I laid low for a long time. Years. Once my hair had grown out, we did a whole makeover and I resurfaced using the name my mother had always called me. The OZ you know of today had been firmly established by then and no one really questioned anything anymore."

"It must've been a relief to be yourself again."

I turned in Coop's arms to face him, to see his reaction. Our legs twined, and our breath merged. "You don't seem as surprised as I thought you'd be."

"I am. I mean, I'd realized you weren't exactly you, and Zaki wasn't at all Zaki. But I didn't know the how, or the when, or the why."

"Zanji passed away a few months before I hired you. Sometimes I still pull Zaki's hologram up and to talk things out with her. But it's really just talking to myself. In case you were wondering who've you been talking to this whole time, it was me. But I'm guessing you knew that, too—given your attitude with Zaki was always a bit put out."

"I was put out. You only went through Zaki when you didn't think I would agree with you, when you didn't trust me to support you. I hated talking to him, knowing you were hiding from me behind a mask."

"I'm sorry. I should've trusted you."

"I understand now. I understand everything now. Why you've never left the island. I'm sorry it took this to make me come. I should've just come. I love you so much, Ozma Zamirah Aziza Zaki."

"I love you more, Michelangelo Amadeus Cooper. But, um…what happens on the island stays on the island, right?"

Coop let out a deep, rumbling chuckle as he pulled me closer to him and kissed my temple. "Don't worry, Presh. Your secrets are safe with me."

For a long time we held each other close, closer than I'd ever been to anyone. Our naked bodies were nothing compared to how naked our souls had become. No more secrets, no more masks, no more lies.

Chapter Thirty-Five

Aziza

I awoke as the sun started to come up. I loved the pastel colors of the morning, soft blues and pinks, the air crisp and fresh, the temperature maybe even a little cold. Our fire had dwindled to just some glowing embers.

"You didn't wake up to stoke the fire, sleepyhead," I said, chiding Coop. Stretching my back, I smiled at feel of his warm body next to mine. I turned, tucking my face into his chest. "Wakey wakey."

Coop didn't stir.

"Wake up." I scrambled to my knees and shook his shoulder. Nothing. "This isn't funny, Sharky!"

He was breathing, his pulse was strong, but his eyes stayed closed and he was completely unresponsive. Immediately I contacted Marakata to get the helo en route with medical personnel, then hustled us both back into our swimsuits.

I cradled his head in my lap as we waited. Kissing his face, I begged and pleaded with any and every God who would listen. Then when the helo landed and the medical team carried his body off on the stretcher, I didn't hesitate to jump in with them. I didn't look back at the little island where the fire had died out. I didn't even look forward as the helicopter banked to the southwest taking us toward Brazil. I only looked at Coop.

My heart had shattered, not into tiny pieces, but into large, sharp shards. They cut into me with every beat and breath. I feared Coop would never open his eyes again and anything worth loving would be lost behind those eyelids, drowning in their deep blue depths.

But *my* brain still functioned, and with it I would move heaven and earth and all the fucking stars in the sky for him. Just like he trusted me too.

* * * *

Two days later
Amazonas, Brazil

I paced nervously in the waiting room, paying little attention to full jungle outside of the windowed walls surrounding the modern, luxurious space. Taking the moniker of medical tourism to its fullest, the clinic seemed more resort than hospital. In my short but completely stressed-out time here, I'd seen much of what Coop had told me about how special the place was. The balance of various medical beliefs and practices working together was inspiring. The staff, whether tending to purely cosmetic procedures or life-saving ones, were equally gracious and caring. It was definitely worth protecting.

I turned, tripping over Titan, who'd been pacing right behind me. Sitting in a well-appointed couch group nearby were Leo, Nik, and Thea. They'd come immediately upon hearing that Coop was unconscious. Wolfe and Vivi had arrived as well, just before Coop had gone in for surgery. They were both consulting with a security team. Hayes had never shown up at the island and now was in the wind. We'd also attracted the attention of Alvarez's crew.

"Only easy day was yesterday," Nik said as he came up alongside me.

"You've been there when he's been in bad shape before." I fought the quiver in my chin. "He's going to be okay, right?"

Nik put his arm around me. "Even if he's not, *you* have to be. We'll be here for you no matter what the outcome is."

"Does that mean HR can start your paperwork?" I asked, forcing a smile.

"I'm sure they already have. But yes, as long as you need me and Leo and Thea, we're all here for you."

I tucked into his side hug, but I wouldn't feel comforted until I knew Coop was out of surgery and stable.

"It's going to be a while before we know anything. I'm going to go with Thea to her consult on the Ibogaine."

I nodded. We'd scrambled up a fake passport for Thea, just in case. But as yet none of us had actually gone through any official channels. Which was a good thing, because I had nothing in the way of documentation.

"Maybe you and Leo should grab something to eat?"

My stomach turned at the thought. "I don't think I could get anything down."

"Okay, we'll be back soon."

I nodded again and resumed pacing. This time Leo fell in step with me. He told me stories of Coop when he was young. How tough he'd always been, working on their family's ranch. The antics he'd get into, the fights.

"He taught me some of my best moves. He's tough. Probably the toughest man I've ever known. He'll come through."

"He has to," I whispered, fearing my voice would crack.

"He loves you. No matter what happens, you have that."

What happened to hope? And people telling you everything would be fine, there's nothing to worry about? It was like they'd already accepted he was gone. What else did they know that I didn't? I mean, the doctor had told us the surgery was risky, but he'd also given me assurances and seemed so sincere about Coop's chances.

I made another lap, this time looking out of the window at the lush greenery. The clinic was built high up on stilts and actually hovered in the cloud forest. I stepped outside for some fresh air, walking along one of the suspended bridge pathways. Even though the surgery had just begun, I didn't want to get too far or be gone too long, so I turned back. Scanning the length of a gorgeous building, I realized I could see right into the operating room where Coop was.

Wait. Why were they standing over the middle of his body, marking up his naked torso, not at his head?

Something wasn't right. Before I could assess what they were doing, the surgeon lifted his hands and started backing away, the nurses looked panicked as well. That's when I saw Marco standing in the doorway with his weapon drawn.

I started running, yelling for Vivi and Wolfe. As I pushed back into the waiting room, I screamed for them to follow. "Alvarez is here. In the OR!"

I burst into the operating room with my Sig drawn. "Get the fuck out of here, Marco."

"*Tranquillo, chica.* This is personal."

"Yeah, it's personal for me too." I glared at Marco. If his aim hadn't still been on Coop I'd have taken my shot.

"Your man here killed my father, three of my best men—my cousins—and then he tried to kill me." Marco looked more businessman than a jungle drug lord as he stood there in a pressed linen suit. He even had one of those little white Cuban-style hats to shade his face, though his brown skin was already heavily leathered and his flesh was further roughened with a scar that ran low on his jawbone. "I'm here to convey my appreciation."

Seek revenge, he meant.

Vivi and Wolfe burst in behind me.

"Not going to happen, Marco," Wolfe growled. "Not today. Not like this."

Marco didn't change his stance, even outnumbered. He was willing to die. Which didn't bode well for Coop. But if all he cared about was killing Coop, why hadn't he done it yet?

"Marco. Someone *hired* Coop to kill you. It wasn't us. Maybe we can help each other out. Take care of who hired him for you."

"Oh, I know who hired him. And it *was* you."

"I swear, it wasn't Zaki. While we certainly don't condone your practices, we've never gone after you before. Why would we now?"

"Ask your boy Hayes."

"Scott Hayes? You think Hayes hired the hit? How do you know?"

Realizing I was still pointing my weapon at Marco, I slowly lowered it and set it down on the operating table at Coop's side. Then I stepped between Marco's pointed gun and Coop, silently conveying that he would have to kill me first. I couldn't help but thread my fingers with Coop's limp ones. "Do you really want to make an enemy of OZ?"

Marco kept his gun pointed my way, but relaxed his stance. "All I know is that Hayes has been in our business for a few months now. Why? We've kept the Amazon routes cleared of the real lowlifes. Human trafficking is almost nonexistent in my territory. It's been increasing everywhere else. You'd think Hayes would thank us."

The sound of the machines distracted me and I realized this was not the time or place for us to be having this conversation. Coop was still in desperate need of surgery. I glanced around the bright white operating room for the doctor and nurses, but they'd fled when the guns started coming out.

"Vivi, please find the doctor and get his ass back in here."

Vivi took off. Then Marco muttered, "His hands will be shaking too much. Is that really what you want?"

"Just keep talking. This human-trafficking ring that wants to use your Amazon routes? Does it have anything to do with a company called Ardent, a woman named Seraphina Westin, or an organization called The Sanctuary?"

"All of the above. And I'll tell you something else. That witchy Westin lady, she's the worst of the bunch. The Sanctuary, that's where she retires the women she's trafficked. Brainwashes them to believe she saved them! Oh, I've seen her parading around like a saint. Going on television shows. Meanwhile, I'm the one taking care of her trash. Do you see me getting to go on *Michael Maddox Live*? Do you see me getting *any* respect at all? And the donation money she gets! You know how many drugs I'd have to move to make that kind of money?"

We both turned as Vivi wrestled her way back in, hollering, "Found the surgeon. And look who else!"

She shoved Scott Hayes in with the barrel of her gun.

I grabbed my gun back up and pointed it at Hayes, but kept my body blocking Marco's shot on Coop. "Start talking."

Hayes had that congressional look about him — he was a little portly and he'd gone bald and gray, not that sexy salt-and-pepper gray either. Being from DC, he'd almost always worn a suit and today was no exception. He held his hands out, placating. "Coop is fine. I promise. Let's just put the weapons down and I'll explain."

I turned my eyes to the surgeon for confirmation.

He quickly blurted, "He is fine. He doesn't have a tumor."

I held back the rush of relief coursing through me. "But he was passing out. He's been unconscious?"

"The doctor who diagnosed him was paid to tell him he had tumor and tamper with some medication, that's all," Scott explained. "It was never supposed to go this far."

"Oh, that's all? He's passed out in places he could've *died.*"

"I'm sure he just took a few too many or something. He thought the gummies were cannabis to help keep his anxiety and pain down until the surgery. They were only meant to give him aural migraines."

"You're telling me he's fine? He's going to live?"

"Yes," Hayes assured with a big politician's smile. Like everything would be forgiven now. Like we all could forget this ever happened.

"So what? You used the threat of the tumor to get him desperate enough to take the Alvarez hit?"

Hayes nervously glanced between me and Marco, trying to determine who he needed to lie to more. In the end he split his response down the middle. "We needed to distract Coop—soften Marakata's security—*and* open the Amazon transport routes. That was all it was supposed to be."

"For the emerald. But then Marco survived, so you went with Plan B?"

"I knew if we sniffed around the site, maybe Zaki would worry and bring the emerald back up."

I glared at Scott. A man I'd worked with for years, trusted. I could almost have forgiven him if he'd just tried to steal the Ozma Emerald, but to do this to Coop? Pure evil. And the way he kept smiling at me, like he was so sure I wouldn't kill him. Wouldn't fill his body with bullets. Like he could talk his way out of this room. He'd really never had any respect for me. But that wasn't worth my thoughts right now. Not with Coop still out cold.

"Then what's this all about?" I asked, flagging my hand at Coop's body on the operating table. I eyed the surgeon. "You got your fucking money. What were you going to do? A fake surgery?"

The surgeon glanced uncomfortably at Scott Hayes.

"It wasn't my idea," Hayes said, holding his hands out. "The whole harvesting thing... Look, it wasn't my idea."

Harvesting! My eyes bugged out as I glared at the piece of shit in blue scrubs. The one I'd begged to do everything he could to bring Coop back to me. The one who'd assured me he would do his best. "You didn't take this job to save him, did you? You were paid to harvest his organs?"

At the slight nod of acknowledgment, I shifted, pointing my gun at the surgeon, and pulled the trigger twice. He dropped instantly, while the other players with guns stiffened their semi-relaxed stances to go back hard with their aims.

"Next!" I gritted out, my own barrel now trained on Hayes. For the first time in years, the asshole actually eyed me with the respect I deserved.

"Whoa, whoa. I came here to stop this."

And still he lied. "Try again."

"I swear. Didn't Zaki tell you?"

I shook my head with a laugh, but now was certainly not the time to let him in on what went on behind the curtains on Marakata Cay. I glanced over at Coop, realizing we'd come just in time. His entire torso had been marked up for organ removal, but thankfully no cuts had been made. "Vivi, would you be so kind as to find a nurse not on anyone's payroll, put her on ours, and have her bring Coop back awake safely?"

"On it, love," Vivi said, heading out again.

Wolfe stepped up to guard Hayes. The big Viking had Hayes, who was no small man himself, cowering.

"Good. Yes, let's wake our patient," Marco cooed, reminding me that he was still in the room and why. "I'd much rather Michael Cooper be awake to benefit from the extent of my revenge. It's no fun if I can't torture him."

Shit. I eyed Marco. "How about we make a deal?"

"A deal? And are you speaking for Zaki, young lady?"

Young lady? It happened so often I didn't even show my offense. I simply replied, "I am."

"No, I am. Zaki gave me full authority," Hayes piped up, but the tip of Wolfe's knife in his carotid artery had him clamping his lips.

"Tell you what, I bet Zaki would be honored to speak with you directly," I suggested amicably.

Hayes looked like he was about to throw up.

Marco straightened, honored to finally get to speak with the great and powerful one in 'person'. "Yes, that would be delightful."

"Very well, I'll set it up right now."

Within minutes I'd conjured Zaki up. Marco slapped his thigh and scanned the room as if thoroughly entertained by all of this. The OR with all its implementations and a full wall of windows showcasing the beauty of the rain forest as a backdrop. The dead organ-harvesting surgeon slumped on the floor at his feet. Me, standing guard in front of Coop, who was still unconscious and on a variety of machines. Viking-esque Wolfe with his knife poised to slit Hayes' throat and his Glock trained on Marco's chest. But it was Zaki's hologram that took center of this very strange stage.

Marco Alvarez seemed to think the same, because he tapped the barrel of his gun to his lips and asked, "What is that saying about hell being empty?"

My fingers twitched as I finished the Shakespeare quote for him.

"Yes, Mr. Alvarez," Zaki said. "'*All the devils are here*' now."

Chapter Thirty-Six

Coop

I awoke covered in warm blankets. I blinked, sleepily. The nurse at my bedside explained I was in Brazil and had just come from surgery. I hadn't remembered going in. Last thing I remembered was falling asleep next to my beautiful Zee. I must've gone to Brazil to have the surgery as planned. Maybe some of the memories hadn't quite made it past the surgery, but my memories of Zee were all there in perfect clarity. *Thank fuck.* Now I just had to get back to her.

* * * *

The next time I awoke I was in a private room. Leo was in a chair next to me. "Well, look who finally woke up."

Groggily I asked, "Do I still have a brain or did they take it all?"

"You're able to talk, aren't you?" Leo said with a grunt before flashing me a smile.

"Any idiot can talk."

"Good to have you back, brother."

"Did they get everything? Where's Zee?"

"Zee's—"

"Never mind, I know," I muttered. The nurse had said I was in Brazil, which meant Zee was in Marakata. "I need a phone. I need to call her."

"She's in the middle of something. You gave us quite a scare."

"It's what I do best," I joked, then coughed. I pushed up, repositioning myself, then grabbed the ice water next to my bed. I couldn't believe how good I felt. "How long have I been out?"

"A couple of days."

Before Leo could say more, the door to the room opened and Zee came in. Tears filled her eyes as she rushed to my side. "You're awake! I wanted to be here when you opened your eyes. I wanted to be the first person you saw."

I wrapped her in my arms, hoisting her closer until she was in my lap. "You're here now. That's all that matters."

"Your being alive is all that matters."

Ignoring me, Leo asked Zee tentatively, "So, everything okay?"

Sniffing, she nodded. "Everything's okay."

"With my surgery? I feel great." I lifted my hand to my head, but there were no bandages. "What did the doctor say? Did he get the whole tumor?"

Zee stiffened. "The doctor didn't get anything. But you're fine. You're perfect. I'll explain in a minute. Leo, the jet's ready for us. We're just waiting for Thea to be done with the Ibogaine. If you could let Wolfe and Vivi know."

"Wolfe and Vivi?" Shit, maybe I'd lost more time than I'd thought. I looked around the room and realized I wasn't hooked up to any machines.

"I'll let you all talk." With a curvy grin, Leo slipped out of the room, calling, "Glad you're alive, brother!"

Zee brought me up to speed on my passing out on the island and the whole operating room standoff while I listened in disbelief. But instead of reveling in the fact that I was fine and had no tumor, I asked, "You shot my surgeon?"

"He wasn't a surgeon. He was an organ harvester. He stood there with me going over your tumor and the surgery while I cried. He knew you didn't have anything wrong with you. He knew you wouldn't ever wake up. He knew it was murder. There's no coming back from that in my book. I'm telling you, this Seraphina Westin witch is bad news. She's moved to number one on my shitlist."

"Mine too. Well, right after Hayes, apparently."

"Yeah...Hayes... About him—" Zee started to say before I cut her off.

"And how the hell did you get Alvarez to back down?"

"Actually, Hayes has something to do with that. Might as well cross him off your shitlist."

"No, no, no, I don't care what kind of slick shit he pulled. He's not getting away with this."

"He's not getting away with anything." Zee grimaced. "You have to take him off your list because he's Marco's to take care of. Zaki gave Hayes to him to torture as he pleased."

"Zaki, huh? Always doing your dirty work." I chuckled.

She shrugged. "Marco wanted to negotiate with Zaki, not me. Anyway, Hayes was the one who actually contracted the hit, and Hayes had lied about Alvarez's organization extracting money from the clinic and blocking them from getting supplies. Marco didn't appreciate his character being assassinated like that. He actually cares a lot about the region and has been wanting to clean up his family's reputation."

"Marco Alvarez?"

"Yes."

"How do we know he'll actually kill Hayes?"

"It's already confirmed. Marco and I found we have an enemy in common, one who Hayes apparently had been working with and had some intel on."

"Hayes is a highly trained agent. Why would he share anything if he knew he would be killed either way?"

"An operating room table and surgical tools can be very persuasive. Marco was not very nice to Hayes."

"Shit. But wait, I still don't understand. How was fucking Hayes an even trade for *me*?"

I had to laugh. "Don't worry, Sharky, Alvarez thought you were worth more too. Zaki reminded him that you'd be pissed you didn't get to kill Hayes yourself, which made him feel slightly better. But Marco still felt he was due extra since the men you killed were also his cousins, and then there was still the matter of his father. So to sweeten the deal, Zaki negotiated for Marco to wipe the slate with you as well as step away from the drug trafficking, if Beryl bought this clinic for him and set him up with a charity bundler specializing in the kind of donors who could bring in big contributions. He can make a shit ton more money than with illegal drugs, while providing a great service to his people. It's not a perfect setup, but Beryl retains controlling interest to ensure it is run to our standards, while Alvarez will keep the Amazon region clear of major trafficking of any kind."

"What? That can't be right. Are you sure my brain is really still intact? I'm not understanding any of this. Alvarez is going straight? Marco?"

"I imagine he'll always be a bit bent, and we'll certainly have our hands full working this closely with him. But, yeah, he was eager to break free from the family tradition. He wants to be legitimately respected at a higher level. Zaki reminded him that he already has an exceptional portfolio of legal investments and that the worst of his organization's endeavors actually came from his cousins. Since you took them out, the housecleaning he needed to go straight was practically done for him."

"You seriously got Alvarez to go straight? You really are a wizard."

"Well, Zaki is."

I tilted my head at her. "You are Miss Zaki, aren't you?"

Her lips wrenched, turning down.

"No, *Miss Zaki* isn't really you at all, is it, Presh? In fact, I don't want you to carry the name of that man anymore, even if I'm the only one who knows. Shit, I wasn't planning to do this now. A hospital room isn't romantic and I don't have the ring on me. But now that my brain is fine, medically speaking, I don't want to waste another second living this life without you." I took her hand in mine. "Aziza, you are my best friend, my ride or die, my deepest love, and my best fuc — "

"Sharky!" Her eyes, pearling with tears, popped as she swatted my shoulder.

"*Fine*, I won't drop an f-bomb in my proposal." I grinned, flashing my dimples. "But I'm just being honest, because from here on out, between us, it's always going to be the truth." I brought her hand to my lips and kissed it. "And the truth is, I love you more than I ever imagined was possible. Will you do me the honor of becoming Mrs. Cooper?"

Zee pushed her tears away and kissed me hard. "Of course, yes! I love you more than anything." She pulled back and grimaced. "But I do have one more secret before I can accept a ring."

Oh boy. "Let's hear it, Presh. Lay it on me."

She leaned in close to whisper in my ear. "I've never been a fan of the color green. So, please, don't you dare get me an emerald."

Epilogue

Ophelia Protocol
Aziza

Michael *freaking* Cooper, my amazing husband, spun me around as he kissed me. Wasting no more time, we'd arranged for the ceremony to take place immediately after landing from Brazil. Django and Mickie made sure I looked like a princess, while Vivi dressed me in a simple, elegant gown. But the best part was saying our I dos on my favorite beach on Marakata Cay while surrounded by my Oztralian family.

Before our kiss even ended, the party started with DV8 and Lil' BayBay playing and everyone cheering.

As Coop set me down, he said, "I hope you liked the ring."

I admired the beautiful princess-cut diamond flanked by two dark sapphire stones on my finger. He'd had it made six months ago, when he'd been in the Mediterranean. The sapphires were for the ocean, but I loved how they matched his eyes. The cut would always remind me of Baba's nickname for me. "I love it. It's perfect for me, just like you are."

"Thank God Nik grabbed up our luggage before getting in the helo, because I sure as hell wouldn't have wanted to go on another treasure dive so soon."

Nik, Thea, Leo, and Titan, of course, all surrounded to congratulate us first. It was hard to believe these sweet souls had only been a part of my life for a few days. To me they were already family.

I hugged Thea extra-long. She'd been quiet and reflective on the plane as she'd processed what she'd learned from the Ibogaine session. "Are you okay? We haven't had a chance to talk much about how the therapy went."

"I think I'm going to need your help," she said quietly.

"You've got it. Anything at all. What's going on?"

"My sister Amanda Gale, Mandy—she's alive. I remember everything."

"We'll find her. Don't worry," I said, hugging her again. As we pulled apart, I noticed a stir of activity in the crowd, people looking and pointing to the sky. "What's going on?"

I turned, spotting a plane in the distance with a trail of puffy white shooting out behind it.

"Looks like a skywriter," Leo said. "Haven't seen one of those since I was a kid."

"Coop, did you plan this?" I asked.

He held his hands up and shook his head. "Not me. Vivi maybe?"

Vivi had done most of the work planning the impromptu wedding, while I'd scrambled to respond to all of Zaki's correspondence. Which had included calming Marguerite's fear that Zaki had died because he hadn't eaten any meals in a week. I'd felt a twinge of guilt convincing her that he'd gone on a cleansing fast and I'd simply forgotten to let the kitchen know. I really was getting tired of deceiving people I cared about. Coop assured me we'd figure out a way to kill OZ off while still retaining my rights and our organization's integrity. He was determined to help me get out from under all the lies and secrecy.

"Wasn't me, love," Vivi said as she congratulated me with a hug and kiss to both cheeks. "Security mobilized when it came into our airspace. But it appears to just be a skywriting plane. Maybe someone from one of the nearby islands practicing?"

"Zaki doesn't believe in coincidences," I said out of habit.

We watched each letter form, S U R R E trying to guess what it would say.

"Surrender? How ominous," Coop said as he casually sipped from a beer bottle the guys had brought out to him. Despite his relaxed attitude, he'd made quick eye contact with Nik, Wolfe, and Colt. They all had their heads up and on a swivel to ensure there were no other surprises.

"There's more," I murmured as the small plane looped. T H E... From the corner of my eye I saw Thea's face pale and Nik's jaw flex. "Vivi?"

"On it, love," she said, and I knew she was contacting Gray to find out who exactly had contracted the skywriter. Soon the plane disappeared, leaving only its threatening message to hang in the air above the emerald island.

'Surrender Theadora.'

I turned to Thea, but she just stared at the message.

I gently put my hand on her arm. "Do you know what it means?"

"No, but I know who it's from." She turned to look me in the eye. "Seraphina Westin."

* * * *

"So much for going straight to the honeymoon bungalow," Coop laughed as we headed into the war room. I eyed the table and Coop chuckled. "Careful, Presh, I just might."

Unfortunately, Nik, Wolfe, Vivi, Thea, Leo, and Titan were already filing in behind us. I sighed, then flicked on the power and proceeded to conference in with Gray.

"Congratulations, Mrs. Cooper. Let me see the ring," she cooed and I complied. "Gorgeous! Great job, Coop! And that kiss you planted on her, whew! Hotter than Georgia asphalt."

"You saw that, huh?" I laughed. As Coop grabbed me around the waist and pretended to do it again. I swatted him away. "Sharky, stop."

"*Never*," he hissed in my ear, before narrowing his eyes as Wolfe sat in his chair. "Excuse me while I kick this kid's ass."

I grimaced as Wolfe scrambled to move. Turning back to Gray, I said, "Since you watched on live feed, I guess you know why Vivi called and why we're here."

Gray nodded as she sipped from the straw in her oversized insulated cup. "Yes, ma'am, oh, and I've got scuttlebutt for you as well."

"Go first, while we're waiting for Zaki and few others to remote in."

"Guess who your next guest to the island will be?"

"I have no idea," I said, a little shocked by the realization. But I had been kind of preoccupied. "You'll have to tell me."

"It's no fun when you've been offline for a few days. Coming, in just two days, is the one, the only, Miss Olivia Austin. And before you ask, no, I didn't reach out to her. She'd heard from a friend of a friend that maybe OZ could help fish her sister out of a cult. We were so right!" She punched her fists over her head in victory.

"Cults give me the creeps," I said with a shiver.

"I know! Oooh, look what just came in. I'll give you three guesses as to which company hired the skywriter."

"The production company for the reality show?"

"Winner winner chicken dinner, she's back, folks!"

"How *many* sweet teas have you had?"

"A few. My eyeballs are floatin'. We better get this meeting started before I spring a leak."

I turned to see everyone had settled in seats or were standing and waiting. I couldn't help but notice Leo had gone pale. "Everything okay?"

"Did you say *Olivia Austin* is coming here?"

"Yeah! Are you a fan too?" Gray asked before taking another sip.

Coop's deep laugh rang through the war room before he slapped his brother on the back. "Oh, he's her *biggest* fan."

I ran my hands along my chair arms. "Well, without further ado, it's time we bring in OZ."

I glance across the table at Coop, and he shook his chin, then lifted his hands. "Everything on the table, Zee."

"But..." I stared back at him. Mad, scared, unsure. I gripped the armrests, digging my fingers in to keep them steady.

"It's going to be fine." Coop scanned the room, then held his warm gaze on me. "We're all family here. It's the only way to be free of it. Just jump. Fly. You know how."

I slid my hands to the table and slowly pulled the curtain back on the behind-the-scenes reality of OZ. As I revealed the truth to those closest to me, I felt immense support and relief. Freedom. I glanced back to Coop, whose smile fed my soul. I mouthed, '*Thank you.*'

'*Love you, Presh.*'

'*Love you.*'

"Not to interrupt the lovefest," Nik grunted, "but there's some psychopath witch trying to intimidate Thea. What the hell are we going to do about it?"

I pulled in a deep breath. "We're going to infiltrate Seraphina Westin's cult, and this mission, which you have no choice but to accept," I said as everyone chuckled, "will be...Ophelia Protocol."

Want to see more like this?
Here's a taster for you to enjoy!

Unbreakable Heroes:
Under Control
Zoe Normandie

Excerpt

Carrick

"Moose, hold up. I haven't cleared the area," Delta called out to the man jumping out of the passenger side of the armored black SUV.

Former Navy SEAL and decorated war hero Carrick Byrne tilted his head back, giving Delta the usual 'don't even start' expression.

"Relax, big rig. This is just a little 'find and retrieve' contract," Carrick said in a skeptical voice tinted with the slightest Irish accent as he leaned back into the idling SUV. "I don't think we need to worry about one little girl."

Delta narrowed his brown eyes, and a lock of his slicked-back dark-blond fell onto his unimpressed face. "She's been on the run for years. Don't underestimate her."

Carrick looked around with obvious sarcasm at the fact that they were literally about to walk through a park on their way to finish the job. Glancing back,

Carrick raised his eyebrow to his friend, recognizing the face of someone who wanted to punch him.

"Come on. How much trouble could one chick cause?"

"Your client seems to think she can cause a lot of trouble," Delta reminded him. "And our intelligence suggests the same. She's slippery, Carrick — and I don't think your client is very forgiving."

"Don't overdramatize this," Carrick warned. "This is a nothing contract."

The two strong, opinionated men exchanged looks before Delta backed off, seemingly knowing that at the end of the day, Carrick was the CEO of Sea-to-Sky Security.

"Have it your way," Delta said, leaning back. "You're the boss."

Moving away from the SUV, Carrick slung his old black hockey skates over his shoulder, heading toward the rink. He flipped up the collar of his black work coat, even further concealing his identity. He had a target to follow. Years of urban reconnaissance and black ops had given him more than enough tactical training to handle the job.

Popping a black baseball hat on and smoothing back his black hair that was peppered with gray, the dark Irish-American moved stealthily.

Delta took off behind him with gusto, but Carrick didn't care. He just needed to get the job done and over with, then move on to the next one. It should be in and out — quick and easy. Those were the types of cases Carrick needed to build his client base and his reputation as the premiere private security firm in LA.

And, damn it, he was going to do the best job he could — because after losing everything that mattered to him, this new business venture was all he had left.

Carrick focused on the scene before him. The crowd had thinned. It was growing quiet. As he came up to the skating rink, a young couple passed him on the other side of the pathway leading out of the park. They seemed happy — in love. His only instinct was to scowl, and he pulled down the brim of his hat farther as he stooped to put on his skates.

The target was on the ice. It was time to get *closer*. *Then retrieve.*

Out on the rink, it was nearing closing time, and everyone was clearing out. He was the only one heading in. *Good.* He needed the space. It was much easier to keep eyes on the target.

At least, that was what he told himself. He wouldn't admit it, but at that moment — Valentine's Day night — he wanted nothing else than to have a reason to be alone — alone and away from everything to do with his life, away from the memories. *Is this my second Valentine's Day alone?* He shuddered, pushing the thought aside. That wasn't something he was prepared to feel.

He didn't have to. The girl was in sight.

Hockey skates on, Carrick moved hard down the bumpy outdoor ice — as hard as the restrictive leather strap of his shoulder holster would allow. Wearing a pistol was like wearing boxers. He did it every day, no matter what. It had come to feel like a second skin.

Keeping his eyes on the ice, not on her, his blood pumped to his engorged muscles and a sated grin crossed his lips. There were very few things in life that served to alleviate his stress — hockey being one. The other was a similar cardio-exhausting exercise that elevated his endorphins, pumped his blood and left him satisfied and spent.

Pushing forward, he observed her—the lone woman skating in the opposite direction, once again nearing his position. Her long brown hair had escaped her pink toque, and her warm breath visibly illustrated her panting chest, even from afar. Carrick had to admit that her form was more than pleasing to look at. Athletic and swift—he didn't doubt she could give him a run for his money in a race, but he kept his gaze down. He made sure to give her enough space so that he wouldn't scare her away.

Danica Petrova.

As she was skating past him, he stole one glance of her face, locking eyes. He *had* to see her face in person. All he'd seen was a picture.

He wasn't disappointed.

Her red cheeks flashed at him and her eyes sparkled. *So youthful and full of life.* What he'd seen in a blink of an eye held the promise of an eternity of pleasure as he took in her beautiful face.

But then, in an instant, just as her body floated by him, her skate hit a groove in the ice, an unmistakable sound—and common. Turning immediately, he thrust forward and reached out, catching the young woman as she fell. He quickly heaved her back onto her skates, rescuing her from a hard fall. As he held her, she fluttered her dark lashes at him, enchanting and stunning him.

"You okay?" he asked, looking her over, hoping she hadn't been hurt.

"I'm okay." A sweet, feminine voice escaped her full lips.

Holding her close, he realized that her eyes hadn't been sparkling. They were wet.

Has she been crying?

"I just caught an edge," she explained, like she'd been caught doing something wrong. "Thank you."

As she made to push away from his arms, he realized that he had been still holding her all this time. *I never let her go.*

She frowned as she probably realized the same thing. He released his grip on her thick sweater, letting her float back a foot into her own space. Silence filled the rink. Their gazes did not break, and she continued to blink at him, likely assessing him, given the look in her eyes.

There was something distrustful about the way she was evaluating him. Her body language screamed that she was scared and threatened that she was about to run. Before thinking, he threw out his hand, just knowing she was just about to pop smoke and disappear—and knowing he couldn't allow that. His client had warned him that she was a runner—and that she could slip out of any situation.

His client had also warned him of the importance of not letting her go.

"Carrick," he introduced himself, keeping her there.

She took his hand, though hers remained limp, and she retracted it right way. Clearly, she didn't know what to make of him—but her manners shone through.

"Dani."

Cute. She seemed very sweet, and not at all like the client had described. That was the first thing that brought on his suspicion that something might be wrong and not as he'd been led to believe.

"Nice to meet you," he replied with a little more meaning than he'd expected.

She responded slow and shy, her voice cracking, "I really do appreciate you saving me from the fall."

"Forget it." He shrugged as instinct urged him to back off a little.

But the caveman inside him couldn't take his eyes off her. Lithe and pert, she almost glowed under the soft lights. There was something different about this target. She continued averting her gaze, looking down at the hard ice and shaking her pretty heart-shaped face.

Something was brewing in his mind that he was unwilling to accept, and his strategy shifted. This was not how he'd planned the operation to go, but he had to adjust on the fly — right?

Carrick checked his watch and turned in the direction she was going. "Heading this way? Last five minutes."

He motioned, nearly regretting it as he did. Really, he knew better. They didn't have time for leisurely skating.

"I was." Her words poured out nervously, responding to his invitation. "But…"

"You aren't anymore?"

"I mean, I am." She toyed with her gray sweater buttons as she looked away, seemingly just as conflicted as him. She was a smart little coyote, and he wondered if she was ready to bolt.

She is definitely *ready to bolt.*

"Well, let's go then." He took the lead, pushing off the ice and gliding away from her.

If there was one thing Carrick was good at, it was controlling a situation. After a pause, there was the distinct sound of skates on the ice behind him, and she caught up to glide alongside him. He'd been sure she would follow — had just known it.

A sense of intrigue tugged at his senses as a cold burst of wind blew her long brunette locks across her shoulder.

So he decided to lay it on thick.

"Looks like you've got tough luck tonight," he said.

"It certainly wouldn't have been the worst thing to happen to me on Valentine's Day." The rebellious words seemed to slip from her mouth, and she glanced up with an embarrassed expression.

"That sounds like a good story," he replied.

Her wide gaze betrayed discomfort. The effect? He was able to observe her eye color more closely. They were a lighter brown, but mixed. *With green? Like camouflage.* He'd never seen a color like that before.

He continued looking around. "We must be two sad cases — out here alone on Valentine's night."

She brought her gloved hands together, rubbing them and offering him a shy smile. "*Or*, we must both just love skating."

He couldn't help but smirk, his chest flexing, "Guilty. I'm a hockey guy."

What the hell am I doing? He wiped the smile off his face, feeling like an idiot. However, it seemed her guard was lowering — and in return her shy tiny smile grew a bit.

"I can't believe you...*caught* me."

"Come on. I couldn't let you take a nosedive." He shrugged, pumping harder down the ice.

She kept up, showcasing just how good she was on blades.

She cocked her head and offered the slightest grin, tepid and testing. "You have quick reflexes."

He shrugged again. "Yeah, when I need to."

Built from years of Special Forces tactical training.

She shook her head again in apparent disbelief, then looked away. It was almost like she didn't believe someone *would* save her.

The bumpy ice on the rink was overdue for maintenance, which tended to be the case at the end of the skating day. There weren't many rinks in California — and fewer outdoor ones. Her skate caught an edge again, which she was too distracted to see. As she yelped and almost fell, he lunged instinctively, grabbing her against his body one more time.

"Christ." He exhaled.

Holding her in his arms again, he gazed down on her young, golden face. She bit her lip as she glanced up at him. He was aware of his great height and wide frame, which could be intimidating for some, especially when he was on skates.

"Want to keep going?" he asked, offering his arm. "Or should we head off?"

Danica grinned up to him, making him wait far too long before she answered, her glittery, innocent gaze flickering left and right. Never before had he wanted someone to take his arm so badly. As much as he hated to admit it, he had her exactly where he wanted her. He was forcing her to make a choice. It was going to play into the job nicely.

"One more round." She grinned her little smile, but her cooperation was tentative at best.

She slipped her hand in the crook of his elbow, only to then avert her gaze from his. The flush in her cheeks grew, and he guessed it was more than just the cool night wind coming in off the Pacific Ocean.

Comfortable silence found them briefly as they pushed along the ice side by side. She never let go of his arm, and for the first time, it felt like they were skating *together*. Something stirred inside him that hadn't been there before.

"How long have you been skating?" he asked, propelling the conversation forward.

"Oh, for as long as I can remember," Danica began, revealing more and more. "I grew up on skates and dreamed of becoming a figure skater."

Again, the admission was followed by caution that flashed across her eyes. She didn't want to share much, but she *was*. She recoiled slightly, as if realizing her mistake, and tried to create space between them until he decided he wouldn't let her. He didn't want her to withdraw.

Changing the tempo, he pushed her out a little from him, allowing her hand to slide down his forearm and slip to his just as he twirled her around on the ice. It was so smooth, so natural—like they'd been skating together for years. He didn't miss the wide smile that crossed her lips.

"It never hurts to dream," Carrick said as he pulled her back into him, running his gaze over her form for the hundredth time, his curiosity at maximum.

What does Danica want? What does she do? Questions sprang to the front of his mind. *Why did my client lie to me?*

"I have no shortage of dreams." Her sweet smile betrayed a longing, and it was clear she noticed the way he was looking at her.

"What do you do for work?" He pressed on as he ushered them farther down the ice.

"I'm a nurse."

"At the hospital?" His gaze caught the city worker beginning the process of closing the rink.

"No, at a family clinic," she replied.

"What else?" he probed. "Tell me more."

She let out a low laugh, as if in disbelief he would even say that. "I think it's time to go."

Then she let her hand slip out of his arm, gliding one perfect white skate in front of the other on her way to leave the rink. As he followed, he couldn't keep his eyes off her, watching her closely as she moved. It was like he'd never met a woman before, never seen one. If he were a wiser man, he'd notice that his chest didn't feel as tight as usual for the first time in too long.

If he were a wiser man, he'd notice that he'd grown very distracted.

"What about you?" She cut into his thoughts as she held on to the wall of the rink, stepping one foot through the gate. "Are you...?"

If it weren't for the sound of a man shouting as he sprinted toward them, Carrick would have caught what she said after that. The shouting was unmistakable, and for a second he felt like he could kill Delta for the interruption.

Danica snapped her eyes open like a doe caught in the headlights, clearly frightened by the six-foot-five man running up to the gate. Delta grabbed onto the side of the rink with his meaty SEAL-build as he spoke to Carrick in low tones.

"Moose, there's a situation. We have to go."

About the Author

Brooke Taylor lives and writes from her country home in Oklahoma where her pets are a constant, but happy, distraction. When she's not reading or writing, she enjoys horseback riding, going to the lake, and traveling.

Brooke has worked extensively in the travel industry, from dude ranches to ski resorts to cruise lines. Her many overseas adventures include sky diving in New Zealand, scuba diving with sharks, sailing through hurricanes, and having her tent attacked by wild animals in the Mara game reserve in Kenya. Due to current health insurance rates, Brooke is letting her characters do most of the risk-taking from now on.

Brooke loves to hear from readers. You can find her contact information, website details and author profile page at https://www.totallybound.com

Home of Erotic Romance

Sign up for our newsletter and find out about all our romance book releases, eBook sales and promotions, sneak peeks and FREE romance books!

Made in the USA
Monee, IL
16 May 2022

96496077R00198